"Heavy stun! Aim for center mass!" Behind her, Dastin aimed his weapon half a second faster than Tan Bao and Hesh.

As Nimur let the misshapen husk of Ysan's body fall in a heap, the wounded Wardens struggled to get up. A few of them started to aim their lances once more at Nimur.

All the Wardens' heads twisted one-hundred-eighty degrees in a fraction of a second. The breaking of their necks sounded like old-fashioned firecrackers.

Then there was nothing between Theriault and the demonic force once known as Nimur.

"Fire!"

Four blue phaser beams screamed through the darkness and slammed into Nimur. Their combined force launched her backward several meters and knocked her onto her back. For a moment, the crackling electricity on Nimur's hands ceased, and the fire in her eyes dimmed. Then her eyes flared white and a brutal, invisible blunt force struck Theriault.

She and the rest of the landing party landed in a tangle of limbs, all of them stunned and groaning in pain. She blinked to clear the spots from her purpled vision and staggered to her feet. With her phaser clutched in her outstretched, unsteady arm, she looked for any sign of Nimur.

The fugitive was gone.

Behind her, Dastin rubbed the back of his head. "Is it over?"

Theria[...]
this is jus[...]

Read more adventures of the starships
Endeavour and *Sagittarius* in the saga of

STAR TREK®
VANGUARD

Harbinger
David Mack

Summon the Thunder
Dayton Ward & Kevin Dilmore

Reap the Whirlwind
David Mack

Open Secrets
Dayton Ward

Precipice
David Mack

Declassified
(anthology)
Dayton Ward, Kevin Dilmore,
Marco Palmieri, David Mack

What Judgments Come
Dayton Ward & Kevin Dilmore

Storming Heaven
David Mack

In Tempest's Wake
Dayton Ward

STAR TREK®
SEEKERS

SECOND NATURE

DAVID MACK

**Story by
David Mack and
Dayton Ward & Kevin Dilmore**

**Based on *Star Trek*
created by Gene Roddenberry**

POCKET BOOKS

New York   London   Toronto   Sydney   New Delhi   Arethusa

Pocket Books
A Division of Simon & Schuster, Inc.
1230 Avenue of the Americas
New York, NY 10020

This book is a work of fiction. Any references to historical events, real people, or real places are used fictitiously. Other names, characters, places, and events are products of the author's imagination, and any resemblance to actual events or places or persons, living or dead, is entirely coincidental.

First Pocket Books paperback edition August 2014

POCKET and colophon are registered trademarks of Simon & Schuster, Inc.

For information about special discounts for bulk purchases, please contact Simon & Schuster Special Sales at 1-866-506-1949 or business@simonandschuster.com.

The Simon & Schuster Speakers Bureau can bring authors to your live event. For more information or to book an event, contact the Simon & Schuster Speakers Bureau at 1-866-248-3049 or visit our website at www.simonspeakers.com.

Cover art and design by Rob Caswell

Manufactured in the United States of America

10 9 8 7 6 5 4 3 2 1

ISBN 978-1-4767-5307-2
ISBN 978-1-4767-5312-6 (ebook)

Dedicated to the memory of actor
Michael "Kang" Ansara

Historian's Note

This story takes place in August 2269, a couple of months after the *Starship Enterprise* returns from a rescue mission at Camus II ("Turnabout Intruder") and approximately six months after the destruction of Starbase 47 (*Star Trek Vanguard: Storming Heaven*).

Whom the gods love dies young.
—Menander, Greek dramatist (341–290 B.C.)

1

Gazing into the eyes of her infant daughter, Nimur almost forgot for a moment that calamity was stalking her. The baby girl gazed up at Nimur with innocent delight, her golden eyes opened wide to drink in a world whose every detail was new to her. Nimur stroked her hand over the downy silver fuzz that covered her newborn's teal-colored scalp, then traced the paths of pale yellow spots that ringed the girl's ears and met at the nape of her neck before continuing down the center of her tiny back—the same coloration and pattern shared by all Tomol.

Kerlo, the girl's father, placed his hands on Nimur's shoulders. "She needs a name."

Nimur craned her head back to smile at her mate. "I was thinking of 'Tahna.'"

Her suggestion conjured a bittersweet smile from Kerlo; it had been the name of one of their dear friends who recently had been claimed by the Cleansing. "If you like, yes." He sat down beside Nimur and tickled the baby's tummy and the bottoms of her plump feet. Tahna squeaked and cooed, then flailed her tiny limbs as a broad smile lit her face. A grim cast overtook his lean, handsome face. "Have you thought about who we'll name as—"

"I don't want to talk about it yet." A glare from Nimur gave Kerlo pause.

It took him a moment to regroup. "We can't put it off."

"Why not?"

"Because we don't have much time left—either of us."

It was too painful for Nimur to face head-on. She had always known this day would come, that this was the cruel shape of her life, as it was for all Tomol. So had it been for countless generations, all but preordained, stretching back to the time of the Arrival.

"I only just birthed her, Kerlo. I can't give her up yet."

"No one says you have to. But we need to choose her Guardians." Kerlo circled around Nimur and kneeled in front of her. He rested his hands upon her knees, a gentle and comforting gesture. "It took us so long to have a child, Nimur. Almost too long. We can't afford to wait any more. We need to make a decision."

Nimur hugged her infant gently to her chest, then rocked slowly forward and back. The selfish part of her wanted to spend every waking moment reveling in her beautiful child, and in her wildest fantasies she imagined being able to watch Tahna grow up and become independent. But that was not the way of things. That was a dream born of delusion, a specter of false hope.

She kissed the baby's head. "What about Chimi and Tayno? They'd take care of her."

Kerlo was noncommittal. "I don't know them. But if you trust them, so do I."

A twisting sickness churned in Nimur's gut. Deciding to whom she and Kerlo would give up their precious child, the last proof they had ever lived, made her ill. Despite ages of tradition, it felt like a crime against nature, against her very essence, to surrender to such a demand. All she could do was salve her conscience with empty declarations of hope.

"They'll be kind to her, I think." A foolish optimism sprang up inside her. "Should we try to have another?"

The mere proposition made Kerlo blanch. "At our age? Nimur, we've both passed our seventeenth sun-turn. Conceiving new life at our age is forbidden."

"*At our age?* Kerlo, look at us! We're better and stronger than we've ever been!"

He shook his head in stern refusal. "You know the law as well as I do."

"The law, the law, *the law!* Nothing but words scratched on a rock!" She clutched his arm and squeezed it. "You and I are real! Our lives"—she nodded at Tahna—"*her* life, is real."

"So are the lives of everyone else we know." Kerlo slowly lifted his hand and pressed his jade-colored palm to Nimur's face. "Think of the Endless, the ones who defied the Wardens. Remember how much pain they caused? Do you want to do that to everyone we care about?"

Nimur closed her eyes. Shutting out the world around her was easier than facing a future in which she had no place. "Can we talk about something else?"

Kerlo stood and paced around their hut, which they had inherited from a long line of Tomol who had come and gone before them. "We need to get ready for next year's crop rotation. And not a moment too soon, if you ask me. The north field needs a fallow season. But what I'm really worried about is irrigation. Last year was the driest I've ever seen, and the scribes say it was one of the driest on record. If we don't get some decent rainfall next spring, I don't think the tubers will make it to harvest season. We might have to pull them in the summer before—"

His voiced faded over the last few words, then he fell silent.

The sudden gulf of quiet was split by Tahna's frightened wailing.

Nimur clutched the infant closer in a futile attempt to comfort her, but the maternal gesture only made the baby's cries louder and more shrill.

Kerlo plucked the infant from Nimur's hands and retreated across the room, then edged backward through the doorway to the bedroom they shared. He made no sound, but his face was marked by the same brand of horror that split the air in Tahna's panicked shrieks.

"What is it? What's happening?" Nimur's questions were acts of denial, a refusal to accept what she had long known to be inevitable. Kerlo grabbed up a walking stick of jungle reed and brandished it like a weapon. Still, Nimur refused to believe that this moment, whose arrival she had dreaded most of her life, was at last upon her.

She turned toward a crude mirror propped up in the corner and saw the horrible truth.

Her eyes burned with the crimson fire of the Change.

It was the destiny of all Tomol, if they lived past their seventeenth sun-turn. None escaped the Change. It came on without warning and, within a single arc of Arethusa's twin moons, turned all whom it afflicted into fiends of flame and suffering. No prayer, no sacrifice, no offering could spare a Tomol from its baleful touch—and now it had laid its burning hand upon Nimur.

She fled from the hut and she ran, without direction or destination, into the sultry embrace of the jungle. Her feet followed familiar trails—around the great menhirs of the first Tomol, past the sacred Caves of the Shepherds, and over the Peak of Shadows. Thick foliage snapped as she sprinted through it, breaking each leafy embrace with a twist of her body. The erratic patter of her footfalls was lost beneath her frantic tides of breathing and heaving sobs of panic. She crested the steep-faced cliff and fell to her knees on a rocky ledge.

Rage coursed through her. *Why? Why do our lives have to end when they've only just begun?* She hid her face in her hands as she wept. There was no path left to her now but the Cleansing, a willful descent into the ancient blue fire. She would be expected to give up her only child, her future, her hopes and dreams . . . her life. All to satisfy a law no one could overrule.

A defiant streak inside her compelled her to deny the high priestess and her Wardens the satisfaction of condemning her to the holy flames. *I could leap from here and dash myself on the rocks,* she told herself. She stared down over the edge, at the angry sea tearing itself across jagged stones where the cliff's base met the water, and she knew she could never do it.

The sea beckoned, but Nimur knew that no matter how strongly she felt the ocean's call, her path lay in the Well of Flames. Every instinct she possessed told her that her daughter needed her alive—but every lesson she had ever been taught told her the hour of her death was at hand.

2

Senior Chief Petty Officer Razka waved a slender, web-fingered hand at the glistening cocoon that stretched from deck to overhead in the corner. "You can't tell me this is regulation."

It was a fair statement. If pressed, Lieutenant Commander Vanessa Theriault would have to concede the ship's lead field scout had a point. The svelte, red-haired first officer of the Starfleet long-range scout vessel *Sagittarius* leaned at a slight angle to look past Razka at the freshly spun shell of silk. All she could muster was an awkward shrug. "It's . . . *different*."

A low hiss signaled the lanky Saurian's displeasure with Theriault's assessment. "Spoken like someone who no longer shares quarters." He had been assigned to Compartment 10 with the ship's two newest crewmembers: an Arkenite science officer, Lieutenant Sengar Hesh, and a Kaferian helm officer, Ensign Nizsk. It was the latter who had caused the Saurian noncom such dismay. Despite his seniority as a member of the ship's crew, in this instance Razka had the misfortune of being the lowest-ranked occupant of the berthing space, and therefore had the fewest options. He crossed his scaly arms. "What if I awaken tomorrow in a tomb of silk?"

Theriault skewered Razka with a scowl of reproach.

"Raz, you know Kaferians don't eat flesh. Their diet consists almost entirely of fruit sugars."

His vertically slit eyelids blinked slowly, an affectation Theriault recognized as a sign of distrust. "So they say. But on my world, anything that spins a web should be feared."

"That's not a web, it's a cocoon. Or, to be more precise, a hibernation sac."

"I see no significant difference."

"The former is for capturing prey. Nizsk uses that for a sleeping bag." Theriault suppressed her growing frustration with the discussion. "Look, I'm telling you: It's harmless."

The scout folded his elegant hands behind his back and leaned down, close to the Martian-born human woman's face. "Then perhaps she could move into your quarters."

"That's not happening."

"I see no reason for you to refuse."

"I'm the XO. That's all the reason I need." She poked her index finger against Razka's narrow but rock-hard chest and nudged him backward, out of her personal space, with firm but gentle pressure. "You've never been squeamish before. Do insectoids creep you out *that* much?"

He motioned for Theriault to step inside ahead of him. "Go wake her up."

"Excuse me?"

He gestured at the massive cocoon suspended in the corner. "If you wish to discover the root of my objection to sharing my quarters with the ensign . . . I invite you to rouse her."

It was an odd challenge, one that sparked Theriault's curiosity. Her admittedly limited knowledge of Kaferians told her there should be nothing to fear, but a more primitive node of her psyche kicked into gear upon hearing Razka's suggestion. It sounded like a trap, and that got her blood pumping and her adrenaline flowing. Regardless, it would be unbecoming a first officer to shrink from the dare of a noncommissioned officer. She edged past Razka. "All right, then."

The Saurian followed her inside, but he lingered at least a few paces behind the trim young woman. Every quality of hesitation, every reservation telegraphed by his body language, implied that he knew something she didn't about what was to come. She eyed him with suspicion, then stepped up to the cocoon and listened for any sign of activity from within. This was Nizsk's scheduled rest cycle. As Theriault suspected, all was quiet inside the silken shell.

She took a breath and made two gingerly taps on part of the cocoon that had dried to form a chitinous and slightly tacky patch. Within seconds there came a scratching sound from inside the cocoon, and then a fracture split the tall, cigar-shaped sac from base to tip. Two thick grayish green claws poked through the split at chest level and pried the cocoon open.

As the sac was cleaved in twain by Nizsk's emergence, a torrent of pungent, gelatinous goop spilled out of the cocoon. Razka backpedaled ahead of the nose-wrinkling slime, but all Theriault could do was watch it submerge her booted feet up to her ankles as it spread across the deck. The Kaferian helm officer and navigator stepped out of her hibernation sac glistening with the fluid, which dripped and oozed off her, adding to the mess underfoot.

Mandibles slowly flexing, Nizsk turned to face Theriault. The Kaferian's native language, which to human ears was an impossibly fast series of clicks with barely any variance in pitch, was instantly parsed by the universal translator Nizsk wore around her neck. The device rendered her words in a pleasant, rich feminine voice. "Yes, sir?"

Theriault lifted one foot from the sea of goop. It pulled free with a disgusting squelch of broken suction. "Ensign, what is this that just poured out of your sleep sac?"

"Regenerative jelly, Commander. It repairs damage to my exoskeleton, keeps the plates and connective ligaments supple, and purges bacteria and contaminants from my spiracles."

The first officer eased her foot back down with a soft squish. "And does this happen every time you retire for a sleep cycle?"

"Yes, sir. It's an involuntary function of my exocrine system."

"I see." A slow nod was followed by a reluctant turn to face Razka. "My apologies, Chief. There was nothing about this in her personnel file."

Razka lurked just outside the open doorway, whose slightly raised lip for the sliding door's guide track was all that held back the leading edge of the slime flood. "Apologies do not interest me, Commander. I should not have to trudge through these secretions to reach my bunk—even if they are the product of an officer's glands."

"Fair enough."

Nizsk's translator conveyed a tone of deep regret. "Forgive me, both of you. I did not realize I had imposed such an inconvenience. I have never been asked to share quarters before."

Theriault combed her fingers through her hair while she considered the situation. "The bad news is, this is a really small ship. We have nowhere else to put you."

Razka hissed. "You could give her your—"

"Hush." The first officer turned back toward Nizsk. "We can't put you in the cargo bay, since we sometimes have to depressurize it. Besides, we need all the storage space we can get on this boat." She looked back at Razka. "Any other complaints I need to be aware of?"

He shook his head. "No. Just this."

"Fine." She slogged out of the muck-filled compartment. "I'll have the master chief put a vacuum-powered drain in the deck by her cocoon."

As she passed the lead scout, he asked, "And what of that repugnant smell?"

"Beg some incense off Taryl, or learn to use a mop." She slapped the tall reptilian's shoulder as she stepped past him into the corridor. "I can't solve *all* your problems, Chief."

The silicon bearing had a mass of only a few dozen grams within the artificial gravity field inside the *Sagittarius,* but to the part of Lieutenant Sengar Hesh's mind that levitated the bearing by forcing subtle changes to its wrinkling of space-time, it felt like a ponderous weight.

Suspended by the force of his admittedly limited telekinesis, the metallic sphere rotated slowly. The Arkenite science officer sat cross-legged against the forward bulkhead of the *Archer*-class scout ship's cargo bay and smiled at the distortion of his reflection on the metallic sphere's brilliant surface. The image of his three-lobed head bent around its curved exterior, rendering his likeness in the stretched perspective of a funhouse mirror.

Telekinesis was an uncommon talent among Hesh's people, but even among the tiny fraction of Arkenites with psionic abilities, his own gift was considered minor, at best. He had never succeeded in manipulating anything with a mass greater than a hundred grams. Some of his classmates at Starfleet Academy had dismissed his special knack as naught but a "parlor trick." To him, however, it was a source of comfort, a way to focus and relax his mind all at once. Whenever he felt his mental acuity deteriorating, his nerves fraying, or his mood souring, he tried to make time to get away and recover his mental and emotional balance by training his mind on a singular feat of simple levitation.

A sharp gasp—the opening of a pressure hatch—interrupted the soft thrumming of the ship's engines and broke Hesh's concentration. His silicon bearing dropped to the deck with a dull clang and rolled away from him, toward the shaft of light beneath the now-open ladderway to the main deck. As he uncrossed his legs and stood to pursue the escaping ball bearing, someone's shadow eclipsed much of the light spilling down from the main deck. At first it was not clear who it might be, since all the personnel aboard the *Sagittarius* wore the same kind of olive-green coverall as their standard uniform. Each jumpsuit boasted a number of utility pockets on its torso and legs and bore the ship's insignia patch—a bow-and-arrow graphic—on the right shoulder. No rank insignia adorned the uniforms. Their only unique details were their respective crewmember's surname (or equivalent) stitched on a rectangular patch above the left breast.

Hesh caught up to the rolling silicon bearing and scooped it up. He turned and recognized the person on the ladder as engineer's mate Petty Officer Second Class Karen Cahow. The fair-haired, tomboyish young human woman flashed a warm smile at him as she bounded off the ladder. "Hey, Hesh. Whatcha doin' down here?"

"Just thinking." He pocketed the bearing with a casual pass of his hand over a pocket on the leg of his coverall. "I find the cargo bay more conducive to meditation than my quarters."

"Tell me about it." Cahow strolled past Hesh and opened a shipping container that was secured to both the deck and the port bulkhead. "I gave up trying to read in my bunk between shifts. Every time I turn around, the doc's spritzing everything in her war against germs, or Taryl's humming some song she's got stuck in her head."

Hesh nodded in sympathy. "I suspect that would test one's patience."

"The worst part is, Taryl couldn't carry a tune if you put a handle on it. I mean, that girl is tone-deaf. My worst nightmare would be hearing her try to sing a shower duet with Threx." Cahow reached deep inside the reinforced polymer crate and rooted around with casual abandon. The resulting clamor pained Hesh's pointed ears, which were even longer and more sensitive than those of a Vulcan. Cahow emerged from the crate with a high-tech widget clutched in one fist and closed the bin with her free hand. "So, when I need to get away, I usually tuck in over there"—she gestured aft with the widget—"by the plasma conduit. Warmest spot on the deck. Plus it lets me see anyone coming down the ladder before they see me."

"Most clever."

"So. Whatcha been thinkin' about?"

"Pardon me?"

She narrowed her eyes and kinked one brow into a suspicious arch. "You've been down here for a while. Hide much longer and Theriault's gonna send out a search party for you."

He recoiled in offense. "I am not *hiding*. And let me remind you that you're speaking to an officer." A deep breath restored a measure of his composure. "But even if our ranks were the same, my private ruminations are just that—*private*."

Cahow raised her hands against his rebuke. "Whoa, sorry if I crossed a line, sir. It's just that, well, this is a really small boat. We don't usually pay much attention to things like rank."

Suddenly self-conscious, Hesh looked away from Cahow and adjusted his *anlac'ven*, a lightweight headset with two slender protrusions that flanked his face and tapered inward toward his prominently jutting chin. The device helped Arkenites retain their balance in non-aquatic environments; most of their civilization on Arken II existed on ocean platforms, and the Arkenite inner ear had evolved to feel at home riding the rise and fall of waves in the open sea.

The young petty officer reached out and placed a hand on Hesh's shoulder. "If I'm prying again, I apologize, but . . . are you okay?"

He nodded. "I am. For the most part, at any rate." He considered how much was appropriate to confide to a subordinate, especially one with whom he had served for only a few weeks. "I think the best description for what I am feeling is 'homesick.'"

"We all get that way from time to time. When I first enlisted, I missed home like crazy."

Her frankness inspired him to share a bit more. "For an Arkenite, the separation is even more painful. It is not merely the absence of familiar people and places that pains me—it is being without my *sia lenthar*." He saw her brow furrow in confusion, so he elaborated. "My bond-group. The *sia lenthar* is the fundamental social unit of Arkenite culture."

"Like a tribe?"

"In a sense, but larger and more diverse. A *sia lenthar* earns esteem through diversity. The earliest ones were very homogenous; they tended to comprise many individuals of the same profession, such as hunters, agrarians, or artisans. But as different groups merged, or as members of some groups married into others, the knowledge and experience of the various packs became dispersed throughout the world. Today, the larger or more unusual the membership of a *sia lenthar,* the greater the pride its members feel. Mine, the Taldan *sia lenthar,* counts many of the most esteemed artists, scientists, and philosophers among its numbers."

"Sounds like a cool way to organize a society."

"It has its benefits." Courtesy mandated he reciprocate her interest. "If I might inquire, what world do you call home?"

She grinned. "Nowhere and everywhere. I'm a child of the stars—born and raised on starships. Except for boot camp, I even did most of my Starfleet basic training on starships."

"So you have no native culture?"

Cahow looked up and around. "This is it, sir. Space is my home, and Starfleet's my tribe." A mischievous smile played across her face. "Mind if I dole out a bit of advice?"

"If you must."

"If your idea of a great *sia lenthar* is something big, diverse, and full of uniquely talented individuals, you could do a lot worse than Starfleet—and the *Sagittarius*." She slapped his back as she stepped around him and headed for the ladder. "There's an old Earth saying: 'Home is where the heart is.'" She set her free hand on the ladder and paused. "Think of this ship as home, and us as your kin, and you'll never be homesick." Counsel dispensed, she tucked the widget into a leg pocket on her coverall and started climbing.

Hesh had never considered the possibility that aliens might be accepted as members of a *sia lenthar,* despite the similarities between the Federation's ethos and that of the Arkenites. Would his native *sia lenthar* accept one composed of off-worlders? Could he?

Watching Cahow ascend, he realized she had given him something new to think about.

• • •

"Helm, assume standard orbit." Captain Clark Terrell leaned forward in the command chair and cupped his left hand over his right fist. The image of the jade-green ringed planet on the main viewscreen grew slowly larger as the *Sagittarius* cruised toward it. At the helm, Ensign Nizsk gradually slowed the ship from full impulse to semi-geosynchronous orbital velocity. Terrell swiveled his chair right, toward the new Arkenite science officer, whose three-lobed head was limned with blue light from the sensor hood. "Sensor readings, Lieutenant?"

Hesh answered without lifting his eyes from the azure glow. "Nereus Two is a Class-M world. Equatorial diameter, eleven thousand nine hundred seventy-five point twelve kilometers. Axial tilt, nineteen point four one degrees. Gravity is approximately point nine one *g*. The surface is eighty-seven percent water, a freshwater ocean with a median depth of less than two kilometers. The majority of its landmass consists of a tropical archipelago of volcanic islands."

Theriault sidled up to Hesh and peeked over his shoulder at the sensor readout. "Are you picking up any signs of artificial power generation? Or broadcast signals?"

"Negative, Commander." Hesh moved over to give the first officer a clearer look at the hooded display. "Our instruments detect abundant life readings, but no sign of technology."

"Abundant life is right," Terrell said. "I've never seen a planet so green."

Lieutenant Commander Sorak, the one-hundred-twenty-year-old Vulcan third-in-command, who months earlier had switched his billet from lead scout to senior tactical officer, rotated his chair toward Terrell. "The planet's chromatic uniformity appears to be the result of robust aquatic vegetation, Captain."

"You don't say."

The exchange of dry sarcasm for dry detail drew a smile from Theriault. "If you like seaweed salad, you've come to the right place."

"I'm not so sure we have." Terrell was confounded by the sensor readings. "Didn't the long-range probes indicate high-level energy signatures on this planet?"

Theriault moved to an auxiliary console and keyed commands into the library computer. Seconds later, the display above her head scrolled with information. "Yes, sir. But those readings were taken from a significant distance. There might have been interference or a subspatial lensing effect that triggered a false positive."

Hesh shot a nervous look at Theriault and turned toward the captain. "Sir, I reviewed the scans that led us here. I saw no evidence of interference or subspatial lensing. With all respect to Lieutenant Commander Theriault, I am certain those initial readings were accurate."

Terrell wanted to believe Hesh. "All right, Lieutenant. If the earlier readings were correct, where are those power signatures and subspace communication signals now?"

The young Arkenite frowned. "I don't know, sir." He turned his solid-green eyes toward the main viewscreen, now dominated by the emerald-hued world's northern hemisphere. "But I have enough confidence in the original scans to recommend that we set down to conduct a planetary survey."

Theriault turned and stepped toward Terrell. "Sir, we

need to watch our step if we land on the surface. Sensors confirm there's a small humanoid population on the largest island."

That sparked Terrell's curiosity. "Are they intelligent?"

"No idea," Theriault said. "But judging from the lack of industrial pollution or radio signals, I think we ought to consider the Prime Directive to be in full effect."

It was sound advice. "Agreed. Sorak, where can we set down safely?"

The Vulcan reviewed a scan of the planet's primary island chain. "There is an uninhabited isle located approximately fifteen kilometers west of the main island. It is far enough away that if we approach it from the west, we can land without risk of being seen."

Theriault seemed satisfied with that recommendation. "That works. Then we can use one of the new amphibious rovers to make an underwater approach to the main island."

"Be careful, Number One. Even a seemingly primitive culture can be dangerous—especially when you're a stranger on *their* turf."

She acknowledged his warning with a pointed finger. "Will do."

He trained his cautionary stare on Hesh. "As for you, Lieutenant: Resist the urge to study every last speck of life you find. Our chief objective is to confirm or falsify the power readings our probes detected. Don't make contact with the natives if you can avoid it."

"Understood, sir."

Terrell opened a channel to the engineering deck with a jab of one dark-brown thumb on a red button built into his command chair's armrest. "Bridge to engineering."

The chief engineer's voice replied through the overhead speaker. *"Go ahead, bridge."*

"Master Chief, be advised we're making planetfall in five minutes."

"Go for it. We're tight as a drum."

"Glad to hear it. How long to rig Vixen for amphibious ops?"

"Thirty minutes by the book. Ten if you need a miracle."

"Save the miracles for a rainy day, Master Chief. Thirty's fine."

"Roger that."

"Bridge out." Terrell closed the channel. "Mister Sorak, relay the landing coordinates to the helm. Ensign Nizsk, take us in, slow and easy." Brimming with hopeful anticipation, Terrell leaned forward until he was literally on the edge of his seat. "Let's see what's down there."

3

"Please, Ysan, there must be a way. I'm not asking for much, just another turn of the red moon."

Nimur watched Ysan's face, desperate for any sign of mercy. The high priestess, who was only a few red-moon-turns younger than she, shook her head. "The Shepherds' warning has always been clear. As soon as the Change comes, the Cleansing must follow within three days."

"But I feel the same! I haven't changed."

"You will." Ysan was sad. There was pity in her eyes. Like all Tomol, she had seen this too many times before. "Ignoring the Change is dangerous—for you as well as the rest of us."

Filled with a toxic storm of rage and fear, Nimur paced. "I've read the glyphs, too. The Shepherds said the Cleansing had to follow within *nine* days."

Ysan shifted beneath the weight of her vestments, an ancient cloak of brilliant feathers woven with bark-thread. It was a majestic-looking garment, a riot of color that commanded attention. Pulo, a former high priestess Nimur had known, had once confided that the cloak was extremely uncomfortable; its woven mesh was rough and scratched the skin, and in the sultry heat of Suba's lush jungle and the blaze of its sun-splashed beaches, it was oppressively warm. The priestess frowned. "The law has been amended over time to suit our needs."

"Whose needs?"

"The people's." Ysan reached out and clasped Nimur's hand. "All our lives depend on this shared responsibility. We owe it to one another."

The argument, which for so long Nimur had accepted as gospel, rang hollow now. She pulled her hand free of Ysan's. "All I want is a few days. I can resist the Change that long."

"Maybe you can. Maybe you can't. If I grant you this time, and you've guessed wrong, there's no telling how many would pay the price in blood and stone. I can't take that chance."

Why was there no reasoning with her? When did the world become so inflexible? Or its laws so absolute? Nimur forced herself to stop pacing and drew a calming breath. "Ysan, there must be some other way. The Shepherds left us so many glyphs that we've never translated. I'm sure there's a solution there, a secret locked in the stone, if only we—"

"You think we've never looked for it?" Ysan glared at Nimur as if she were an insolent child. "Countless lives have been spent trying to unravel the Shepherds' riddles, Nimur. If there is a cure for the Change trapped in the stone, more generations than we can count have gone to their Cleansings without finding it. The hard truth is that there is no way to slow the Change—it's only gotten faster over time. And there is no cure." She stood from her cushioned pallet to face Nimur. "You need to stop chasing fantasies, Nimur. It's time to make yourself ready."

Nimur's anger burned a bit hotter. "You mean it's time I surrendered."

Ysan shrugged one shoulder. "If you can. To be honest, I've always been afraid of what would happen when this day came. You've always been a rebel, ever since we were young."

"And you were always the dutiful child." Nimur turned her back on Ysan and looked out the open doorway of her hut. "How would you see me meet my end?"

"With a measure of dignity, perhaps." The priestess stood beside her in the doorway. "Have you and Kerlo chosen your daughter's Guardians yet?"

She shook her head. "We can't decide." A tear shed half in anger rolled down her cheek, and she palmed it away. "Or maybe I just don't want to."

"Who are you considering? It's a sacred charge, Nimur, not one to be—"

"I'm aware of that." She was insulted that Ysan thought it necessary to remind her of how vital it was for her and Kerlo to name Tahna's Guardians. Because most Tomol went to their Cleansings after only seventeen sun-turns, while their offspring were still quite young or, in some cases, newly born, it was necessary to choose a pair of younger Tomol, typically around the age of ten to eleven sun-turns, to assume parental responsibilities for one's children until they became old enough to tend to their own basic needs. Inevitably, when the Guardians were old enough, they produced offspring of their own—at which point, their adopted charges often assumed the mantles of obligation as Guardians for some older Tomol's orphans.

"If I have to choose someone to take care of Tahna," Nimur said after reining in her temper, "I guess I might ask Chimi and Tayno."

"They would be good choices, I think. How does Kerlo feel about them?"

"He likes them." It was a white lie; Kerlo had met the youths only in passing. He knew next to nothing about them, but he had no reason to dislike them. He was willing to consent to them as Guardians for Tahna based on nothing more than Nimur's suggestion. With the approval of the priestess, the matter was all but settled. "How soon can we perform the Bonding?"

"If Chimi and Tayno are willing, we can do it tomorrow."

A sad nod. "Yes, all right." Nimur felt as if she were pantomiming her acquiescence, playing a part whose lines she knew all too well despite not believing a single word she said.

Ysan laid a hand on Nimur's shoulder and ushered her out of her hut. "Good. Now, go home and talk this over with Kerlo, then get some sleep. Tomorrow, I'll come with you both to talk to Chimi and Tayno and secure their pledge." The priestess held Nimur and gently turned her around to face her. "This is the right thing, Nimur. The best thing. I promise."

In the distance, barely visible through the endless green of the jungle, Nimur saw the glow of the Well of Flames, an azure inferno that never dimmed, never ceased, and waited to devour all Tomol who lived, or who would ever draw breath. Seeing its blue truth, she knew in her heart how much a priestess's promises were worth. She slipped free of Ysan's hand again.

"Thank you, Holy Sister. Good night."

• • •

By the time Nimur returned to her own hut, her fury had swelled into a rising tide. Her head was hot, as if with a fever, but she didn't feel light-headed or ill: She was energized.

She entered to find Kerlo sitting cross-legged on the floor in front of the baby's cradle. His spear was a bridge across his knees; he rested one hand on its shaft. On his belt he wore his sling and lizard-skin pouch of sharpened stones. Strapped to his left ankle was his onyx hunting knife. His torso was clothed in layers of old leather, a collage of weathered pieces passed down for generations as the garb of a hunter. His armor and weapons were humble compared to those of the Wardens, but they were well cared for and had been tested and proved many times over.

He watched Nimur enter and tightened his grip on the spear until his knuckles blanched. "Did Ysan approve of Chimi and Tayno?"

"She did." She stared at his bone-white hold on the spear, then looked him in the eye. "Is something wrong?" He didn't answer, so she asked another question. "What are you afraid of?"

"I'm just following Ysan's advice."

"She advised you to hunt small game inside our hut?" He refused to take the bait—not a smile or a laugh, not even a sour look. Just his stone-faced vigilance. She tried to step around him. He swung his spear into her path with alarming speed. She stepped back, irritated. "What's the matter with you? All I want to do is nurse her. She must be hungry by now."

His spear was unwavering. "Keora nursed her already."

"Keora?" Primal urges quickened Nimur's pulse. "Why was *she* nursing *my* baby?"

"It's for Tahna's protection. You know that, Nimur. You nursed Jenica's baby boy when she Changed, remember?" There was a pleading note in Kerlo's voice. Nimur sensed he was afraid he would have to fight her, as if she were nothing more than some mindless, wild animal that had blundered into their home. He shooed her with the spear. "Don't try to touch her."

It was madness. Yesterday he had loved her. They had seen the universe in each other's eyes and made a perfect child together. Now he treated her like a sworn enemy. "Kerlo, what are you doing? I'm still me. Can't you tell I'm the same person I was yesterday?"

He shook his head. "Your eyes are burning. It's only a matter of time now."

More nervous energy welled up inside her, adding to an excruciating sensation of pressure for which she had no means of release. Impelled into motion by her own anxiety, she stalked back and forth in front of Kerlo while wringing her hands. "This makes no sense! Can't you see that? Why would we turn into monsters just when we reach the peak of our abilities? No other creature in nature does that. Do they? Name one. I can't think of any. Not on land, or in the air, or in the sea. So why would we be any different?"

Kerlo parroted the sacred words of the Shepherds. "We are in this world but not of it."

"How do we know that? Because someone told us so? Did any of us every try to find out the truth for ourselves? Did any of us ever think to ask?"

She lunged toward Tahna, hoping to slip past Kerlo, but he swung the spear and blocked her path again. She backed off as he sprang to his feet.

No matter where she moved, he kept the spearhead pointed at her throat. "Don't try that again. The part of me that still loves you doesn't want to hurt you."

"No, you just want me to throw myself into the fire."

"The Cleansing awaits us all."

"Maybe I want more." He recoiled as she said that, so she pressed on. "What if the Change isn't something to be feared? What if we were lied to, Kerlo? What if this is all some stupid mistake? Why not let someone finish the Change, just to be sure?"

His stare narrowed, and he kept his spear on-target. "Many have tried, Nimur. We've all been to the Valley of the Endless. There are only three ways that we end: blood, fire, or stone."

"Those could be statues. Crude works of art left to melt in the rain. You've never seen anyone die by stone. None of us have. No one for a hundred generations, if ever."

"Something to be thankful for."

"No, something that should make us ask why we believe whatever we're told." She untied the knot at the shoulder of her dress and showed a bit of her chest to Kerlo. His attention snared, she affected her most alluring tone of voice and inched closer to him. "Look past the Change, Kerlo. It's still me. The one you loved. The one who loves you. All I want—"

She snared the shaft of the spear and tried to wrest it from his grasp. He lunged forward and twisted the weapon, lifting the back end of the shaft. It hit Nimur in the side of her face, and her vision doubled for a few seconds. She let go of the spear and fell to the ground, wailing and pressing her hands to the bloody wound. By the time she opened her eyes, Kerlo had scooped up Tahna and fled the hut. He vanished into the arms of the night as she turned to follow the sound of his footsteps.

Nimur let out a primal howl of pain and wrath as she staggered to her feet. Her whole life was being ripped from her—her future and her past, her family and friends. All her choices were being made for her now. Even so simple a privilege as mothering her infant was to be denied, all because some eldritch power had awakened inside her, some energy without a name. For this, she was expected to step over the edge of oblivion and cast herself into the flames.

She tore the decorations from the walls of her hut and flung them outside, into the darkness. Screaming and crying, she ripped apart her other dresses, all of Kerlo's clothing, the bedsheets—anything made of fabric. What she couldn't shred with her hands she cut apart with stone cooking knives. The bowls and jewelry she crushed underfoot. For minutes that felt like forever she was a whirlwind of destruction, laying waste to all she had ever made or owned.

When her indignation was spent, and its borrowed strength abandoned her, she crumpled to the dirt floor inside the hut, surrounded by the broken pieces of her life, and wept like a child.

There was nothing left for her now but the fire.

4

A low bump and a brief tremor reverberated through the interior of the *Sagittarius* as the ship set down on the planet's surface. Theriault felt the main ladder's rungs vibrate as she descended it to the cargo deck, which doubled as a garage for its rovers. The small, unarmed vehicles were used most often for planetside exploration. Because the *Archer*-class scout had only a single transporter pad, its landing parties tended to rely on the rovers for traversing short distances rather than asking the ship for site-to-site beaming. Officially, rovers were designated for moving personnel, equipment, supplies, and collected samples. Unofficially, they were also fun to drive.

Theriault stepped off the ladder to find three of the ship's four engineers huddled around the rover they'd dubbed Vixen. It and its twin, Blitzen, had been added to the *Sagittarius*'s equipment loadout during its recent repairs at Earth Spacedock. They had replaced its original rovers, Roxy and Ziggy, which had been lost in action several months earlier, during a classified mission to an ancient statite situated inside the emission axis of a pulsar known as Eremar.

Noting the concerned looks on the engineers' faces, Theriault decided a gentle inquiry was in order. "S'up, guys?"

"Just a few last-second tweaks," said Master Chief Petty Officer Mike "Mad Man" Ilucci. The chief engineer was shorter than average for a human male, thicker in the middle than Starfleet regulations preferred, and as scruffy as a junkyard dog. He activated a sonic tool that filled the air with its oscillating sing-song whining. "Vixen needs a bit of fine-tuning."

Crewman Torvin, the youngest member of the ship's crew, rolled out from underneath the amphibious rover. The Tiburonian's large, finlike ears were daubed with grime, and his olive coverall was stained with industrial chemicals. "Ventral water seals fixed, Master Chief."

The first officer accused Ilucci with a single cocked eyebrow. "The water seals?"

The chief engineer's face settled into a put-upon scowl as he looked around for someone else to take the blame. Torvin wisely rolled back underneath the rover. Facing Ilucci from the other side of Vixen, his thick-bearded, long-haired Denobulan hulk of a senior engineer's mate, Petty Officer First Class Salagho Threx, held up his hands. "Don't look at me, Master Chief."

Behind Theriault, the rest of the landing party descended the ladder, one at a time. Science officer Hesh arrived first, followed by nurse Lieutenant Nguyen Tan Bao and Lieutenant Faro Dastin, who had joined the crew a year earlier as its tactical officer, but now served as a field scout. The men gathered behind Theriault while the chief engineer hemmed and hawed.

The XO crossed her arms. "Master Chief? What's wrong with the rover?"

"Nothing. Well, not anymore." He surrendered the

truth. "We were doing a routine pre-mission check, and we found out the water seals weren't as tight as they should be."

Theriault eyed the rover. "Meaning what, exactly?"

When the chief engineer hesitated to answer, Threx spoke up. "The crew cabin would've flooded within twenty seconds of submersion."

The landing party exchanged anxious looks. Ilucci was quick to add, "But we fixed it."

Dastin grinned. "Well, okay, then. I'm just *brimming* with confidence now."

"Good thing I brushed up on my CPR techniques," Tan Bao said.

Hesh poked at the edges of the rover's open, gull-wing doors. "You brought them aboard in parts, yes? So, would you classify this as a design problem or an assembly problem?"

Ilucci suffered the snarky remarks with fading patience. Theriault threw him a rhetorical lifeline. "Ignore them, Master Chief. Just tell me this: Is the rover good to go?"

"Yeah, it'll get you there and back."

Threx averted his gaze as he rolled his eyes. "As long as you don't hit anything, get torpedoed, or break the windshield."

Ilucci shot a deadly look at his right-hand man. "Hey, ray of sunshine: Shut up."

Torvin scuttled back out from under the rover. "The MHD propulsors check out, Commander. Once Vixen's in the water, she'll be quick as lightning and quiet as space."

"Good to know, Tor. Thanks." The crewman's eagerness to please never failed to amuse Theriault. Magneto-hydrodynamic, or MHD, was hardly a new propulsion technology. It had been invented nearly three centuries earlier as a stealth technology for submersible naval vessels. Nonetheless, it was always a good idea to keep as low a profile as possible when venturing into uncertain situations, such as a potential first contact with an alien culture. The first officer turned to Dastin. "Do you need to brush up on the controls for aquatic operations?"

The young Trill shook his head. "No, I'm good to go."

"Okay. Final equipment check." Theriault faced Tan Bao. "Medical tricorder and medkit?" He nodded, so she turned toward Hesh. "Standard tricorder and sample collection vials?" Another silent confirmation. She checked her own pockets as she continued. "Everybody make sure you've got a communicator and a fully charged type-one phaser." The rest of the landing party followed her example and nodded their affirmations. "All right. Dastin's driving, and I've got shotgun. Let's pile in and move out." The others climbed inside Vixen while Theriault paused to give Ilucci a friendly pat on his arm. "Thanks for prepping our ride, Master Chief."

Despite his best effort to hold a gruff frown, a smile played at the corner of his mouth. "For you? Anytime." He glowered at Dastin. "Sure you want to let Mister Fabulous drive?"

"Why wouldn't I?"

"I saw him wreck two shuttles and a hoverbike on shore leave. The man's a menace."

"I don't think we have anything to worry about." Just then, Vixen's engine surged to life with a *vroom* so loud it made Theriault and the engineers wince. Torvin, whose Tiburonian eardrums were hypersensitive, yowled in pain as he covered his ears with both hands. Through the rover's windshield, Theriault saw Dastin laughing like a child with a new toy. Abashed, she faced Ilucci's trademark *I told you so* look. "Maybe you should leave a light on for us, Master Chief. Y'know—just in case."

"Will do." Ilucci walked over to the control panel for the cargo deck's ramp. Torvin and Threx moved to the other side of the deck, well out of Vixen's path.

Theriault got inside the rover, closed the passenger-side door, and double-checked that it was securely sealed. She gave Ilucci a thumbs-up. He returned the gesture and, with the pull of a lever, opened the ramp.

A sliver of light appeared near the overhead as the ramp angled downward, and then the gap widened to reveal the golden radiance of daylight. After a few seconds, Theriault's eyes adjusted to the brightness of natural sunlight, and she was able to appreciate the off-white sand of the beach, the viridescent waves of the sea, and a majestic blue yawn of sky on the horizon.

Ilucci windmilled his arm, signaling Dastin to move out. The field scout eased the rover into motion and steered it down the ramp onto the beach. Once they had cleared the ramp, he turned toward the crashing surf and slowed to a smooth stop. "Final systems check. Activating onboard navigation system." He keyed some buttons on the armrest between him and Theriault. A small screen set into the dash switched on and displayed a simple map over which was superimposed a digital compass and a range-to-target readout. "Navcomp checks out."

Theriault opened a comm channel to the *Sagittarius* while Dastin finished his routine review of the rover's other basic systems. "Vixen to *Sagittarius*. Do you copy?"

Captain Terrell answered. *"Roger, Vixen."*

"All systems are looking five-by-five. We're ready to head for the big island."

"Acknowledged. As soon as you dive, we'll head back to orbit. Just give a holler when you're ready to dust off and come home."

"Will do, sir."

"And Number One? Be careful out there."

"Roger that, sir. Vixen out." She closed the channel, checked the fastener on her seat's safety harness, then pointed her arm seaward. "Mister Dastin, all ahead flank. Dive!"

The Trill grinned and stepped on the accelerator. "Aye-aye, Skipper!"

Vixen plunged headlong into the breaking waves and sliced through them with ease. As the sea washed over the rover's canopy, Theriault caught a blurred glimpse of the *Sagittarius*, already airborne and making a steep climb back toward space. Then all she saw was an eternity of emerald ocean and deeper-green shadows as Dastin piloted them away from shore into open water, on a heading for the planet's only populated island.

She peered down at the thriving underwater ecology that surrounded them. She was sure that Nereus II would be a marine biologist's dream come true—but all she could think about as she stared at the endless aquatic splendor was how quickly it would kill her if the engineers had missed any of the rover's faulty water seals during their hasty last-minute repairs.

And I call myself an optimist.

The wind was sweet with the perfumes of new blossoms, but Nimur was too bitter to savor them. All she wanted was to hold her child during the Bonding ritual, but neither Kerlo nor Ysan would permit it. Her only part in the ceremony, it seemed, was to parrot the words of the high priestess, who recited the ancient words from memory.

"As I prepare to Cleanse myself in the Eternal Fire of the Shepherds . . ."

"As I prepare to Cleanse myself in the Eternal Fire of the Shepherds," Nimur repeated.

"I name Chimi and Tayno as my child's Guardians, and I grant to them my sacred and irrevocable trust, in accordance with the Law of the Shepherds."

Nimur echoed the words of the priestess, but they felt like nothing more to her than hollow sounds, noises without meaning. As soon as the oath was spoken, Kerlo handed Tahna to the young pair of Guardians. Chimi cradled the infant in her arms, and then Tayno embraced them both, adding his support. Ysan accepted from her disciple Seta a bowl of vermillion paint that had been mixed from crushed berries and fired clay. The high priestess dipped her thumb into the paint and used it to draw glyphs of consecration on the foreheads of Tahna, Chimi, and Tayno. The three of them were Bonded. No matter what protests Nimur or Kerlo might make, Tahna was no longer their child; she belonged to her Guardians now.

Ysan touched Chimi's and Tayno's chins and spoke to them in a soft voice. "Go now, and make your home her home. Guide her, teach her, and protect her. As the Shepherds have willed."

"As the Shepherds have willed," the two youths said, and then they walked away, down the trail that led back to the village.

The high priestess returned to Nimur and stood in front of her. "It's time."

A dozen Wardens emerged from the jungle's shadows and formed a circle around the Well of Flames. Their arms and legs were bare, but their feet were shod in high-wrapped sandals, and their torsos were protected by ornate armor crafted from lightweight but nearly impenetrable stone, made in ages past by methods long since forgotten. Each Warden wore a unique headdress that evoked the image of a jungle creature: majestic birds of prey, terrifying reptiles, or fearsome beasts of claw and fang. Each mask was decorated with the appropriate details of feathers, scales, or fur. But the Wardens' true symbols were their weapons of office: the Lances of Fire. A Warden who held a Lance was protected as if by the invisible might of the Shepherds themselves and could unleash the Cleansing Fire anywhere, with only a single word.

Even though Nimur knew that beneath their ceremonial armor the Wardens were mere flesh and blood, just Tomol like her, she also knew better than to underestimate them. Only the strongest, fastest, and bravest Tomol were chosen to act as Wardens. Their commitment and loyalty were tested constantly, and a candidate who failed even a single trial of character was deemed unfit to serve as a defender of the faith and the people.

Two of the warriors flanked Nimur while Ysan and Seta met another couple who were surrendering their two tiny children to Guardians. Unable to witness another family's sundering, Nimur turned to face the Well of Flames. The blue crucible was just over a stone's throw away, but even at that distance its heat was intense enough to sting her face.

All paths lead to the fire. It was an old homily, one that priestesses had told to young Tomol since time immemorial. *This is the way of all flesh.*

A lifetime of indoctrination told her this was the natural order of life. She didn't want to shame herself, or Kerlo, or Tahna—but was disgrace truly worse than death? By what measure? *Was that just a lie someone made up to persuade us to go quietly to our doom?* She refused to accept that. All her life she had been taught that it was not just the fate of all Tomol to be Cleansed, it was their sacred duty, for the sake of all who lived, and all who would come after. But if the rationale was a lie, did it matter how many times it had been told to her? How could simple repetition transform a lie into the truth? And why was it forbidden even to ask the question? How could the priestesses know the answer to a question that was never asked?

Ysan returned to Nimur. In her left hand she held the bowl of crimson paint. She dipped her right thumb into the pigment and began inscribing glyphs onto Nimur's face. "These symbols of the Shepherds will protect you on your journey into the next world."

Nimur said nothing. Was she supposed to thank Ysan? As she watched the priestess cover her arms and the backs of her hands with the symbols of the Shepherds, all she wanted to do was run, flee down the road to the village, steal back her baby, and escape the island.

Shame and despair rooted her in place. There was nowhere to go; she knew that as well as everyone else did. Suba was a large island, but it had no place in which she could evade the Wardens for long, especially not if she meant to take Tahna with her. For a moment she entertained the delusion that she might try to reach one of Arethusa's other nearby islands. There were several that had been visited in generations past but had never been colonized, partly because none of them had proved as verdant or arable as Suba, and partly out of fear that Tomol living anywhere other than Suba might succumb to the Change before they could be Cleansed.

As soon as the notion of flight entered her head, she dismissed it. *I wouldn't survive a sea journey alone, and definitely not with Tahna. And even if we outran the Wardens, how would I find another island without a map? Or know which ones had food and clean water?*

As the priestess painted glyphs down Nimur's left leg, another phalanx of Wardens escorted six other Tomol, four males and two females, who also exhibited the fiery eyes that marked the onset of the Change. The six were already painted from crown to toe with the sacred glyphs. To Nimur's surprise, her fellow condemned looked serene, as if they not only accepted the inevitability of their predicament but in fact welcomed their imminent endings. She envied them their peace even as she resented them for it.

Soon, their families and friends would gather to say their farewells and pray to the Shepherds to guide the spirits of the Cleansed. Nimur wondered what she would say when her turn came to step into the Well of Flames. Would she beg for mercy? Shout curses? Impart some final gem of wisdom for which she would always be remembered? Or just whimper with fear and regret before diving into the midnight-blue inferno?

In a few hours the sun would set on Suba and on her life, and she would have her answer.

Navigating underwater, even at shallow depths, was one of the most disorientating tasks that Faro Dastin had ever been compelled to learn. By comparison, learning to fly shuttles in both atmosphere and low orbit during his years at Starfleet Academy had been easy for the young Trill. There was a freedom to flight in which he reveled, and despite the few minor similarities between aerospace and nautical piloting, the latter had always felt uncomfortable to him.

Because it's backward, he decided. In the air or in space, all the pressure was inside the vehicle, which made maneuvering through such environments as high altitude or vacuum feel effortless. Several dozen meters beneath the ocean's surface, however, there was already considerably more pressure on the ship and its crew than Dastin felt comfortable contemplating. Underwater, every action felt like a struggle against the elements.

He also disliked the limited visibility. Even in relatively clear coastal waters such as those between the islands of Nereus II, the refraction, scattering, and absorption of light from the surface made it difficult to accurately gauge distances. Ranges were easy to underestimate in exceptionally clear water and even easier to overestimate in turgid conditions; objects directly ahead might seem to move more slowly than those crossing one's field of vision.

For all those reasons, he had little choice but to navigate by instruments. It was tempting to look up and simply trust his eyes to show him the way, but whenever he compared his guess to the hard data from the sensors, his instincts proved unreliable. It was like flying in a thick fog, or through heavy cloud cover, or inside a thick gaseous anomaly; in those environments Dastin knew not to trust his inner ear's perception of direction, elevation, or velocity. But at least in those cases he wasn't being lured by an aquatic mirage.

He checked the readouts again, just as a precaution. Vixen's depth was twenty-seven point two meters, a bit deeper than Dastin had intended to go. The clinometer indicated he had unwittingly nudged the nose downward, easing them into a half-degree dive. A quick adjustment brought them back up to twenty-five meters, where he leveled their path. Then he glanced at the navcomp display and made some minor tweaks to keep them on a direct course for the big island.

Theriault leaned forward and squinted. "Dastin? What's that?"

"What's what?"

She pointed. "That wavy wall of dark green ahead of us."

"I think that's called 'seaweed,' sir."

Hesh leaned forward between the front seats. "Forgive me, but I believe that is actually a forest of kelp." He held up his tricorder, which gave off a high-pitched tone as he made a scan. "And it appears to be a particularly robust variety."

Dastin looked over his shoulder at Hesh. "Since when are you a marine biology expert?"

"Arkenites are a semi-aquatic species. Though we can work in terrestrial environments, we prefer to spend at least part of our time in—"

Dastin raised a hand. "Thanks, I get the point." The Trill scout shook his head at Theriault. "Nothing to worry about, sir. According to the navcomp, we're only a few kilometers from shore. We'll breeze through the seaweed and be on the beach in no time."

Hesh struck an anxious note. "I would strongly urge you to circumnavigate the kelp."

Dastin would have been happy just to ignore the Arkenite, but Theriault turned to hear what the man had to say. "Why, Hesh?"

"In my experience, kelp of that size and circumference tends to pose a hazard to aquatic navigation. It can snag on any protruding piece of a vehicle, and its fronds can clog intake valves such as those on our MHD. Also, kelp forests often serve as habitats for apex predators. While that might not be a concern for a large submersible vessel, a craft as small as this rover could sustain significant damage if attacked by a large enough ichthyoid, crustacean, or cephalopod."

The red-haired first officer arched an auburn eyebrow at Dastin. "Faro?"

"It's just seaweed." Outside the rover, the edge of the kelp forest loomed large. "Watch. I'll show you." He opened the throttle on the MHD and charged the rover through the first few meters of fronds. "We'll slice through these weeds like a knife through—"

Vixen slammed to an abrupt halt. Its nose pitched sharply downward, and then the vehicle listed hard to port. Dastin switched the MHD into reverse and opened the throttle. The rover jerked and shuddered. Multiple firings of the maneuvering thrusters rocked the amphibious vehicle slightly, but whatever had snared it was holding on with a vengeance.

Theriault folded her arms and affected a deceptively stoic mien. "You were saying?"

"I can get us out," he said, though he wasn't sure it was true. "Might take a few minutes."

"Take your time." She made a show of checking her neatly trimmed and unpolished fingernails. "It's not as if the rest of us have jobs to do."

In the backseat, Hesh continued scanning with his tricorder. "How very interesting! This species of kelp behaves like an aggressive creeping ivy, attaching itself to any—"

"Please stop talking," Dastin said.

"Don't listen to him," Theriault said. "Please tell us everything you can about the kelp."

"Belay that, Hesh. If I hear one more word about the kelp, I'll flood the cabin."

Hesh looked taken aback by the conflicting orders.

Tan Bao sighed. "I hate when Mommy and Daddy fight."

The Arkenite switched off his tricorder. "May I make a suggestion?" Theriault skewered Dastin with a pointed look, so the Trill gave Hesh his grudging nod of consent. "If I recall the schematics of this rover correctly, it should be possible to transmit a low-level electrical pulse through the outer chassis by decoupling the ground circuit on Bus B beneath the forward passenger-side floor panel, and then purging the MHD capacitor. Such a discharge should be more than sufficient to provoke the kelp into retracting and releasing its hold on us."

After a moment spent considering the idea, Dastin had to concede it was rather ingenious. However, he had no intention of admitting that to Hesh. He opted instead for verbal deflection. "When did you have time to study the rover's design schematics?"

"Last Thursday, during lunch."

Theriault opened the panel at her feet. "Let's get on with it." She decoupled the ground circuit in a matter of moments, then sat back. "Okay, Faro. Purge the capacitor."

He keyed in the purge command. Tiny forks of white static electricity jumped and danced across the exterior of the rover. Just as Hesh had predicted, the kelp let go of the rover, which bobbed for a few moments and then righted itself, once again free to navigate.

Dastin clapped his hands. "All right! Nice team effort!"

"It sure was," Theriault said. "You got us stuck, and Hesh got us out."

"That's not what you're gonna say in your report, are you?"

"We'll see. Set course for the second kelp on the right, and try to shut up till morning."

5

Vixen's battery-powered motor was whisper-quiet as the rover threaded its way free of the kelp forest and surfaced from beneath the waves. The crystal-clear view of the ocean floor gave way to the momentary blur of water sheeting across the windshield. It cleared quickly as the canopy's transparent coating of hydrophobic sealant repelled even the tiniest drops of moisture, which beaded and fled across the rover's curved nose. Theriault squinted against the sudden return to daylight untainted by the surreal filter of the sea. Her eyes adjusted quickly and took in the white-sand beach backed by a dense wall of verdant jungle beneath a violet dusk sky.

She nudged Dastin with her elbow. "There's a small gap over there. Is it big enough?"

He gave it a critical look. "Yeah, that'll work." He stopped the rover. "You guys should bail out here. Once I back this into the brush, getting out's gonna be a pain."

Theriault looked over her shoulder at Hesh and Tan Bao. "You heard the man." She unfastened her safety harness and released the lock on her door. It lifted open, letting in a chorus of animal sounds from the wilderness ahead—whoops, croaks, buzzing, and roars galore.

Hesh and Tan Bao opened the rear hatches and got out of the rover. As soon as they and Theriault were clear, Dastin closed the rover's open doors with a few taps on the master console inside the vehicle. The rover rolled forward a couple of meters, made a sharp turn back toward the ocean, then halted. Theriault watched Dastin shift Vixen into reverse and guide it into a narrow break in the jungle's dense foliage, provoking a noisy fluttering by unseen creatures.

An oscillating, high-pitched shrilling turned Theriault's head. Hesh was scanning the area with his tricorder while turning in a slow circle. He noted the first officer's stare and apparently took it as a cue to report. "I'm picking up a broad range of life signs, Commander. Countless species of flora and fauna. Some appear to be similar to avian, reptilian, and mammalian forms known on other worlds. Others . . . do not."

"Thanks, Hesh. That was almost informative."

The Arkenite science officer turned away to mask his embarrassment, so Theriault turned toward Tan Bao. The nurse was gathering samples of small berries, leaves, and bark from plants and trees along the jungle's edge, and sealing each new discovery inside a clear vial for return to the *Sagittarius,* where he, Hesh, and Doctor Babitz would no doubt pass the hours between star systems running tests and analyzing biochemical data with meticulous precision. Fearing that he might tell her what he was looking for amid the leaves and fronds, Theriault opted not to ask.

Dastin slithered out of the rover through its barely open driver's-side door. He held a rolled-up bundle of camouflage netting in one hand. It took him less than a minute to drape the lightweight mesh atop the rover. Then he adorned the netting with bits of local foliage and flowers, until the vehicle was all but undetectable to the untrained eye. Admiring his handiwork, he looked very pleased with himself. "Whaddaya say, Commander? Not bad, eh?"

"I've seen worse." Theriault knew better than to feed Dastin's ego; it was large enough already. She'd made the mistake of complimenting him on his new beard a few months earlier, and the preening young scout had crowed about his "awesome whiskers" for weeks afterward.

I'm not going through that again.

She whistled once, summoning the landing party to her side. "Dastin, make sure you get a tricorder lock on the rover's position. If we need to leave in a hurry, I don't want to hear any excuses about not remembering where we parked."

"All set, boss." The Trill held up his communicator. "I synced the transponders. Plus, I left some clues in the camo that'll help me find our ride in a hurry."

"Okay, good. Hesh, do we have a fix on the nearest settlement?"

The Arkenite checked his tricorder before he answered. "Yes, sir. Bearing nine-one, range three point five kilometers." He faced the jungle and pointed with an extended arm. "Less than a hundred meters inside the jungle, there are well-established trails that lead to the largest agglomeration of humanoid life signs."

Dastin looked dubious. "I'd suggest we stay off the trails, Commander. If we parallel them, there's less chance of an unplanned encounter with the locals."

Theriault nodded in agreement. "Good idea." She looked at Hesh. "I don't suppose you've picked up any sign of the energy readings that our probe detected on this planet?"

Hesh pursed his small, thin-lipped mouth into a pin-stripe frown. "No, sir. So far, I am unable to confirm any readings consistent with artificial energy generation, signal transmission, or other forms of advanced technology. Likewise, the only atmospheric pollutants I can detect appear to be the product of a nearby geological phenomenon, a crater that acts as a vent for a long-burning pocket of natural methane. However, I have set my tricorder to monitor the most common range of power and communication frequencies. If there is any change, I will report it."

"That was a lot of words to say 'no,' but thank you for being thorough." Theriault checked the settings on her phaser. "Everyone set phasers to light stun, but keep them holstered unless we're threatened. This is supposed to be a recon mission—not contact or combat."

The other members of the landing party did as she'd instructed, verifying their weapons' settings before returning them to their inconspicuous pocket holsters along the waistbands of their jumpsuits. Satisfied that everyone was ready, Theriault nodded inland. "Okay. Let's go."

Entrusted with the duty of walking point, Dastin felt his way through the alien jungle with all his senses at once. He attenuated his balance as his feet found purchase in the soft mud beneath the roots and decaying vegetation that carpeted the ground, and he breathed deep the tropical climate's sultry musk, floral perfumes, and animal odors. The landing party's footfalls squished softly on the damp ground behind him, while the trees around them echoed with the warbles and shrieks of wild animals sending up warning cries at their approach.

Dastin knew well enough that he needn't fear the creatures he heard at a distance. He saved his dread for the ones that moved nearby with lethal silence, their passage marked only by fleeting shadows, faint tracks, or momentary traces of their scent in the air.

Sunset's violet glow soon dimmed as dusk faded into night. The landing party skulked from the sheltering darkness of the jungle to crest a steep incline. Dastin dropped to all fours to traverse the last couple of meters, and the others emulated his caution. The team spread out, flanked him, and crawled four abreast to the top of the ridge. Together they peeked over the rocky edge at the vale far below.

Primitive-looking huts huddled along the edges of a maze of streets that crisscrossed the area, which was more developed than Dastin had expected. Several wide paths radiated from the village's center and extended in many directions into the jungle and across the island, as if this village were the hub of a great wheel. Small fires burned in the middle of intersections throughout the village. Plumes of smoke climbed from a handful of crude chimney pipes that pierced the huts' thatched roofs, and the ruddy glow of firelight flickered within many of the structures.

Theriault studied the scene with a sharp eye. "Dastin? How many people do you think live down there? Eight hundred? Nine?"

The scout put his specialized training to work, estimating at a glance the number of dwellings and how many humanoid occupants each could likely support. "More than that. I'd say at least twelve hundred, and no more than fourteen hundred."

Science officer Hesh fiddled with his tricorder. "Those numbers would be consistent with these humanoid bio-mass readings, Commander."

Tan Bao looked confused. "Then where the hell is everybody?" He tilted his head toward the village. "Less than a third of those huts look occupied, and the roads are all but empty."

Hesh checked his tricorder, then pointed at a cerulean glow nestled in the jungle some distance away. "Bearing zero-one-one, range one point six kilometers." He adjusted his tricorder. "Several hundred humanoids are gathered around the crater I mentioned earlier."

His report made Theriault apprehensive. "So that blue light is burning methane?"

"Yes, Commander. A great deal of it."

The first officer thought for a moment. She directed her next question at Dastin. "How long would it take to get us close enough to that crater to see what's going on down there?"

"No offense, sir, but why would we want to?"

"Just playing a hunch. I'm thinking they might be up to something that could cause the energy readings that drew us here."

Her suggestion left Hesh wide-eyed and befuddled. "Forgive me for doubting your hypothesis, Commander, but I am unable to conceive of any process by which a natural methane burn could produce an energy signature powerful enough to be detected by one of our reconnaissance probes."

"I never said it made sense on its face. I just said I have a hunch." She turned her green eyes toward Dastin. "So? How long to get us sideline seats at the crater?"

Dastin struggled to discern a safe path to the pit of fire from their current position. "Looks like we can follow the edge of this ridge back down into the jungle, then shadow that trail over there to the crater. Barring disasters, we can be there in about twenty minutes."

"Then let's get moving."

The order was given, and Dastin wasted no time or breath debating it. He guided the landing party along the ridge line, which sloped gradually downward until it was swallowed by the jungle. Beneath the lush canopy of the forest, darkness reigned. As the last traces of daylight vanished, the black expanse of the jungle came alive with a mad cacophony of noise—the sawing music of insects, the throaty growls of animal hungers, and shrill cries that sliced through the primitive gloom. Dastin did his best to remain silent amid the clamor, to emulate the quiet surety of a predator in the night, only to feel betrayed by the labored breaths of his comrades, who struggled to keep up with him as he blazed a trail toward the crater.

As they neared the tree line, the heavy pulse of low drums resounded through the night like a titan's heartbeat, and the light of the crater's blue fire became bright enough to silhouette the great throng of people who encircled it. Dastin stopped and held up a closed fist to tell the others to halt. Despite his signal, they ran into each other like bumbling cadets.

"Smooth," he whispered over his shoulder.

Theriault reproved him with a poisonous glare. "What do you see?"

"The creepiest town meeting in history." He beckoned Hesh forward and pointed at the crowd encircling the crater. "Check this out. Looks like some kind of ceremony."

The Arkenite made a silent scan of the natives with his tricorder. "The female in the feathered robes appears to be leading whatever ritual is being carried out."

Dastin squinted to pick out details. "What about the ones wearing the big headpieces?"

Hesh sounded baffled. "What of them?"

"What are those weapons they're carrying?"

The entire landing party eyed the armored natives who ringed the throng. Tan Bao shrugged. "They look like spears."

"No." Dastin shook his head. "Those aren't blades on the end. They're too bulky, and they have no piercing tips or cutting edges." Something about the natives' pole-arms troubled him. "I can't say why, but I don't like the look of those things."

Hesh checked his tricorder again. "I detect nothing unusual about them."

"Well, do me a favor and keep an—" He saw the armored guards prod certain individuals toward the pit of fire. "What are they doing?"

Theriault's jaw slackened with horror. As the landing party watched, the armored guards with the pole-arms and ornate headdresses ushered toward the pit a young man whose body was painted with peculiar symbols—and they nudged him over the crater's edge. He screamed for only a few seconds as he fell—and then a gust of golden fire roared into the black sky, and the only sound was the snap and crack of the cyan flames, and the steady tempo of the drums.

"I'm starting to think coming here was a bad idea," Theriault muttered.

Dastin respected the XO's gift for understatement. "That makes two of us."

Hesh sidled up to them and thrust his tricorder toward Theriault. "Commander, I've made an interesting discovery."

"More interesting than people being sacrificed to a pit of burning gas?"

The science officer pointed at the tricorder's display. "Sir, all the natives I've scanned are no older than their late teens. This appears to be an entire civilization of children."

Tan Bao telegraphed his dissent with a furrowed brow. "Let's not jump to conclusions, Hesh. There are lots of species that look young to us even after they've attained full maturity. The Fesarians of the First Federation, for example, or the Nimmilites of—"

"I am not saying these people *appear* young." Hesh was adamant. "Look at these scans of their cellular structure, their DNA, their telomeres, their mitochondria. The subjects gathered here range in age from newborns to their late teens. The eldest subjects, by my estimate, are no more than eighteen years of age, and are in the physical primes of their lives." He nodded toward the pit. "And I suspect it is no coincidence that they are the ones being sent to their deaths."

6

The night stank of burning flesh. Chanting voices snaked between the steady tempo of the drums, a hymn to the sacrifice. Nimur had seen more than a hundred Cleansings, but only now, poised at the precipice of her demise, did she feel the full weight of it. Each beat of the drums, each haunting incantation—they were invitations to step into the flames.

Everyone she knew stood gathered in the outer circle, bearing witness to the ceremony. Between the observers and the sacrifices stood the Wardens with their lances, and the priestess with her feathered raiment. On the far side of the Well of Flames, two Wardens ushered forward Derym, the next person to be Cleansed. The reed-thin young man's face was blank, his eyes aflame but empty. It was as if he had been drained of his will to live. Without any sign of resistance or hesitation, he walked in slow, even strides toward the fire. Then, with the single-mindedness of a moth drawn to a torch, he stepped over the edge and fell facedown, arms outstretched, into the blue inferno. A jet of flames shot upward as the abyss consumed him.

Nimur wrinkled her nose at the sickly, charnel odor that belched from the Shepherds' merciless crucible. The reek passed quickly, carried away on scorching gusts of brutal heat.

And the drums beat on. Their rhythm coursed through Nimur until their cadence held sway over her heartbeat and left her head swimming. She swayed like a reed in the breeze. The chanted words were as much a mystery to her now as they had been all her life; they were not composed of Tomol words; they were the prayer of the Shepherds, passed down verbally from priestess to disciple, one sunturn after another, since the time of the Arrival. No one knew what they meant, only that they were meant to be recited during the Cleansing.

So it had always been, and so it would remain.

On Nimur's right was Teolo, a young woman she knew but with whom she had never been friendly, partly because she had envied Teolo's beauty and effortless grace. Next to her, Nimur had always felt plain and clumsy. When they both had reached the age for choosing a mate, Teolo had enjoyed a surfeit of handsome suitors, while Nimur had counted herself fortunate to capture the attention and affection of the simple but kindhearted Kerlo.

Now they stood together on the verge of annihilation. Despite the abundance of natural gifts with which Teolo had been born and lived, tonight she was doomed to meet the same end as Nimur. In the fire, the two of them would be equals at last.

The young beauty hesitated at the crater's edge and cast her final glance at Nimur, of all people. Behind the blaze of power in her eyes was a fathomless sorrow, and Nimur understood it all too well. Teolo grieved, just as she did, for the lives they might have led.

A Warden nudged his lance into the small of Teolo's back. She crossed her arms over her chest as she fell, comforted only by her own lonely embrace, and vanished into the blue death.

The night's other candidates all had been Cleansed. Ysan and two Wardens moved toward Nimur in a solemn slow march. All that remained now was for the priestess to bless Nimur with the Benediction of the Cleansing, offer her the forgiveness of the Shepherds, and send her to walk the last path of all flesh. She heard Ysan and the Wardens halt behind her.

"Sister? Are you ready to be Cleansed?"

Nimur turned and faced Ysan—and felt her fear become fury. "No."

Ysan stood her ground. "There is no other way, sister."

"Not for you." She made no effort to mask her threatening tone.

The Wardens spoke the ancient words that sparked the fires in their lances.

Savoring the heat of confrontation, Nimur realized she had a new sense of the world around her, a new awareness. Other beings gave off tangible but invisible auras, and if she turned her mind to the task, she could alter the shape of those energies. With a single violent impulse, she turned the two Wardens' life-forces inward and away from herself.

The two hulking defenders flew backward, helpless leaves riding a harsh wind.

Nimur backhanded Ysan and laughed as the priestess crumpled into a defensive curl.

A collective gasp sounded from the witnesses, and the other Wardens leveled their weapons at Nimur. She pushed back with a thought driven by rage. A shimmering

ring of distortion appeared around her and rushed outward, knocking the Wardens and witnesses off-balance. As the assembled Tomol stumbled and fell, Nimur charged forward and confronted Chimi and Tayno, who huddled over the swaddled, bawling infant Tahna.

"Give her to me."

The two youths could not have failed to understand the implicit threat behind Nimur's demand, but instead of obeying, they shuddered and closed their eyes.

Nimur ripped the wailing infant from Chimi's arms and dashed toward the jungle.

The tree line was still many strides ahead of her as she heard the angry whine of lances preparing to fire. A Warden shouted, "Stop running and put down the baby!"

She was only seconds away from cover, from the shelter of foliage and darkness, but she knew she would never get there in time. No matter how fast she ran, she could never outrun a blast from a fire lance.

Then flashes of red light cut through the night, searing past her on both sides while filling the air with a piercing shriek. The crimson beams left a strange odor in the air, like the smell after a lightning storm, and when their screeching ceased, all she heard behind her were screams.

Golden blasts tore past her as she barreled into the forest. Pulses of fire from the Wardens' lances lit trees on fire and kicked up great fountains of short-lived sparks.

More red pulses flew out of the jungle in the opposite direction, forcing the Wardens to abandon their pursuit and harassment.

Nimur didn't know what had attacked the Wardens, or if it had acted on her behalf. All she knew was she had to keep running—because all that Suba had left for her now was death.

"Commander? She's coming right at us."

Theriault barely registered Dastin's warning. She was still processing the sight of two armored guards being hurled backward as if by the hand of God. "What was that? Telekinesis?"

Despite the drama unfolding in front of them, Hesh focused on his tricorder's display. "Unknown. But I'm picking up high-power energy signatures from all the guards' weapons."

The desperate, fleeing young woman plucked a crying infant from the arms of two younger natives, leaped over them, and continued her mad dash toward the landing party's concealed position in the jungle. Her fear shone through her eyes, which Theriault realized for the first time were ablaze with an inner fire unlike any she had ever seen.

Tan Bao reached for his phaser but stopped himself from drawing it. "What do we do?"

Theriault wanted to give the order to lay down suppressing fire and cover the woman's escape, but she knew that was forbidden by the Prime Directive.

Behind the escaping young woman, several armored guards scrambled to their feet and aimed their lances at her back. It took all of Theriault's willpower not to shout out a warning.

Red beams blazed from concealed positions nearby in the jungle and slashed through the night to slam into the armored natives. A few quick volleys streaked past the woman, felling half a dozen of her pursuers with each volley, and sowing chaos and terror in the unarmed crowd that had surrounded the pit of burning natural gas.

Frightened natives ran every which way, obstructing the warriors from returning fire with any accuracy. Wild shots tore into the jungle, igniting blazes and peppering the jungle floor with ephemeral sparks. The landing party hit the deck, pressing themselves facedown into the dirt to stay below the barrage, which was as fierce as it was random.

Tan Bao asked Theriault through gritted teeth, "Who's shooting?"

"How the hell should I know?" A near-miss ricocheted off the stump of a fallen tree next to her. Sparks rained down on her as she covered her head with her arms.

Prone against the fallen tree trunk, Dastin winced as another volley of golden fire screamed past overhead and was answered by ruby-hued blasts from the jungle. "Those are Klingon disruptors. I'd bet my beard on it."

Silence fell upon the jungle. In the aftermath of the firefight, the animals all had fled or gone quiet, leaving the nocturnal wilderness eerily bereft of its natural ambience. Without the sonic camouflage of combat or fauna, the fleeing woman's footfalls were crisp and distinct— and without a doubt closing in on the landing party's position. From the clearing around the pit came shouted orders and the bustle of warriors readying a search team to breach the tree line.

Remembering her own directive to avoid contact with the natives, Theriault whispered to her team, "Fall back to the ridge line, single file."

The landing party started to get up. Dastin said, "Belay that! Down!" They all dropped back to the muddy ground and took whatever cover they could find.

The patter of the woman's footsteps was matched by several more from nearby. All the footfalls slowed, as if those responsible for them had just noted their mutual proximity.

Common sense—not to mention Starfleet basic tactical training—dictated that until the risk of detection had passed, the wisest course of action in this situation was to stay quiet and out of sight. Unfortunately, Theriault was eager to know if Dastin was right about the weapons being Klingon disruptors, and, if so, what they were doing here. *Just keep your head down,* she told herself, over and over again. Then her curiosity trumped her caution. She crawled forward and lifted a wide leafy frond to steal a peek at the encounter transpiring only a few meters away.

The green-skinned, silver-haired native woman in a crudely woven dress had halted in the middle of a narrow trail. She turned in a slow circle, one way and then the other, her eyes and ears searching the darkness around her even as she hugged the whimpering infant to her chest.

Burly figures emerged from the shadows around her. One stepped onto the trail less than two meters from Theriault, which had meant she had nearly collided with him by accident. In all, she counted six figures. The one in charge approached the woman with empty hands held at chest height, palms out. His deep, rasping voice had the telltale reverb of one processed through a universal translator. Thanks to the flickering light of a nearby burning tree, Theriault noticed the man's dramatic cranial ridges and well-groomed facial hair.

Nimur recovered her wits and challenged her saviors' leader. "You are not Tomol."

"No, we're not. We are Klingons." He extended one gloved hand to the woman. "I am Commander Tobar."

The woman eyed Tobar and his men with naked suspicion. "I am Nimur."

"Nimur, we have come to help you."

Three armored warriors from the pit sprinted into view, several dozen meters behind the impromptu meeting on the trail. Tobar lifted his chin toward the interlopers, and one of his men turned, fired his disruptor pistol, and stunned the approaching trio. Then Tobar smiled at Nimur. "We can take you far from here, to a place where you will be safe. Come with us."

The commander had taken care to phrase his statement as an invitation. Why was he being so solicitous? Since when did Klingons ask for anything instead of taking it by force?

Nimur was slow to grant her trust. "Where can you take me that I'll be safe?"

"Somewhere your kinsmen can never follow. A place called Qo'noS."

"I've never heard of that island."

Tobar put on a humble aspect. "As I said, it's very far from here."

None of what Theriault was hearing made any sense to her. *Qo'noS? Why would they take her to the Klingon homeworld? What do they want with her?*

Aggressive shouting from the village filtered through

the jungle, followed by the rapid beat of war drums. It sounded to Theriault as if the natives were rallying, and that the panicked crowd would soon regroup as an angry mob.

On the trail, Nimur looked away toward the growing clangor, then cast an appraising eye on the Klingons. "Very well. Take me to Qo'noS."

"As soon as our ship comes back, we will," Tobar said. He motioned to one of his men to take point and lead them away, into the jungle, on a northeasterly heading. Then he draped an arm over Nimur's shoulder and guided her away. "Until then, we'll keep you safe."

Theriault watched the Klingons slip away into the night, and then she scuttled backward through the underbrush. Her landing party awaited her with anxious stares.

"I've got good news and bad news."

Tan Bao asked with reluctance, "What's the bad news?"

"Dastin gets to keep his beard. Those *were* Klingon disruptors that shot the natives, and it was Klingons who fired them. They intercepted the woman who fled the ceremony, and they plan on taking her back to Qo'noS as soon as their ride comes back for them."

The Trill scout frowned. "So what's the good news?"

"I lied. There isn't any."

Hesh looked up from his tricorder. "I have a fix on the Klingon landing party, Commander. They are moving away on heading zero-one-nine."

Dastin and Tan Bao traded inquisitive glances, and then both men looked at Theriault. The scout asked, "Orders, Commander?"

Theriault was torn. "We're supposed to avoid contact. On the other hand, we have standing orders from Starfleet to investigate all covert Klingon military activity in the sector."

Hesh said, "If I might offer an observation?"

"Go ahead."

"My tricorder continued scanning during the Klingons' firefight with the natives," the science officer said. "Some of the energy readings from the native soldiers' weapons are on the same frequency as the one we were sent to find—albeit at a much lower power level. However, this is our first evidence that the energy readings reported by our probe are accurate. To abandon our investigation now would be premature."

"Y'know," Dastin said, "if we think those energy readings are worth checking out, so might the Klingons. Maybe they helped that woman 'cause they know something we don't."

"Good points." Theriault weighed the risks against her objectives and made her decision. "Dastin, take point. Follow the Klingons, but keep us at a safe distance—I don't want them hearing us and setting up an ambush. Tan Bao, watch our six—make sure the natives don't jump us from behind. And Hesh"—she smiled approvingly at the Arkenite—"keep on scanning with that tricorder, Lieutenant." She pointed forward. "Stay sharp and tread softly, gents. Move out."

7

Violet waves of pain lingered like echoes inside Ysan's head. She had been unprepared for the invisible assault Nimur had unleashed; the closest comparison the priestess could imagine was being struck by an ocean wave of unexpected strength and slammed beneath the waves, pummeled by the weight of the water into the jagged rocks, coarse sand, and broken shells. Something warm tickled her upper lip. Ysan wiped at it with the side of her hand, which came away smeared with bright green blood. Probing gingerly with her fingertips, she realized the blood had spilled from her nostrils.

Around her, the Wardens stirred and let out muffled groans. The ones who had been struck by the red lightning bolts from the forest sported smoldering divots on their armor. A few lay groaning on the ground, their headdresses knocked off and their lances at their sides. Fear stirred inside Ysan; she had never seen or heard of anything that could overpower Wardens that way. Whatever had done this, it seemed to be helping Nimur—and that could only mean trouble.

Ysan found her staff and used it to help herself stand. She was on her feet while most of the stunned Wardens were still on their knees, bellies, or backs. "Get up!" Her command galvanized the humbled defenders, who struggled to stand and assembled in front of her. She directed her questions at Kitraan, the eldest Warden, whose mark of office was the most ornate of the headdresses, a plumed serpent with great fangs. "How many hurt? How many dead?"

"None dead, and none so badly hurt that they cannot avenge."

His answer pleased her. "Have you ever seen the likes of that red lightning?"

"No. I was going to ask if the Shepherds ever wrote of such a thing."

"No, they did not." Ysan saw her bruised and dust-shrouded disciple stumble toward her. The priestess-in-training tripped and almost fell until Ysan caught her. "Seta! Are you hurt?"

"Dizzy." The younger girl pressed one hand to her forehead. "Hit my head when I fell."

Ysan inspected the injury. "The skin is not broken, and the swelling is slight. You'll feel better soon." Satisfied her appointed successor was not in imminent danger, she returned her attention to Kitraan. "Did you see who threw the red lightning?"

"No. But I am certain there must have been more than one attacker."

That was unwelcome news, but Ysan kept her tone neutral. "How many?"

"At least three, perhaps as many as six."

Seta stepped forward to stand at Ysan's side. "Why would they help Nimur? Is it possible they're other Tomol, maybe ones who've already Changed?"

It surprised Ysan to hear her best pupil ask such a foolish question. "If her rescuers had been Changed, we would all be dead. No, I don't know who they were, or why they helped her. None of that matters as much as the fact that Nimur must be found and brought back to finish the Cleansing before she completes the Change."

Kitraan reacted with cool pragmatism. "How long do we have to bring her to the fire?"

"Maybe a day," Ysan said. "Perhaps less. It's hard to say. Summon all the Wardens and task them to the hunt. Nimur is already showing signs of the powers that follow the Change. It's only a matter of time until the madness takes her. We can't risk letting her live that long."

Seta struck a fearful note. "How much stronger will she get?"

The disciple's innocent question drew all the Wardens closer; they, too, were eager to know the truth about the threat that now ran loose on their island home. Ysan decided the time for comforting euphemisms had passed. "Much stronger. According to the writings on the Shepherds' wordstone, soon she'll be able to do far more than strike with an invisible hand. All the elements will bend to her command—water and fire, air and earth. She'll be able to see into our thoughts, and from there into the past, and the future. The Shepherds wrote of the Changed trampling entire cities underfoot and laying waste the world before this one. But this world is all we have left, and we are its only caretakers. It falls to us to find Nimur and to Cleanse her—before she destroys us all. . . . Kitraan, I want you and your Wardens to set your weapons to their deadliest strength. If Nimur will not surrender and consent to be Cleansed, do whatever you must to stop her and bring her back here to face the fire's judgment."

Kitraan sounded troubled by the order. "What of the infant she abducted?"

"Spare it if you can, but capturing Nimur is more important. Do you understand?"

A single, slow bow of Kitraan's masked head signaled his acceptance of her decree. He turned and barked orders at the other Wardens. "Weapons to full! Order by pairs and fan out! Find Nimur, take her down, and bring her back here! Move!"

The Wardens spoke ancient words to activate their lances, whose bulbous heads crackled with blue lightning. Then the defenders split off into pairs and scattered out of the clearing. Some charged down the trails while others blazed new paths into the jungle. In less than a minute, only Ysan, Seta, and a handful of shocked witnesses from the village remained near the Well of Flames. Ysan gently gripped Seta by her shoulders. "We need to calm the others' fears and get them to go home and stay inside."

"What are we going to tell them?"

"The truth. Nimur gave in to fear, and she ran. Now the Wardens are going to bring her back to finish her Cleansing, as they always have."

"And what if they can't? What if it's already too late?"

Ysan sighed with grim anticipation. "Then you and I will have to invoke the power of the Shepherds—and condemn Nimur to the ranks of the Endless." She started walking back to the village and beckoned Seta to follow. "Come with me. There is much I have yet to teach you about the Shepherds, and all our lives might depend on what you learn tonight."

Fury had turned to fire inside Nimur's head. She felt as if her thoughts themselves were boiling and her free will was cooking off as steam. Her vision blurred even as her new senses turned the black night red in response to its suddenly omnipresent energies.

Tobar and his men were dull shadows in all that glory, ashen figures that shed more heat than light into this rarefied plane of existence to which Nimur had just become privy. He and two of his men moved ahead of Nimur, clearing a path for her. The other three followed her—one guarding against pursuit while the other two hurried to erase all signs of their passage.

All her life, Nimur had lived on this island, but its jungle had never felt more stifling than it did at that moment. Every breath was a labor, every step a struggle. All the familiar sounds of the night submerged beneath a rush of white noise that Nimur soon realized was the pounding of her own heart and the ebb and flow of her own shallow breathing. She clutched her daughter to her chest. It took all her concentration to neither drop Tahna nor smother her.

Her feet grew heavy, and her balance faltered. Unable to distinguish objects from their doppelgangers as her vision doubled, she caromed off one tree and ran headlong into a low branch that blocked her path. The impact knocked her onto her back and left her reeling as her terrified infant wailed in her arms.

Swarthy hands closed like vises on her arms and hauled her upright. "Keep moving," said Kergol, one of Tobar's subordinates. "And silence that whelp. Or I'll do it for you." He gave Nimur a rough push to force her back into motion, following the trailblazers.

She stumbled forward but said nothing. Another throaty cry from Tahna drew baleful looks from the strange warriors, and Nimur suspected Kergol's threat to harm Tahna had not been an idle one. Knowing it was best for all of them to keep Tahna from giving away their location to the Wardens—who, she had no doubt, were tracking them—Nimur pulled one strap of her dress off her shoulder to expose her left breast and let the infant feed. As she'd hoped, the hungry child nursed eagerly, putting a momentary end to her caterwauling.

The return of relative quiet seemed to placate the Klingons. They pushed on, their pace faster than what Nimur was accustomed to. Wherever they had come from, she realized, it must be not unlike Suba, because they all seemed quite at home in the steamy heart of its untamed jungle. Even the growls and hisses of nearby predators did nothing to slow the Klingons or change their path. They moved through the night as if they knew they had nothing to fear from it.

"Can we rest soon? I need water."

Tobar sneered. "You can rest when we reach shelter." He looked away from Nimur as if she weren't even there, to speak to one of his men. "Kroka, has the *Voh'tahk* answered yet?"

Kroka pulled a small metallic device from his belt and with a flick of his wrist opened its delicate-looking cover. He eyed it for a moment, then closed it and put it away. "Not yet."

"If you don't hear from them in the next two hours, hail them again."

"Yes, sir."

No one spoke as the group trudged through the dense undergrowth. Nimur worried when she noticed that the ground sloped gradually upward. The longer they walked, the more tiring it became thanks to the slight but unrelenting uphill grade. Nimur quickened her pace to catch up to Tobar. "Where are we going?"

He seemed bored of her. "To a defensible position, just up the hill."

The jungle thinned as they climbed. When Nimur glimpsed a familiar rock formation silhouetted against the pale orb of the rising blue moon, a sick chill traveled down her spine. "Not the caves!" She grabbed Tobar's sleeve, forcing him to stop. "We can't go into the caves!"

"Of course we can. And we will." He pulled his sleeve from her hand and kept walking. "There's only one way in, and the entrance has a clear line of sight down the hillside."

"Only the priestess and her disciples are allowed—"

"Quiet!" Tobar turned on her like a wild animal, teeth bared. "An hour ago, you were ready to kill your holy priestess to save your scrawny neck. I don't care what silly superstitions you used to believe in, little girl. *Play time is over.*"

His refusal to heed the warning made no sense to her.

Couldn't he see the wild energies gathering like a halo above the hilltop? Was he so blind that he couldn't see that the Shepherds' wordstone had been roused? "We can't hide in the caves. The priestess and her disciples will be coming soon, and they'll bring the Wardens in force. This place isn't safe!"

"We're not afraid of your soldiers' puny fire-sticks. Now, do as you're told."

Nimur seethed. As her rage flared she felt the fire of the Change blaze within her, gaining strength and sharpening its focus. The more the power within her awakened, the angrier she became. But her fear of attracting the Shepherds' wrath remained.

She turned back and ran. Behind her, Tobar roared, "Stop her!"

The three Klingons bringing up the rear tackled her. The crushing impact left Nimur growling and Tahna screaming. A fist slammed into Nimur's face. One of the Klingons wrestled Tahna from Nimur's hands, then another flipped Nimur over and bound her wrists.

As they rolled her onto her back, Tobar stepped over her and stood astride her. A fleeting, sadistic smirk crossed his face. "Ready to follow orders now?"

She couldn't conceal her hatred. "I thought you were here to help me."

"We are. As long as we help ourselves in the bargain."

She spat at him. He laughed and wiped her spittle from his chest. "You have spirit. I respect that. But I won't put up with disobedience." He beckoned Kergol. The younger Klingon stepped into Nimur's line of sight; he held Tahna in his burly bare arms. Tobar cracked a sinister smile at

Nimur and maintained eye contact with her as he gave his next order.

"Lieutenant Kergol: If the prisoner runs . . . if she disobeys another order . . . or does anything to give away our position to the natives . . . break her baby's neck."

8

Silent and single file, the landing party pushed through walls of vines in stealthy pursuit of the Klingon expedition. Each of them had one hand open and free to force past branches and other obstructive vegetation, and one hand gripping a compact phaser.

Theriault had put her faith in Dastin's tracking skills to keep them heading in the right direction because she didn't want her people to risk giving away their own position with the glow from their tricorders' displays. She moved in careful steps, well aware of the Klingons' reputation for exceptional hearing. Then she remembered the Klingons were also reputed to have superlative olfactory senses. *I guess we'll just have to hope we're downwind of them.*

Ahead of her, Dastin was barely visible. She perceived him and their surroundings as little more than the ghosts of shapes haunting the pitch-black night, profiles limned by brief, broken gleams of dark-blue moonlight that slipped through the jungle's canopy. It was so hard for her to see even a meter ahead that she almost ran into Dastin's back when he stopped, raised a fist to signal the landing party to halt, and dropped to one knee.

The first officer recovered her balance and crouched beside the scout. She dropped her voice to the softest hush she could manage. "What is it?"

He lifted his index finger, cueing her to wait a moment. Then he cupped a hand over his mouth and whispered back, "They stopped. Twenty meters ahead. I hear an argument."

That sounded promising. Dissent in enemy ranks was often useful. "Details?"

Dastin shook his head. "Can't make out the words. Just the tone."

Tan Bao inched up behind Theriault and Dastin. "Are we heading uphill?"

"Yes," Dastin said. "Have been for about half a klick. Based on the maps we made from orbit, I'd say we're heading toward the large hill in the northeastern part of the island."

That caught Hesh's attention. "Commander, I reviewed the geological profile for this island before we left the ship. Our scans showed a network of caves beneath that hill."

"Artificial or natural?"

"Unknown. The scan was inconclusive. To answer your question with any degree of confidence, I would need to make a more detailed survey of the caves."

"Well," Theriault said, "if the Klingons use them for cover, you might get your wish."

Dastin hissed to silence the others. Theriault strained to hear anything from the Klingons, but all she heard was the nocturnal chorale of the jungle. The Trill scout pivoted back toward the landing party. "They're moving again. Uphill, straight toward the cave entrance."

Theriault looked ahead. "All right. Let's stay with them, see what they're up to."

"I'd advise against that," Dastin said. "The Klingons are using the caves for cover for a reason: because it works. With just two men inside the entrance, they could hold it indefinitely. Our only approach is over open ground. They'd cut us down before we got within ten meters."

"Great." Theriault looked back at Hesh. "Did our scans show any other entrances?"

"As I said, they were inconclusive. There are several locations that might offer alternative points of ingress to the cave network, but without visual confirmation of their existence—"

"Forget I asked. Dastin, what if we used our tricorders and phasers to bring down some of those loose boulders from higher up the slope?"

The Trill sounded confused. "To do what? Block them in?"

"If need be. Or at least to create some new cover for a frontal assault."

"Trapping them inside won't gain us anything. It'll guarantee we have no way of seeing what they're doing, and they have more than enough air in those caves to last for weeks. Plus, we have to assume they have a ship either close by or coming to get them—which means they could get beamed out of there and we'd have no way of knowing it."

It was still too soon for Theriault to give up. "Tan Bao? Could you use your medical tricorder to generate the Klingon equivalent of delta waves?"

"You mean to put the guards to sleep from a distance, like a chemical-free anesthetic?"

"Exactly!"

"Sure. If I knew anything about Klingon neurochemistry. Or their sleep patterns. Or what even a baseline Klingon brainwave looks like. Or their susceptibility to subaural frequencies."

"In other words . . . no."

"Not a chance."

"You're no longer my favorite member of the landing party."

"Imagine my disappointment."

Dastin cut in, "Wait, does that make *me* your favorite by default, or are we treating this like an open position? 'Cause no offense to Hesh, but I really think seniority should count here."

"Guys, you know that part of the mission where I get fed up and shoot all three of you? We're coming up on that pretty damned fast."

Hesh tapped Theriault's shoulder. "Commander?"

"I mean it, Hesh. We need to figure out a plan to get inside the caves before we—"

"*Commander.*" The Arkenite's tone was urgent. "We are *not alone.*"

Theriault turned and looked back, then up and around. Dastin and Tan Bao did the same, and soon they all were looking at the same thing: a crescent formation of the armored warriors they had seen at the pit of fire. Their massive headdresses caught the cerulean moonlight with every feather, every scale, and every tuft of fur, and their jeweled faux eyes shimmered in the darkness. Most daunting of all, however, were their lances. The pole-arms, which earlier had looked so primitive from a distance, now crackled with pale blue electricity. Even from a few meters away, they presented a palpable threat.

In a low voice, Theriault said to the landing party, "Phasers down. Now." She led by example, slowly placing her own weapon on the ground while keeping her empty hand up, where the natives could see it. She waited until Hesh, Dastin, and Tan Bao had laid down their own phasers, and then she slowly stood.

The warriors' lances followed her every movement.

She kept both hands up in front of her and took a step forward. "Um, hi. My name is Vanessa Theriault. My friends and I are from the United—"

A flash of light and heat blasted Theriault onto her back. Stunned, all she could do was listen as the natives opened fire on the rest of the landing party.

Not cool, she decided as her consciousness faded, and she sank into the dark's waiting embrace.

9

Clark Terrell found a lot of things to like about serving on a small ship such as the *Sagittarius,* but its onboard menu was not one of them. The crew had no end of nicknames for the scout ship's galley. The engineers' current favorite was "The Unholy Mess," while the officers tended to refer to the communal dining area as "Pre-sickbay." One thing everyone agreed upon was that the Starfleet-approved bill of fare programmed into the food synthesizer left much to be desired.

So it was that Terrell, while making a hit-and-run foray to the galley for a quick lunch, found himself surprised by the sight of Master Chief Ilucci carefully setting plates full of food on the open compartment's four tables. At a glance, Terrell saw that each table was arranged with the same six prefabricated meals—but only one set of utensils per table.

Terrell crossed his arms and leaned in the doorway. "Planning a feast, Master Chief?"

"A science experiment."

If there was one thing a Starfleet career had taught Terrell, it was to be alarmed whenever an engineer was doing something odd and chose to refer to it as *an experiment.* "Dare I ask?"

"Threx and I have a little bet with Razka."

"Let me skip ahead, Master Chief. Is the end of this story an eating contest?"

"Not exactly." Perhaps sensing Terrell's silent disapproval, he added, "Not directly."

"Chief, don't make me use a court-martial to get a straight answer."

The engineer scratched his whiskered chin. "It's a . . . well . . . a not-puking contest."

"Duty compels me to ask you to elaborate, even though I really don't want you to."

A shamed nod. "Yeah. You see, Razka said that Saurians never vomit. But I know he's just talking out his gills, because I've seen Saurians hurl before, more than once. So has Threx. So, we made a bet with Razka that we could make him puke. And he made a counter-bet that he could make me, Threx, *and* Torvin boot before he did."

"Hence the display of pending gluttony I see before me."

"Yes, sir."

"And afterward?"

"Sit-ups."

Doing his best not to imagine the aftermath of the engineers' ill-considered wager with the ship's lead field scout, Terrell moved toward the food synthesizer. "Mind if I grab a chicken sandwich and a coffee before you boys paint the decks?"

"Be my guest, sir."

"Too kind." Terrell reached into his pocket and fished out a yellow data card that was programmed to deliver his least-un-favorite lunch. Half a second before he could insert it into the food synthesizer's input slot, the ship's alarm whooped, and the bulkhead panels flashed yellow.

"Captain Terrell, please report to the bridge," Sorak said over the intraship comm.

Terrell stepped over to a nearby bulkhead comm panel and opened a response channel. "On my way." He closed the channel and pocketed his meal card. "So much for lunch." He stole a parting look at one table's row of condiments on his way out of the galley. "Mind the hot sauce, Chief. It's twice as mean the second time through."

Leaving the chief engineer to his preparations, Terrell hurried through the main deck's ring-shaped corridor along its starboard side, passing the hatch to the ship's sole lifeboat, two compartments of crew quarters, and his own cabin on the way back to the bridge.

The door slid open at Terrell's approach, and as he strode onto the bridge, Sorak stood from the center seat and began delivering his report. "We detected an encrypted subspace comm signal on a Klingon military frequency, sir. It originated on the planet's surface."

Terrell pivoted into his command chair. "Can we decrypt the message?"

The white-haired Vulcan stood to the right of the captain's chair. "Not yet, sir. It's a newer cipher, one we've not seen before." He glanced at the image of Nereus II on the main viewscreen. "Captain, if Klingon military personnel are on the planet's surface, it stands to reason they would have one or more support vessels nearby."

"If so, why aren't they in orbit? Why leave a team on the surface without backup?"

Sorak pondered that. "Difficult to say. A desire to maintain a low profile, perhaps? It might also be that the personnel on the ground are a long-range reconnaissance team. The Klingons have been known to let their scouts explore new worlds autonomously and summon starship support only when it's required, for combat or exfiltration."

Terrell swiveled his chair toward the science console, which was crewed at that moment by Ensign Taryl, a female Orion who served as one of the ship's field scouts. "Ensign? Is it possible the energy readings our probe detected were Klingon comm signals?"

The green-skinned woman, whose black hair had been shorn to an efficient but still becoming pixie cut, looked up from the sensor display and shook her head. "No, sir. The power readings our probe detected were not consistent with any known Klingon technology."

"At least we can rule out mistaken identity, then."

Sorak lowered his voice. "Orders, Captain?"

The sudden change in the situation left Terrell feeling anxious. "Not many good options."

"Assuming the Klingons on the surface have requested starship support," Sorak said, "we can either stand our ground and meet their ship in orbit, or we can take evasive measures and assume a stealth profile in advance of their arrival. How do you wish to proceed?"

Terrell stifled a grim chortle. "You were at Jinoteur. Remember how well *that* encounter with the Klingons went?"

The memory elicited a somber nod from the Vulcan tactical officer. "Very good, sir. An excess of caution it will be, then." He raised his voice. "Helm, rig for silent running. Ensign Taryl: Find us someplace nearby to hide. And act with haste, please. Time may be a factor."

The crew set to work, and Terrell breathed a low, weary sigh.

Here we go again.

10

Vanessa Theriault awoke to many pairs of golden eyes radiating malice. She was on her back, lying on the ground, looking up at faces that gazed back with hostility. All she could do was hope that, like many humanoid species Starfleet had encountered through the years, this one reacted positively to seemingly common benign gestures and expressions. She mustered a feeble smile and hoped it would be seen as friendly. "Um . . . hello."

Masked warriors responded by pointing their pole-arm blaster weapons at her. The young alien female in the great cloak of feathers—the leader, Theriault surmised— wore a stern expression that seemed ill-suited to her pretty, yellow-freckled, pale-green face. "Quiet."

Through the forest of legs that surrounded Theriault, she saw other warriors use their weapons to nudge Dastin, Tan Bao, and Hesh back to consciousness. None of the other members of the landing party had their tricorders, so Theriault slowly and subtly pressed her arms close to her sides and confirmed that her tricorder, communicator, and phaser also were missing. She turned her head away from the rest of the landing party and glimpsed their equipment gathered in a pile near a small fire. A native warrior in a quasi-feline headdress inspected one of the phasers.

Panicked thoughts fluttered through Theriault's mind.

Don't press the trigger. Please don't press the trigger. She masked her unease as best she could while imagining the young warrior vaporizing himself with a careless sequence of pokes and pushes.

The girl in the cloak of feathers paced along the feet of the landing party, who had been set parallel to one another in a dusty jungle clearing. Her discerning eye passed from Theriault to Dastin, then from Tan Bao to Hesh. "You are not Tomol. Who are you?"

"Friends," Theriault blurted.

Her outburst brought feather-girl back to her. "That remains to be seen." The girl threw a narrowed glance at the three other members of the landing party, then trained her suspicions on Theriault. "The others follow your example. Are you their leader?"

"Yes." Volunteering information might be a risk, but Theriault wanted to bridge the divide of mistrust that lay between her and the natives. "My name is Vanessa. Vanessa Theriault." She pointed at the other members of the landing party and named them in order. "That's Faro Dastin, Nguyen Tan Bao, and Sengar Hesh."

Some of the girl's ill will abated. After a moment, she replied, "I am Ysan, the High Priestess of the People. Why have you come to Suba?"

"Suba? Is that your name for this world?"

"It's our name for this island. This world we call Arethusa." The question must have struck the priestess as odd, because her dark suspicion returned. "Why are you here?"

"My friends and I are explorers. We travel to different places looking to meet new people and learn new things. We come in peace and mean harm to no one."

Dubious whispers passed among the masked warriors. Ysan silenced them with a raised hand and a fierce stare. She softened her mien when she faced Theriault again. "Then why did you and your friends attack us and help Nimur escape the Cleansing?"

Dastin interjected, "That wasn't us."

Theriault aimed a wide-eyed glare at the Trill scout and hoped he would intuit her unspoken command: *Shut your mouth and keep it that way.*

Ysan did not seem convinced by Dastin's protestation of innocence. "An odd claim, since your weapons seem to be the ones that felled so many of our Wardens."

Lying was a calculated risk, but one that Theriault felt might be justified under the circumstances. "What weapons?" She sat up as the priestess pointed at the pile of tricorders, communicators, and type-1 phasers. Theriault feigned confusion. "Those aren't weapons."

"Really? Then what are they?"

"Trinkets. Nothing more than fancy boxes and—"

The screech of a phaser beam cut her off. The warrior in the feline headdress had succeeded in firing one of the compact phasers, unleashing a blue beam that sheared a thick branch off a nearby tree, leaving behind a smoldering stump.

Ysan fixed Theriault with a withering look. "You were saying?"

"Okay, *some* of them are weapons. The jungle's a dangerous place, you know that."

Another young female Tomol joined the group studying the landing party's equipment. As the teenaged girl picked through the pile of high-tech Starfleet gear, the priestess stepped between Theriault and the other woman. "Where are you from?"

"A place far away."

The priestess looked at Hesh, with his pinched Arkenite features and peculiar three-lobed head. Next her gaze lingered on Tan Bao's eyes, with their pronounced epicanthic folds, and his drooping mustache. Then she raised an eyebrow at the pale brown spots that framed Dastin's face and trailed down his neck and under the collar of his olive jumpsuit, a common cosmetic feature among Trill (and also Kriosians, Theriault had learned). The variety in their physical appearances seemed to intrigue her as much as it confused her. If she thought the landing party's members hailed from three different species, she said nothing to betray her suspicion.

Just then, one of the communicators in the pile of confiscated equipment beeped. The cat-masked Warden reacted by aiming his captured phaser at it and firing.

A white flash vaporized the beeping communicator.

The priestess was furious. "Kolom! Put that down! Now!"

Startled, the Warden hesitated a moment, looked at the phaser in his hand, and then he lobbed it back into the pile with the rest of the landing party's confiscated hardware.

Theriault was grateful the phaser hadn't gone off while pointed at her or a member of the landing party. *I just hope that call from the ship wasn't for anything important.*

Ysan pointed at the scorch mark on the ground where Theriault's communicator had been only moments earlier. "What was that?"

Recalling the rules of the Prime Directive, Theriault chose her words with care. "A tool for talking to people far away. That beep meant that someone wanted to talk to me."

"How does it work?"

"I can't even begin to explain it to you."

The younger female Tomol moved to stand beside Ysan. "We're wasting time."

"Patience, Seta." Ysan nudged the fragile-looking teen behind her. Then she looked at Theriault with a steely quality in her gaze, one that seemed out of place in a person so young. "We need to find Nimur, the one who escaped. Where did you hide her?"

"That wasn't us."

"Who else could it have been?"

Theriault was still debating how much to tell the Tomol when Dastin made the decision for her. "It was the Klingons. They have weapons like ours. We saw them attack your Wardens and help your friend escape."

All the Tomol turned their attention on Dastin. Pole-arms were subtly angled in his direction, and Ysan moved to loom over him. "Where did they take her?"

"The northeast part of the island." Dastin pointed, though Theriault had no idea how the scout could have any idea in what direction he was gesturing, since dawn was hours away and they had all been moved while unconscious. "Six Klingons took your friend there."

Ysan and the other Tomol appeared energized by Dastin's news. Then the priestess's manner turned menacing. "And these Klingons are friends of yours?"

Hoping to regain control of the dialogue, Theriault answered first. "Far from it. We have a long history with the Klingons—most of it less than friendly, some of it bloody as hell."

"Then you are enemies?"

"At the moment? More like rivals."

"I fail to see the distinction."

Theriault waved off the semantic debate. "Not important. What matters is, we don't want to let the Klingons get away with your friend any more than you do."

"Why not?"

As Theriault struggled to concoct a diplomatic answer, Dastin said, "Doesn't matter. If they want something, we want the opposite. So for now, that makes you and us friends."

The priestess remained wary. "You presume much." She turned her back on Dastin and spoke to Theriault. "Help us bring Nimur back to the Well of Flames for her Cleansing, and then perhaps we will call you friends."

Theriault tilted her head at the landing party's equipment. "We'll need our things back."

"After you have led us to Nimur."

The first officer's tone was firm. "No, before. Without our tools, we can't help you."

"Please, there is no time to waste arguing. We must bring her back to—"

"If there's no time to waste, I suggest you give us our tools and let us get to work."

"You may have the talking boxes and the ones with straps, but not the weapons."

"It's all or nothing," Theriault insisted. "I won't be held hostage with my own weapon."

Ysan glanced at the hardware on the ground, then at the landing party. "If we give you all your tools, will you help us bring Nimur home to complete her Cleansing?"

"If Nimur attacks us, we'll defend ourselves. We won't help you attack her, but we also won't stop you from doing so. We'll help you find your missing friend, and we'll do whatever's necessary to protect you, your people, and ourselves from the Klingons. Agreed?"

The terms did not seem to please the priestess, but after a moment's thought she nodded. "Very well." She beckoned the younger Tomol female, who on closer inspection Theriault estimated was no older than fourteen or fifteen years of age. "This is my eldest disciple, Seta. She's going to come with us, as will a company of my strongest Wardens."

"Fine by me." Moving with caution so as not to upset the Tomol, Theriault stood and dusted off her jumpsuit. As she got up, the rest of the landing party followed her lead. Once they had regained their feet, Ysan signaled her Wardens to stand aside and let the landing party take back their tools—minus the vaporized communicator. Theriault and the others made quick work of slinging their tricorders over their shoulders and tucking their phasers and communicators back into the custom-fitted pockets on their jumpsuits.

Theriault made sure the Tomol could hear the orders she gave the landing party, so no one would have reason to think she was hiding anything. "Hesh, run a scan and try to get a lock on the Klingons. Make sure they haven't moved since we got captured." As the Arkenite scientist worked, Theriault turned to explain the situation to Ysan.

"The devices with straps are used for finding people and things, and for studying things. My friend Hesh is going to use his to help us lead you to your friend."

"I understand." Ysan nodded to her Wardens, who fell in behind her. "You and your friends will stay in front of us. I strongly recommend none of you draw your weapons without good reason—or else my Wardens will teach you new kinds of pain."

"Noted." Theriault signaled the landing party to move out. As soon as her back was to the Tomol, she vented her frustration and anxiety with a roll of her eyes.

Something tells me this ain't the beginning of a beautiful friendship.

11

"You need to let me go."

Nimur's warning went unheeded. The Klingons were gathered around a rock they had heated with beams from their handheld weapons, and they were feasting on the raw flesh of small rodents they had captured with simple snares set inside the caves. It made no sense to Nimur that, as much as the Klingons enjoyed the stone's warmth, they wouldn't use the red-hot boulder to cook their food. It was a peculiar choice, but one she could accept—except that they refused to use it to cook the skinned rodent carcass they had tossed to her.

She crouched in a nook of the cave tunnel, secured in place by a chain attached to her by a ring of metal that had closed as if by magic once its ends touched each other. The chain was anchored to the floor by a ring on a metal rod that she guessed the Klingons must have put there, because she had never heard of such a thing being in the caves—not from any of the priestesses or disciples she had ever known. Being tethered was an insult to her pride, an indignity she wouldn't inflict upon an animal, much less on a fellow thinking creature.

Tobar and his men joked in their guttural native tongue, and then he sent two of them to relieve the pair guarding the caves' entrance. The man left behind with Tobar was not like the others. He was slimmer and quieter, and his forehead was smooth rather than ridged. His cohorts called him *Quch'Ha*. Only Tobar showed him the courtesy of calling him by his name, Tormog. Nimur had no idea why Tormog didn't look like the other Klingons, even though he spoke their language, wore their clothes, and ate their food—but she had seen enough teasing by cruel children to understand what defined someone as the prey of bullies. Tormog was a victim.

Hoping to play on some reservoir of sympathy he might harbor in secret, Nimur waited until Tobar stepped away to relieve himself in a nearby empty cave nook, and then she reached out to Tormog with a desperate whisper. "Please, you must set me free."

The *Quch'Ha* sneered at her request. "You must be kidding."

"Please. Release me, or something terrible will happen."

Tormog chuckled. "Wrong. Something terrible will happen if I let you go. Tobar will cut off my head, hollow out my skull, and tell his men to use it for a chamber pot."

On the far side of the glowing boulder, she heard her baby's cry of hunger and fear. "I'm begging you, Tormog. Let me and my baby go. All I want is to reach a distant island and live out my life. It's not so much to ask."

He spit on her. "Don't ever use my name again, you filthy *Ha'DIbaH*." Exuding contempt, he turned and walked back to the rock to bask in its ruddy glow.

Shame and fury burned inside Nimur, and the heat of rage overwhelmed her senses. Close at hand, she felt the life-forces of the six Klingons. Each was distinctive in some way, but all six felt similar to this new sense that had awakened inside Nimur's consciousness.

Other energies swirled around them. Invisible threads of connection and influence were woven into the fabric of the universe, and if Nimur attuned her mind to the texture of those threads—to their peculiar vibrations, their idiosyncratic frequencies—she could tug on them. Some were slack, awaiting a motive force; others were taut and resisted her desires. But the hotter the fires inside her mind blazed, the more of these threads she felt surrender to her will.

Tobar returned and noted the uneaten rodent carcass at Nimur's feet. "Not hungry?"

"Let me go," Nimur demanded. "I won't ask you again."

"Good, because I'm bored of telling you 'no.' Now shut up and let us rest."

The Klingon commander sat down on the hard ground, propped himself against the cave wall with his legs crossed in front of himself, shut his eyes, and went to sleep as if he had not a single care in the waking world.

Staring at him, Nimur felt her hatred flare until it blazed like the fire in the Pit, hot enough to Cleanse one and all, a flame bright enough to burn away a world of flesh and leave only the fury it had spawned.

It would be only a matter of time now until she was free, and then Tobar and his men would pay for their arrogance—as would Ysan, the Wardens, and all the rest.

At last, Nimur understood why the Changed had always been feared, and why since the time of the Arrival they had been condemned to the Well of Flames for Cleansing. She realized what she would become when the Change was over.

She was being reborn—*as the fire*. And when that fateful hour came around at last, Nimur vowed, all those who had wronged her would *burn*.

The only thing worse than marching through a sweltering, overgrown jungle, Theriault decided, was doing so with a deadly weapon aimed at one's back. She was near the front of the single-file line, directly behind Dastin, who walked point. An armed Warden walked between her and Tan Bao, who was followed by Hesh. Another Warden followed the Arkenite, and behind him were Ysan, Seta, and four more Wardens.

Theriault palmed the perspiration from her forehead and pushed sweaty locks of her red hair off her face. She stole a look at the sky. The number of visible stars had decreased, and the heavens betrayed the first hints of blue in the blackness. Dawn was close.

Ahead of her, Dastin slowed, so she did the same. The terrain looked familiar. Noting the uphill grade on which they stood, Theriault surmised they had begun climbing the hill toward the cave entrance. Her morbid curiosity compelled her to wonder what would happen when the Tomol confronted the Klingons; her desire for self-preservation didn't want to find out.

Hesh called out to her, his voice strained by the struggle between the need to whisper and the desire to shout. "Commander? You should see this."

The procession stopped as Theriault turned to look back. Hesh tried to move forward with his tricorder clenched in both hands, but a Warden blocked his way with his lance. The pale, diminutive Arkenite tried to push past the obstacle, but the Warden stood firm. Theriault shot an exasperated look at Ysan, who gestured quick commands to the Wardens. The one who blocked Hesh raised his lance and motioned for Theriault to swap places with Tan Bao. She failed to see the logic in the arbitrary enforcement of the single-file formation, but as a guest on the Tomol's island she didn't think it was her place to argue with their rules.

Tan Bao and Theriault passed each other with sidelong looks, and then she was next to Hesh. She felt the Tomol's stares upon them. "This better be good, Hesh."

"I've isolated a peculiar disparity in the biochemistry of the Tomol and the other animal life-forms we've detected on this planet, both at the landing site and here on this island."

He seemed rather excited about what sounded to Theriault like a rather dry discovery. "And you think this 'disparity' is significant because . . . ?"

"Because if my scans of the Tomol's mitochondria, and my comparative analyses of those mitochondria to those of other fauna on this planet, are both accurate, my findings suggest the Tomol do not share a common ancestor with any extant species on Nereus Two. I concede that without a thorough xenoarcheological study of the planetary biosphere it's impossible to rule out any connection to a native precursor life-form, but I'm reasonably certain the Tomol are not an indigenous species on this world."

It was bigger news than Theriault had expected. "Whoa, slow down. Are you sure?"

"As certain as I can be, pending a more detailed and controlled study."

She lowered her voice and hoped the Tomol hadn't already overheard them. "If they aren't from here, where did they come from?"

Hesh shrugged. "I have no idea, sir. Their genetic profile doesn't match any species previously encountered by the Federation."

"Could they be living here as refugees? Or maybe as prisoners?"

The science officer shook his head. "I have insufficient data to make such a conclusion."

Nothing about Hesh's revelation seemed immediately pertinent to the situation with the Klingons or the missing Tomol woman, but the mere possibility that the Tomol had come to this world from another sparked Theriault's curiosity. "Hesh, listen carefully. Set your tricorder to transfer all its stored readings to the ship in an emergency burst transmission, but do it quietly. I'll try to hail the ship, but in case we can't, I want to make sure the *Sagittarius* has this data."

"Understood, Commander. I'll start the transfer now."

She walked past Hesh, heading back toward Ysan. As she'd hoped, all eyes were on her, and no one paid any attention to Hesh while he futzed and fiddled with his tricorder. Theriault stopped when another Warden pressed the business end of his pole-arm to her chest. She leaned around him to make eye contact with Ysan. "I want to tell you something."

The priestess waved the Warden away from Theriault. "Speak."

"I need to let the crew of my ship know my friends and I are all right. I plan to speak to them using my friend Hesh's talk-box. Will you permit it?"

Now the collective focus was on Ysan, awaiting her judgment. "I will permit it."

"Thank you." Theriault walked back to Hesh and held out her open hand, which he filled with his communicator. A flick of her wrist opened its grille, and she adjusted the device to an encrypted ship-to-shore setting. "Theriault to *Sagittarius*. Do you read me?"

She felt tremendous relief at the sound of the captain's voice. *"Go ahead, Commander."*

"Sir, we've made contact with the local residents on the big island."

Terrell sighed in disappointment. *"And how's that going?"*

She noted the weapons pointed at her. "About as well as these things usually do."

"Wonderful. Any sign of our neighbors?"

Neighbors was Terrell and Theriault's previously agreed-upon euphemism for the Klingons. "Affirmative. In fact, we're on our way to an unscheduled powwow."

He sounded understandably concerned. *"That wouldn't be my first choice."*

"Mine either, sir. But it's not really up to us." She turned away and cupped her hand over her mouth and the communicator. "Hesh is sending up his tricorder data. It seems to imply the natives are anything but, if you take my meaning. Do me a favor and have Doctor Babitz give it a look. I think it might explain what our neighbors are doing here."

"Understood. We'll let you know what we find. Anything else?"

"Negative. Our hosts look anxious to get moving. I'd better go."

"Acknowledged. Keep your head down, Number One. Sagittarius out."

A light on the communicator switched off, indicating the channel had closed. Theriault flipped the grille shut and lobbed the communicator back to Hesh, who caught it—after a second of clumsy half-fumbles—and tucked it back onto his belt. Theriault moved forward, signaled Tan Bao to fall back, and resumed her place in the line behind Dastin. "Okay, Lieutenant, let's go. I want to meet the Klingons while we still have the cover of darkness."

"Aye, sir." Dastin resumed his steady, careful march through the jungle, leading the procession uphill, through tangled walls of flowering vines and hip-deep fronds, to what Theriault feared was now an unavoidable confrontation with the Klingons.

When her pace slowed for a few moments, Theriault felt the jab of a Warden's lance prod her forward. *That does it,* she decided. *If I live through this, I'm gonna let the captain lead all the damned landing parties he wants. Why should I get to have all the fun?*

Cold, hard edges bit into Nimur's flesh as she strained against the bonds that lashed her to the stone floor of the cave. The circle of metal around her wrist looked solid, and compared to her flesh it felt unbreakable—but she knew better. She was learning to see things in new ways.

There were spaces in everything, in everyone. The entire world was more emptiness than form, more void than presence. There was no difference between solids, liquids, and air—they were just degrees of being, octaves on a scale, and only a fool would be blind to that truth.

Even the Klingons, with their ugly laughter and foul odors, were more illusion than reality, from Nimur's point of view. To her eyes they looked like flesh, blood, and bone, but to her mind they were wild energies harnessed into temporary shapes, bundles of earth and water, fire and air, all yoked together with an illusion of will, a cruel joke of consciousness.

They were nothing to her. Mere insects. Vermin. A pestilence to be stamped out.

Clarity returned suddenly. *The heat of the Change is making me mad,* Nimur realized. Each bout of delusion lasted longer than the one before, and filled her with ever-greater intensities of hatred and power. More of her mind was succumbing to its effects with each turn, leaving only one small part of her untouched, unsullied by its irrational fury and primitive cruelty. She feared her next descent into that emotional inferno would be her last.

Tahna's cry split the pre-dawn silence and echoed through the caves. Tobar and his men groaned and cursed. Exhaustion slurred their epithets and left the Klingons blinking through the gray half-light toward the swaddled infant, who lay beside the boulder that once had given off such great heat but now stood cold and dark. Kergol rolled over and threw a stone at the wailing baby. "Shut up, you mewling *taHqeq!*"

Nimur screamed back, "Stop it! She needs to be changed! Let me clean her."

Her protest roused the sleeping Klingons, who sat up to face her. Tobar scratched the fur that ringed his mouth and covered his chin. He asked Tormog, "What is she screeching about?"

Tormog winced as he massaged his own neck. "She wants to tend to her child."

Kergol grimaced at the shrieking newborn. "Why did we let her bring it here? It's going to draw predators—or worse, scavengers." He growled in disgust. "We should just kill it and bury it in the jungle."

"No!" Nimur lunged toward the Klingons, only to have her chains stop her in mid-step. "Don't you touch her! She's mine! Do you hear me? Mine!"

Tobar groaned, then waved his hand. "Fine. I hate that noise. Get rid of it."

The commander lay down, perhaps expecting to go back to sleep, as Kergol lumbered toward the crying baby. Tormog leaped to his feet, blocked the lieutenant's path, and seized the larger Klingon by his arms. "No! We can use the child to keep her under control!"

Kergol swatted his way free of Tormog's grip and shoved him out of his path. "I have other ways of keeping *novpu'* in line. Quieter ways that'll let us get some sleep while we wait for the *Voh'tahk* to pick us up and take us home." He stomped over to Tahna, seemingly oblivious of Nimur's anguished cries for mercy or her furious curses of damnation. The brawny Klingon picked up Tahna with one hand, and drew his dagger with the other.

Then Nimur's world turned white with rage and crimson with death.

For the sake of her child, she let go of the last gentle part of herself and finished her transformation into the monster that the Change had always meant for her to become.

The metal that bound her wrists and ankles broke apart at her mental command; it was easy—all she had to do was imagine all the tiny parts of what made it exist flying apart and never returning, and then the metal was gone.

Taking apart the Klingons wasn't quite so simple—something about their life-force made them more coherent—but she didn't mind. If anything, she enjoyed the challenge. Their bodies, which had seemed so formidable to her only hours earlier, now seemed so fragile. She could pummel them with her thoughts, cast them away like stones into a pond, tear their heads from their necks with the same ease she'd once plucked berries from the bushes on the southern hills.

The two who had been guarding the caves' entrance came running at the sounds of battle. Neither hesitated to train his weapon on Nimur, who reacted twice as quickly. She pictured giant invisible fists clamping shut around the two soldiers, and the Klingons' bones broke like dried twigs. In all her life, Nimur had never heard sweeter music than the sound of a Klingon finally becoming acquainted with pure terror. They screamed in pain; she laughed with glee.

It was ecstasy to her. She and the cave walls both were splattered with the Klingons' dark magenta viscera, and it felt good. It was right and just and so utterly satisfying that

Nimur could not believe she had ever hesitated to kill. She thought of all the creatures whose lives she had ever spared and felt her heart chill with regret. Then she sensed a single Klingon life-force retreating deeper into the caves, fleeing alone into the darkness deep underground.

All my life I could have tasted the sweet thrill of murder, but I was too frightened. She fixed her mind on the desperate Klingon survivor. *Never again.*

Energized by a will to vengeance, Nimur stalked deeper into the caves, down toward the sacred wordstone, her new senses keen, all her thoughts on the joy of the hunt to come.

Behind her, a pathetic wailing emanated from the cave. It was a vexing noise, the sound of fragility. Part of her wanted to silence it, to cut away the last evidence of the weakling she had been. Instead, she answered to a faint, almost inaudible desire, an instinct she couldn't name but felt compelled to obey, and left it behind in the cave, never to be thought of again.

Tears were a thing of the past, and Nimur had turned her mind toward the future—one whose designs she would draw in blood.

12

Pastel hues of daylight slipped through the tiny gaps in the jungle's canopy, a silent herald of dawn's arrival. Dastin halted the landing party and their new Tomol acquaintances. They had reached the edge of the tree line. All that remained between them and the caves was the bare slope, which brightened as the burning edge of daylight crept down from the hilltop, forcing the shadows of the forest into slow retreat.

In the rear of the single-file formation, agitated whispers passed among the Tomol. Two of the Wardens and the disciple Seta huddled around Ysan, who seemed vexed by the need to calm her people. She shushed them and moved forward to join Theriault and Dastin at the head of the group. The priestess said nothing as she shouldered past Dastin, pushed aside a clutch of vines, and stole a look up the hillside. When she turned back, her expression was dour.

Dastin threw a questioning look at Theriault, who just shook her head.

Ysan slipped past them and rejoined the huddle of Wardens. When she returned, her countenance was one of stony resolve. "My people and I will continue alone from here."

Theriault looked worried. "Um, I don't think that's a good idea."

"It is not a subject for debate. Those are the Caves of the Shepherds. They are a sacred place, the dwelling of the wordstone, from which we learn the laws and will of the Shepherds. We can't allow outsiders to defile it."

The holy woman was getting on Dastin's nerves. "No offense, lady, but the Klingons have already defiled it. Matter of fact, you'll be lucky if that's all they do to it. And if your last fight with the Klingons was any measure, I think you'll need our help in there."

"Do you know the fastest route through the caves? Or the safest?" Ysan shifted her ire toward Theriault. "We have protected these caves since the time of the Arrival. Only a priestess, her disciples, and her Wardens are permitted to set foot inside them."

The first officer struck a conciliatory tone. "We understand that, Ysan. And if we had no pressing reason for going inside, we'd be happy to respect your wishes. But Lieutenant Dastin is right: Even in a strange setting, the Klingons are dangerous enemies. And they've had time to dig in and prepare for an attack. I know your people aren't defenseless—far from it. But we have experience dealing with the Klingons; we can help you."

Seta sidled up to Ysan. "She might be right. If these Klingons are helping Nimur, they've put us all in danger." The disciple glanced at the brightening sky. "It might already be too late."

A Warden in a plumed reptilian headdress joined the conversation. "Listen to her, Ysan. The longer we wait to subdue Nimur, the harder it's going to be. Maybe we should let the strangers deal with the Klingons so we can focus all our strength on Nimur."

Ysan winced at the mere suggestion of letting the landing party enter the caves. After a few seconds, she turned back to face Theriault and Dastin. "Will you give us your word that once the Klingons have been dealt with, you won't proceed any deeper into the caves?"

Theriault nodded. "We won't go any farther inside than we absolutely have to."

Her promise coaxed a grudging nod from Ysan. "Then we continue together." She beckoned the Warden in the plumed serpent headdress. "Kitraan. How should we proceed?"

Kitraan pointed to the left of the cave entrance. "There is another trail, one reclaimed by the jungle many years ago, that leads up that side of the hill. It will take some time to clear the path without giving away our movements, but it will let us get above the entrance and approach it without being seen."

"That could work," Dastin said. "But it might be faster to find another entrance." He studied Ysan's face for any reaction as he asked, "Is there another way in or out of the caves?" The priestess didn't disappoint him. Her jaw clenched, and her eyes made a brief, almost involuntary turn downward and toward the east. He caught her eye. "All right, where is it?"

"The low path has been blocked for ages," Ysan said. "Its roof fell in before I was born."

Hesh piped up from behind the three Tomol leaders. "How deep is the blockage?" When they looked back at the unassuming young Arkenite, he continued, "If it's less than fifteen meters, we might be able to drill through it with an industrial phaser."

Sarcasm infused Theriault's reply. "Got one of those in your pocket, Hesh?"

"No, but Master Chief Ilucci could rig one from spare parts and—" He stopped as he noted Theriault's pointed glare, a silent warning not to mention the transporter in front of the natives, who had already seen and heard too much about Starfleet technology as it was. Hesh swallowed and added, "He could send it ashore for us."

Theriault looked skeptical. "Ysan, how long would it take to walk down to the low path?"

"Until midday, at least."

The first officer asked Kitraan, "How long to clear a trail and get above that entrance?"

"Two hours." The Warden looked around, taking the landing party's measure. "Maybe one, if you and your people are stronger than you look."

"All right, we go with Plan A," Theriault said.

Dastin peeked under a frond and felt a tingle of suspicion in his gut, an instinctual sense that something was amiss. "Hang on," he said, arresting the group's departure. He extended one hand to Theriault. "Commander, can I borrow your tricorder? I need to check something."

She lifted the strap of her tricorder and ducked out from under it, then handed the scanning device to Dastin. He checked to make sure its feedback tones were muted, and he began a quick scan of the cave's entrance using multiple settings. The more data he gathered, the more concerned he became. "We might not need to go the long way, sir."

Theriault moved up to kneel beside him. "What're you seeing?"

"It's what I'm *not* seeing. There's no one guarding the

entrance." He showed her the tricorder's display as he cycled through a series of readouts. "Plus, no Klingon life-signs. No humanoid shapes or movement registering on any active sensor frequency. Nothing at all."

She took back the tricorder and tweaked its settings. "Maybe they moved deeper into the caves, to a more defensible position."

"That's possible. But watch what happens when you try to run a deeper scan."

She changed the tricorder's settings. Then her eyes widened. "It's scrambled."

"Exactly. As if it were being jammed."

Theriault shook her head. "No, I don't think so." She beckoned Hesh forward. When the science officer joined them, she passed the tricorder to him. "What does that look like to you?"

Hesh eyed the device's readout. "Natural interference. Most likely produced by high concentrations of fistrium, kelbonite, and trace particles of chimerium in the caves." He recoiled, confused. "But that makes no sense. My initial geological survey of this planet showed no significant levels of those compounds. That would suggest they are specific to these caves."

"Almost as if by design," Theriault said. "If I had to guess, I'd say the Tomol's ancient 'Shepherds' built these caves to be impervious to sensors." She took back her tricorder and switched it off. "Which means that whatever's waiting for us in there, we won't see it coming."

Dastin drew his phaser and flashed an encouraging smile at his XO. "Look on the bright side, Commander. That means it won't see us coming, either."

"If that was you giving a pep talk, you suck at it." Theriault drew her phaser, cueing the rest of the landing party to do the same. "Set for heavy stun and move out."

Weapon in hand, Dastin led the group out of the jungle and up the barren, rocky slope toward the cave entrance. He had no idea what he expected to find inside.

Ten minutes later, he wished he had never set foot inside the caves at all.

Captain Terrell peered over Lieutenant Commander Sorak's shoulder at a pair of tiny red triangles on the *Sagittarius*'s tactical sensor display. Two entities were moving at high warp on a direct heading for the Nereus system, and the ship's computer had tagged them as a potential threat. "Commander? Are those what I think they are?"

"Yes, Captain. A Klingon heavy cruiser and a bird-of-prey. Based on their energy signatures, it is ninety-eight point six percent likely the bird-of-prey is the *Homghor*, and the cruiser is the *Voh'tahk*. Their ETA is two hours and nine minutes."

Terrell admired the Vulcan's stoic detachment, a product of having completed the years-long, emotion-purging *Kolinahr* ritual decades earlier. "Are we inside their sensor range yet?"

"Not for another eleven minutes."

The captain masked his concern and returned to his command chair. "Ensign Nizsk. Have you and Ensign Taryl had any luck finding us a hiding place?"

The Kaferian swiveled her chair away from the forward console, which comprised the functions of flight control, navigation, and operations management. "Not yet, sir."

Taryl turned her chair away from the science console to face Terrell. "We have a few ideas, but they all require us to move out of communications range from the landing party. I'm looking for something that keeps us close but out of sight at the same time."

"Keep looking, but be quick. We need to find cover before the Klingons detect us." As much as Terrell liked to think his crew could master any challenge they encountered, his years in Starfleet had taught him there was no shame in knowing when to retreat—and when to ask for help. He turned his chair toward the communications console, which was manned by Senior Chief Petty Officer Razka. "Chief, what's the *Endeavour*'s last known position?"

The Saurian called up comm and sensor logs on one of his auxiliary screens. "According to her last report, she is still in the Villicus system, completing a survey of the fourth planet."

"Are we close enough to raise her on subspace?"

"Possibly. Let me check." Razka keyed commands into his panel and noted the responses on his master screen. "Affirmative, sir. The subspace repeater her crew deployed is operational."

"Open an encrypted channel and hail Captain Khatami, please."

"Aye, sir." Terrell swiveled his chair toward the main viewscreen while Razka set up the real-time subspace channel to the *Sagittarius*'s companion vessel in the Taurus Reach, the *Constitution*-class heavy cruiser *Endeavour*.

The image of Nereus II switched to the face of Captain Atish Khatami. Behind the youthful, dark-haired Iranian woman, the *Endeavour*'s bridge crew worked with quiet efficiency. *"Clark? This is a surprise. I didn't expect to hear from you so soon after deployment."*

"We're coping with a few surprises here, as well. I hope it's not a bad time."

"Not at all. What can we do for you?"

"We've landed in some hot water with our old neighbors. Apparently, there's more to Nereus Two than we thought."

"How hot is the water over there?"

"We'll find out in two hours."

Khatami angled her chair away from the viewscreen, took a moment for a whispered conference with her first officer, Commander Katherine Stano, then returned to her conversation with Terrell. *"At maximum warp, we can be there in just over two and a half hours."*

"Better late than never. See you then. *Sagittarius* out."

Razka closed the channel, and the main viewscreen reverted to an image of the ringed planet below. Terrell felt sweat bead upon his brow. Help was on the way, but he had no idea if he, his crew, or his ship would still be here when it arrived. "Commander Sorak, take the ship to Yellow Alert. Ensign Taryl, you have nine minutes to find us a place to hide. After that, we'll either have to retreat, or else find a shallow sea on the planet—and scuttle the ship."

Nizsk looked back from the forward console. "Sir, we won't last long underwater."

"Longer than we'll last if we go head-to-head with two Klingon warships."

Something chirped on Taryl's console. The Orion woman silenced the alert, checked the sensor display, and then flashed a wicked smile as she looked up at Terrell.

"Captain, I just found our hiding place."

Daylight didn't reach far inside the caves past their entrance, just far enough that Theriault had time to acclimate her vision to the shadows that lay ahead. She was about to ask Hesh to power up his tricorder to shed some indirect light on their surroundings when her boot sole adhered ever so slightly to a tacky sheen on the cave's floor. Her nostrils filled with the charnel reek of an abattoir—a grotesque mix of blood's ferric tang and the stench of excrement.

"Something bad happened here," she whispered ahead to Dastin.

The Trill lifted his foot and shook it. "No kidding. I think I just stepped on a spleen."

Theriault beckoned Tan Bao. "I hate to do this to you, but this is starting to smell like your department." She waved the svelte Vietnam-born nurse past her.

He inched forward and halted when the smell struck him. "Oh, that's not good."

"I've figured that out. I need you to give me a detailed forensic report."

"Never a dull moment." Tan Bao activated his medical tricorder and moved deeper inside the cave. The glow from the tricorder's display revealed wet splatters of magenta blood and shredded viscera on the cave's walls, ceiling, and floor. He stepped with care, seeking out the few dry patches of ground where he could walk without disturbing any grisly remains.

Dastin and Theriault followed Tan Bao inside. Ysan and Kitraan were close behind them, but Hesh lingered in the entry passage, visibly reluctant to ford the fresh-spilled river of blood. The rest of the Wardens filed past him, spread out inside the cave, and navigated the gore in halting steps. The blue-white glow from the Wardens' lances added to the illumination, revealing the full extent of the macabre details that surrounded them.

Theriault sidestepped some glistening entrails to speak confidentially with Ysan. "What lives in these caves that could do this to an entire squad of armed Klingons?"

The teenaged priestess sounded shaken. "Nothing. This must have been Nimur."

"Nimur? That slip of a girl we saw run away from your pit of fire?"

A fat drop of blood fell from the ceiling and streaked down Ysan's robe of feathers. She winced in disgust and tried to wipe it away, but that only spread the blood farther. "Don't be deceived by her size. She's deeper into the Change than anyone has been in hundreds of cycles. The longer it takes us to restrain her, the more dangerous she'll become."

Hesh walked a slow, wary patrol around the perimeter of the carnage, while Dastin and Tan Bao scrutinized its most gruesome patches. Because the minerals in the cave walls were blocking most active scan functions of their tricorders, the devices could be used only for generating light and making an audiovisual record of the scene. Meanwhile, the Wardens split up and ventured a few meters down the connecting passages, as much to seek out their quarry as to provide a defensive ring for the investigation.

A troubling thought occurred to Theriault. "Ysan? If Nimur wasn't willing to go into the fire before, I'd have to think she'll be even less cooperative now."

"I suspect you're right."

"Well, if she's this strong already, will your Wardens be able to stop her?"

Ysan cast a despairing look around at the shredded flesh and bone. "I don't know."

Tan Bao stood, his expression grave. "Commander? We counted six members of that Klingon recon team, but the"—he struggled but failed to find a euphemism—"*parts* we can account for here only add up to five bodies. I think one of the Klingons made a run for it."

An avian-masked Warden returned in a hurry from one of the intersecting passages. "The stranger might be right, Ysan. There is a blood trail in this passage. It is not Tomol blood."

Dastin hurried to the Warden's side and made his own assessment. "Yeah, this is Klingon blood. Not much of it. Our guy's been hit, but judging from the spacing between these stains, he was running his ass off." The scout looked back at the Warden. "Where does this tunnel lead?"

"All the way down to the labyrinth that protects the wordstone."

"All right, then," Theriault said. "We know Nimur didn't come out of the only entrance. Unless anyone objects, I'd suggest we stick together and follow that blood trail." There were no protests from the Tomol priestess, her disciple, or her defenders, so Theriault continued. "Dastin, stay on point. We can't use tricorders to track in here, and I'd rather not give away our position by shining lights ahead of us, but you'll need some way to follow the blood splatters."

Tan Bao perked up. "Ultraluminol! I can rig a hypospray to disperse it like an aerosol. It'll light up a blood trail like a supernova."

"Good, get it done. Hesh, I—" She looked around, wondering where the Arkenite had gone. She found him crouched in a dark nook at the far end of the chamber. "Hesh, what're—"

A baby's piercing cry split the air and reverberated through the caves.

Hesh stood, cradling the swaddled infant. "She was just lying here."

"That's Nimur's daughter," Ysan said. "Her name is Tahna. Nimur took her."

Dastin looked unhappy to see the child. "And now she's abandoned her."

Ysan summoned a canine-masked Warden with a look. "Matulo, take the child back to the village. Give her back to her Guardians, Chimi and Tayno." The Warden gently took the whimpering baby from Hesh and hurried her out of the ad hoc slaughterhouse. As they escaped to the sunlit world outside the cave and the baby's cries receded, the priestess looked down the dark path that lay ahead. "I doubt the last Klingon is still alive. If he is, he won't be for long." She directed an almost apologetic look at Theriault. "Nimur is not your responsibility; she's ours.

If you and your friends wish to leave us now, we will understand."

Her invitation to bail out drew hopeful looks from the rest of the landing party. It fell to Theriault to be the bearer of bad tidings. "Not until we find the last Klingon. As long as there's a chance he's alive and can answer questions, we have to try to find him."

"As you wish."

Theriault stole a look at Tan Bao's improvised adjustments to a hypospray. "How's it coming? Think you'll get a wide enough dispersal to make it useful?"

"Let's see." Tan Bao pointed the hypospray down the passage and squeezed off a quick pump of the chemofluorescent spray. The short hiss was louder than Theriault would have liked, but it was less likely to betray them from a distance than naked light sources were. Seconds later, a trail of blood spatter extending almost fifteen meters ahead of Tan Bao glowed neon green. "It helps that the air in these caves flows from top to bottom. Means we can spray with the current."

Dastin surveyed the results. "Outstanding. Let's go, before it fades." He followed the blood trail, and Tan Bao walked beside him.

Theriault signaled Hesh to follow the two men, and then she looked back at Ysan. "Stay close. If we find your friend, we'd rather not face her alone."

"We understand." Ysan motioned her Wardens to follow the Starfleet team. "If we did not have to ensure her Cleansing, we would rather not face her, either."

Everyone tried their best to be stealthy as the group descended into the caves, but it was impossible for eleven people treading on gritty stone and patches of loose rock to be silent. *If our survival hinges on setting an ambush,* Theriault realized, *we're all as good as dead.*

Then came manic, taunting cries that echoed and re-echoed through the caves; the sound seemed to come from all directions at once. It was a woman's voice, but Theriault couldn't discern words. Just whooping shrieks and banshee moans. The deeper they plumbed, the louder the sounds became—the only indication that they were getting closer.

Dastin halted the group with a raised hand. Then he pointed at something on the ground. Hesh picked it up. It was a Klingon disruptor pistol, standard military issue—but it was barely recognizable. It had been mangled and smashed, as if twisted and crushed in the gears of a great and merciless machine. The science officer switched the broken weapon to his off hand and then rubbed together the fingertips of his dominant hand. He looked back at Theriault. "Blood."

"Okay. We know the last Klingon survivor made it this far. He might be nearby. Stay sharp and—" Movement on the edge of her vision turned her head.

Nimur was behind them.

"Hello, Ysan."

The fugitive young woman was aglow with strange energies. Her eyes radiated light, as if a bonfire raged behind them. Tiny ribbons of electricity danced between her fingers and crept up her arms. Most alarming of all was her maniacal smile; there was no mirth in it—only malice.

Ysan and her Wardens formed a skirmish line between

Nimur and the landing party. The priestess stepped in front of her people, clearly trying to take charge. "Nimur, this has to stop."

"Came to take me back to the fire, did you?" With a birdlike tilt of her head, she peeked past the Wardens at the landing party. "And you brought new friends for me to play with.".

"Leave them out of this, Nimur."

"But you've already brought them into it. Or, should I say, they brought you. Because from where I was standing, it seems clear they were leading and you were following." Nimur regarded the landing party with a malevolent gleam. "I think that makes them fair game."

The Wardens raised their lances to fire. Then they flew backward, as if swatted away by an angry god—all without a word or even the slightest movement from Nimur.

Ysan drew a long, curved dagger from beneath her robe and lunged at Nimur.

Nimur clenched a fist. Ysan convulsed as she rose several centimeters off the ground. The sickly cracking of her bones was mixed with the wet sound of her body being crushed to a pulp. The dagger fell from Ysan's twitching hand.

Seta the disciple ran toward the landing party. She made it three steps before an unseen force slammed her against one wall of the tunnel and then the other. Bloodied and bruised, the young teen collapsed unconscious to the ground.

Theriault raised her phaser. "Heavy stun! Aim for center mass!" Behind her, Dastin aimed his weapon half a second faster than Tan Bao and Hesh.

As Nimur let the misshapen husk of Ysan's body fall in a heap, the wounded Wardens struggled to get up. A few of them started to aim their lances once more at Nimur.

All the Wardens' heads twisted one-hundred-eighty degrees in a fraction of a second. The breaking of their necks sounded like old-fashioned firecrackers.

Then there was nothing between Theriault and the demonic force once known as Nimur.

"Fire!"

Four blue phaser beams screamed through the darkness and slammed into Nimur. Their combined force launched her backward several meters and knocked her onto her back. For a moment, the crackling electricity on Nimur's hands ceased, and the fire in her eyes dimmed. Then her eyes flared white and a brutal, invisible blunt force struck Theriault.

She and the rest of the landing party landed in a tangle of limbs, all of them stunned and groaning in pain. She blinked to clear the spots from her purpled vision and staggered to her feet. With her phaser clutched in her outstretched, unsteady arm, she looked for any sign of Nimur.

The fugitive was gone.

Behind her, Dastin rubbed the back of his head. "Is it over?"

Theriault holstered her phaser. "I've got a bad feeling this is just getting started."

Oblivion was a comfort; the waking life promised nothing beyond suffering and grief. Loath as Seta was to embrace the light, she knew she had no choice. Its pull was irresistible.

Pain was the disciple's first taste of consciousness. A dull ache filled her skull, and the torn flesh on the side of her face burned at the kiss of a breeze. It hurt to force her eyes open; a bright light made her squint.

"Good pupil response," said one of the strangers, a male with black hair. "Minor concussion, scrapes and bruises. She'll be okay."

Seta held up a hand to block the light. "What are you doing?"

"Tending your wounds. Are you feeling any pain? In your head, maybe?"

"Some."

"I can make it go away, if you'll let me. Won't hurt a bit, I promise." She nodded her consent, and he set to work. He used odd tools that made sounds like music, and he touched one to her throat. It stung for the briefest moment, and then she felt a blissful release from her pain. It was like drinking the milk of the *ulora* root, but it didn't make her drowsy. Another sing-song tool eased the pain of the wound on her face. When she touched it, her skin was whole again.

The female stranger with hair the color of sunset kneeled in front of her. "Seta? Do you remember our names?"

"You are Vanessa. The leader."

"That's right, Vanessa Theriault. The man helping you is Nguyen Tan Bao." She pointed at the two men behind her, the one with spots, and the one with the funny three-bump head. "Do you remember the names of my scout and my scientist?"

"You call them Dastin and Hesh."

"That's right. Faro Dastin and Sengar Hesh." The leader woman patted Tan Bao's shoulder. "Sounds like her memory's good. Any subdural bleeding?"

"None that I can detect." Tan Bao put away his musical tools. "She's good to go." He got up and stepped back to let Theriault talk privately with Seta.

"We need your help, Seta."

"I can't." Seta wished she were anywhere else. That she had never come here. She tried to look away from Theriault, but in one direction lay the twisted corpses of the Wardens; in the other was the mangled body of Ysan. Terror and grief, fury and sadness all collided inside her heart and churned up heaving sobs. She choked them back, fought to deny the terrible memories that she now carried. Tears rolled from her eyes as her sorrow consumed her.

Theriault brushed the tears from Seta's cheek. "I know this is an awful time for you, that you've lost people you care about, in ways too horrible to remember. But you need to find some way to keep going, Seta. Because we need you. More important, your people need you."

"What can I do for them? For anyone? I'm just a disciple."

"Not anymore. Ysan's dead, Seta. That means you're the priestess now."

She fought the notion with wild shakes of her head and squeezed-shut eyes. "No, I can't be. I've only had half the teaching. There are so many mysteries Ysan never showed me."

"I don't know how, Seta, but you need to teach yourself now. Because until you do, you can't stop Nimur—and neither can we. We'll help you any way we can, but you need to let us."

"Why do you care about stopping Nimur?"

"Because I think the Klingons know what she's changing into, and they want to study it. Maybe to use it on themselves, or turn it against others. I don't really know what their game is. What I do know is that powers like Nimur's are too dangerous to let run wild—here or anywhere else. It sounds like the Shepherds your people worship knew something about this, so if we're going to find answers, I think that's where we ought to look first."

The stranger's words made sense. They were the only thing that did right now.

Seta felt hollow and alone as she palmed the last of her tears from her cheeks. *This is how it must be. This is how I must live.* She made herself stand and walked to Ysan's desecrated body. The former priestess's eyes were still open, their lifeless gaze turned toward a sky obscured by endless depths of stone. Seta gently coaxed Ysan's eyelids shut, and then she removed her teacher's ceremonial robe of feathers with tender care. The once beautiful garment was now caked with dust and blood. Seta draped it over herself. Then she untied the scabbard from Ysan's thigh, picked up her fallen dagger, and sheathed it.

Garbed in the robe of feathers, bearing the sacred blade, Seta realized she truly was the new priestess of the people. In her imagination, this was to have been a moment of pride. Instead, it filled her with nothing but dread and regret.

The people need me to be strong. My pain no longer matters. I must think of them.

"I will take you to the wordstone of the Shepherds. It is hidden in a secret alcove, beyond the deepest chamber in the labyrinth. There, the history of the Tomol is written. If answers are what you seek, that is where you will find them."

13

Tormog's back was pressed to the cave wall. He had heard footsteps behind him and presumed the alien woman had found him, despite all his efforts at stealth. How had she tracked him? All he could think of was his blood trail, but that should have made no difference in the darkness. Could a nose as small and delicate as hers be that sensitive? Could her eyes be that keen?

Peeking through the sliver-thin crevasse into the tunnel he had left, he saw flecks of his blood glowing green. He squinted, thinking he might be hallucinating, but the trail's radiance only increased. Primitive instincts filled him with waves of paranoia and a powerful urge to lash out in violence. He called upon his scientific training to quash his animal nature and reason out an explanation for what he was seeing.

Is my blood reacting to particles in the air? My earlier scans didn't detect anything that should fluoresce in contact with blood. Could it be something in the stone of these caves? Maybe, but I can't get a clear scan of anything down here because of the mineral compounds in the rock, so there's no way to know for sure. Is it something the alien woman is doing? That doesn't seem likely—but then, neither did Commander Tobar's head flying off his neck for no visible reason.

Then the explanation walked past him, single file, in olive-green jumpsuits.

He knew they were Federation Starfleet personnel by the patches on the shoulders of their uniforms. Two were human, one was a humanoid with curious spots on the side of his face, and the fourth was an Arkenite. They were escorted by a group of natives. The male human spritzed a fast-spreading mist from a small handheld device. Tormog deduced that the sprayed substance was a chemofluorescent agent that reacted with blood and other bodily fluids.

Now what do I do?

The Starfleeters would soon run out of blood trail to follow. If their point man was even reasonably competent as a tracker, he would soon realize Tormog had doubled back. It would be only a matter of time before they discovered him hiding in this literal crack in the wall.

Then I'll be trapped. He considered the merits of a preemptive attack, but he was in no position to launch an effective ambush. All he could do was hope that they continued far enough past his hiding spot that he could slip out and retreat before they noticed that they'd lost his trail, turned back, and retraced their steps.

Voices led to a commotion. A frantic scramble of activity surrendered to the confused alarms of struggle, and then came screams of agony and fear. Sharp cracking sounds were followed by the heavy, dull thud of bodies falling like dead weight to the stone floor.

A single shout unleashed four screeching phaser beams. The blue light was blinding, and the high-pitched sound of the Starfleet sidearms reverberated inside Tormog's narrow slice in the stone. An unholy wailing echoed outside, and then silence fell, sudden, welcome, and heavy.

The quiet lasted only a few seconds. More talking came next. The voices were lower now, their mood more subdued. After a few minutes, the shuffle and scrape of feet on stone heralded the departure of the survivors. Watching from his shadowy vantage, Tormog counted only the four Starfleet personnel and one native—a young female. She wore the ceremonial garment of the priestess, but she was not the same person he and the rest of his recon unit had seen back in the village. *Looks like someone just earned a battlefield promotion.*

They moved away from him. He skulked from his secret redoubt and peered around a corner. None of them seemed to take notice of him. To his surprise, they were heading not for the surface, but farther into the caves, down a sloping passage into the deepest caverns.

Where are they going?

He was torn between his duty and his impulses. His every ragged nerve screamed at him to return to the surface, where his scanner might function well enough to let him stay a step ahead of Nimur, who had mutated into a crazed engine of slaughter. With open ground and fair warning, even a mere scientist such as himself might stand a chance of surviving long enough to rely upon the aid of reinforcements, whom Tobar had said were already on the way.

Remaining in the caves, literally and figuratively blind to the perils around him, seemed to Tormog like a fool's errand. It made almost no tactical sense. And yet . . . like every other Klingon officer serving in the Gonmog Sector—which the Starfleeters still insisted on calling the Taurus Reach—he had standing orders to investigate and report on all Starfleet activity.

Not only am I the last member of my team left alive, I'm the only one who knows Starfleet is here. His acute night vision watched the last glimmers of light from the Federation team's scanning devices vanish around a distant curve in the tunnel. Plumbing deeper into these catacombs was the last thing Tormog wanted to do, but he knew his career and his life would likely arrive at premature ends if he let the Starfleeters escape his scrutiny. *If I don't find out what they're looking for, and what they're up to, the captain will have my head on a* bat'leth.

Tormog looked back and surveyed the carnage left behind by Nimur. Dead natives lay in a heap, their bodies twisted almost as cruelly as those of his comrades. Broken and bereft of her robe, the priestess Ysan looked to his eye like a piece of smashed fruit.

If I meet Nimur alone, this will almost certainly be my fate.

All at once, the prospect of staying closer to the Starfleeters seemed far more palatable. At the very least, they were a threat that Tormog could understand—and if nothing else, they would make good fodder for the rampaging Tomol woman.

Tormog drew his *d'k tahg* and padded down the tunnel in stealthy, careful pursuit. He knew reinforcements would arrive within the hour, which gave him that long to find out why the Starfleeters were here—and whether they would need to be destroyed.

• • •

Familiar roads had become lost paths from a faded dream. That was all Nimur's life before the Change was to her now—a fleeting vision, a phantasmagoria of half-remembered names and faces. Former rivals and old friends, the Guardians who'd raised her, the ones who had accepted custody of her child. Who were they to her, now that she had become a stranger to herself?

Her feet disturbed a puddle on the trail at the edge of the village. She stopped, looked down at her image on the water's ripple-distorted surface, and waited until it was still.

I don't recognize my own face.

Her eyes were aflame with wild energies, but nothing else about her had changed. So why did gazing upon her reflection feel as if she were staring at a shadow with no owner?

Who am I?

Drifting, light-headed, moving as if by the will of another, she strode down the dirt paths of the only place she had ever called home. Far ahead of her, people she had known all her life, or all of theirs, scurried in a breathless panic at the sight of her. They fled inside their huts, drew the ragged curtains, closed the rain shutters of reeds caked in wax and bound by animal sinew. Mothers snatched up their infants and sprinted out of Nimur's sight. Pairs of young Guardians gathered up their charges and left their hand-crafted toys behind in their haste to flee.

The village looked deserted from the outside, but she knew better. She felt all those eyes upon her from inside the huts. Violet auras of fear hovered like dark halos above each dwelling, signaling the dread with which her return was being met.

She sensed all their minds. They were beacons in the darkness of mere being. In a world of dull matter and lightless emptiness, each spark of consciousness blazed like a sun cresting the horizon. Their light was more than visible; it was tangible. These were embers waiting to ignite.

At the periphery of the village, rushing in from many directions, were all the Wardens. Nimur felt their fear and their anger, their hesitation and their courage. As they energized their lances, she became aware of the source of the weapons' power.

The caves. The wordstone. Of course. I should have known. We all should have.

Her voice shook the ground and rattled the huts as she vented her rage at her kith and kin. "Why are you all hiding? You know me! You called me friend! Now you hide from me? Have we become foes overnight?"

No one answered. The aura of fear darkened, and the Wardens quickened their pace.

Nimur stalked the paths of her youth, hurling her words like stones at the people she had thought loved her. "Why did I believe the priestesses? Why did any of us? The Cleansing is a lie! The Change is not a curse—it's our birthright! Mine, yours, everyone's! The holy ones dare to tell us we can't be trusted with this power, but who are they to take it from us? They send their Wardens to bend us to their will, and they tell us it's because the Shepherds say it must be so. But we can choose our own fates. We don't have to die!"

Only silence and muffled sobs answered her tirade. She was tired of the walls between her and the other Tomol. With a thought she broke them down and cast them away. Entire huts lifted off the ground and launched out of sight, leaving only their bewildered occupants and their orphaned furniture to face Nimur's wrath. "Stop hiding from the truth! You cower and whimper when you should be standing tall and walking this world like gods! Cast off your weakness! Seize the power you were born to wield!"

She marshaled a surge of resentment to sweep aside a cluster of huts ahead of her. Huddled in the suddenly naked footprint of one of them were Kerlo, Chimi, and Tayno, all of them sheltering the infant Tahna. As soon as Kerlo realized they had been recognized, he stood and stepped between the others and Nimur. "Please, don't hurt them. They're our kin now."

"What do you understand about family, Kerlo?" Nimur sneered at her daughter's hapless Guardians. "You're as blind as the rest of them. The priestess tells you to hand over your child, and you don't even *try* to resist. What kind of a father are you?"

Kerlo took a cautious step forward, his hands open and upraised. "This is the way it has to be, Nimur. All of us have our time, and when it draws to an end, we need to think of those we leave behind. It's our responsibility as parents."

"Our duty is to *raise our children*, Kerlo. Not to give them up on demand. Look at me, you fool. Do I look like I'm dying? Do I? I'm stronger than I've ever been, and my power's growing. This is what the priestesses have been afraid of—that we would learn of our own strength. That we would find out we don't really need them. That we would *outgrow* them."

Sadness made Kerlo's eyes glisten. "That's not what they've feared."

"Don't you understand what I'm telling you? We could live twice as long as we do! Maybe three times longer, or four, or even more than that! Instead, we submit to a law that condemns us to birth children we never get to see grow up. A code that dooms each of us to live without ever knowing our real parents. Is this just? Is this right?"

"I don't think that's for us to judge."

"I think it is." Nimur cocked her head at the sound of running footsteps drawing near. The Wardens charged in from all sides, lances leveled and sparking with pent-up fury. A gaggle of villagers pushed in behind the defenders, their mood as fearful as it was hopeful.

Nimur considered retreat; then she decided it was time to make a stand. "We call the source of our legends Shepherds. But do you realize what that makes *us,* Kerlo?" She fixed her former mate with a contemptuous stare. "*Cattle.*"

The cave tunnel terminated at a large chamber that Theriault could see at a glance had been shaped by artificial means. There were clean cuts through solid rock, right angles where walls met, graceful arches over each of its several entrances, and a level floor of smooth marbled stone. In the center of the great room was a well ringed by a carved-granite bench.

Seta picked up a small shard of metal from the well's edge and carried it to the nearest sconce, which was recessed into the wall. She struck the metal against the wall inside the sconce's recess, and it cast sparks that fell and ignited a substance that released rich black smoke. From the odor it cast off, Theriault suspected the fuel was rendered animal fat.

Dastin grew impatient as he watched Seta light more sconces. "Where's this wordstone?"

"In the great cavern." Seta was focused on lighting the eight sconces that ringed the well chamber and seemed annoyed at Dastin's irreverent distraction.

Hesh busied himself shining a light from his tricorder down the well. "I am unable to make a precise scan of the well's depth due to the continuing mineral interference. However, an ultrasonic pulse has registered an approximate depth of one hundred eleven point two meters."

The report drew a skeptical look from Tan Bao. "That's not a precise reading?"

"As I said, sir, it is only approximate." Hesh looked at Theriault. "At this time, I am unable to determine whether the well is dry, but I—" He paused as Tan Bao leaned in front of him and dropped a loose rock down the well. A few seconds later, there was a distant splash. The Arkenite turned a sour frown at the nurse. "How many rocks will tell us if the water is potable?"

Tan Bao clapped his hands clean and walked away. "Just tryin' to help."

Seta lit the last sconce and returned to Theriault's side. "Before I open the way to the great cavern, you all must swear an oath of secrecy. Since the time of the Arrival, only our priestesses and disciples, and a handful of our Wardens, have ever seen this place. If my people were not in terrible danger, I would not be showing it to you now. Do you all swear to keep secret the means by which the entrance is opened?"

Theriault nodded. "Cross our hearts and hope to die." Seeing that the Tomol was perplexed by the human idiom, she added, "Yes, I swear to keep it a secret." Then she aimed prompting looks at the other members of the landing party. Their quick but solemn vows overlapped one another.

Satisfied with the landing party's collective pledge, Seta stepped away from them and faced a blank wall five meters tall by eight meters wide. The teen closed her eyes and raised her arms, and then she uttered a string of words that the universal translator was unable to parse.

"Nchan kaji-mokuu, teon yeshor ukwilena mwongati."

There was a low groan, followed by a loud dry scrape— and the wall started to move. The three-meter-thick barrier slid slowly to the right, revealing a short but broad passage to a vast cavern on the other side. As soon as the wall had moved far enough for people to pass, Seta led the landing party down the passageway and into the yawning expanse that lay beyond.

High overhead, long stalactites hung from the dome-shaped ceiling. Milky pools dotted the floor and lit the cavern with eerie phosphorescent light. The walls and roof boasted colorful striations in an impressive variety of colors. In any other circumstance, Theriault would have expected a trained geologist such as Hesh to be giddy with excitement to study them. Today, however, Hesh's attention was fixed upon the same detail that captivated everyone else.

In the center of the cavern was a flat-topped pyramid composed of smooth stone and a polished, bronze-hued metal. Steps had been carved into all four sides of the pyramid to provide easy access to the impressive metallic object that stood on top of it.

It resembled peculiar sculpture: a thick, blocky base with a pyramidal capstone, from which rose two towering shapes that reminded Theriault of arrowheads; they were perpendicular to and intersected each other, as if one had been shot through the other so that they now shared a common core and tip. Its base was about five meters tall, Theriault estimated, and her best guess was that the metallic structure on top of it stood approximately twenty-two meters tall.

As she and the others walked toward it, her eyes adjusted to the curious illumination cast upward from the chalky pools, and she realized the blocky base of the metal structure was completely covered in raised symbols. She pointed at the object. "Seta, is that—?"

"The wordstone? Yes. There is written the history of our people—how we came to the island of Suba, and the laws given to us by the Shepherds to ensure our survival."

A soft alert tone chirped from Hesh's tricorder. He checked the device. "Commander, my readings are still imprecise due to the interference, but I am certain that my tricorder is detecting a peculiar energy field being generated by that metallic object."

Theriault snapped her fingers, halting Dastin, Tan Bao,

and Seta. She turned toward Hesh. "Can you get a clear reading on that energy signature?"

"Yes, sir. Just a moment." He tinkered with his tricorder while everyone watched him. If the weight of their attention bothered him, he gave no sign of it. He looked up, his mien confident. "I have confirmed this is the energy signature detected by our probe. This is the power source we came to find. It is definitely synthetic and the product of a technologically advanced culture—though I am unable to tell you much more than that. Its inner workings are a mystery."

"Then let's go have a closer look," Dastin said, continuing toward the pyramid. Tan Bao looked at Theriault for direction. She motioned for him to follow Dastin. Seta trailed close behind the two men, determined not to let them mount the sacred wordstone without supervision.

Theriault resumed walking behind them, and Hesh stayed close beside her. She kept her voice down as she issued her next order. "Set up a datalink to the *Sagittarius*. Upload that energy signature and all the visual data you can record about this thing. Then have the ship's computer compare it against all similar artifacts in the memory banks."

"Aye, sir."

Seta skipped ahead of Dastin and Tan Bao and led them up the closest set of stairs to the structure. Theriault and Hesh followed a few strides behind the others. The new priestess turned and wore an embarrassed grimace. "There are still parts of the wordstone I don't know how to interpret. Ysan was going to teach me, but . . ." She let the thought pass unspoken.

Dastin ran his hands over the raised glyphs that covered almost every available square centimeter of the structure's massive base. "This is incredible. I've never seen anything like it."

Tan Bao circled the structure and studied its tens of thousands of symbols. "Reminds me of the Egyptian hieroglyphs, or the Tammarchian pictograms."

Something about that didn't sit right with Theriault. "I don't think so. Not enough variety in the symbols. It's not as complex as those systems. And it's not like kanji, either. There's something deceptively simple about all of it. And it reminds me of something I read, but I can't quite remember what."

Seta pressed her hands against one of the glyphs and closed her eyes. "Do you want to hear the parts of the wordstone that I know?"

"Yes," Hesh said, quick to answer for the group.

"Long ago—more than a hundred thousand sun-turns by our current calendar—was the time of the Arrival. That was when the Shepherds brought us to Suba. We were only a few, the last of our kind. The Shepherds spared us the fate of our ancestors, who were destroyed by the evil of the ones who spoke in fire, the dark gods they called Shedai."

The mere mention of the now-eradicated Shedai raised the hackles on the back of Theriault's neck and drew a wide-eyed stare of rapt attention from Tan Bao.

Eyes still shut, Seta continued. "When the ancient Tomol grew too strong for the Shedai to control, the dark gods poisoned our people with the horror of the Change. It turns us into monsters. It gives us great powers, but it also drives us mad. A Tomol who completes the Change becomes insane and irreversibly violent. Our forebears laid our first homeland waste.

"Nothing can stop the Change. Sometime around our eighteenth sun—for some it comes before, for others it comes later—it begins. The first sign is always the same: The eyes burn with the fire of the Shedai. After that, the end comes within days.

"For the sake of our survival, it was decided that all who show the first sign of the Change would sever their ties to the living: dissolve bonds of marriage, give up custody of children to new Guardians, and surrender willingly to the Cleansing."

Dastin was clearly unsettled. "You mean they jump into that pit of fire."

"Yes. Only by the Flame of the Shepherds can the afflicted be Cleansed."

At the risk of inviting bad news, Theriault asked, "What happens if someone completes the Change now? Someone like Nimur?"

"Then the wordstone is meant to protect us." Seta turned a worried eye on the looming metal structure. "But Ysan never taught me how to summon the power of the stone. In ages past, the wordstone was able to snare and trap the Changed by turning them to stone. We call those prisoners of the wordstone the Endless. There are a few in the valley on the far side of the hill. But I have never seen it used. No one remembers the last time a Changed became Endless."

A beep from Hesh's tricorder turned all eyes toward the Arkenite. He checked the device's display, then hurried to stand beside Theriault. "Commander, have a look at this."

He handed her the tricorder but said nothing else. As soon as she saw the display, she understood the reason for his discretion. The memory banks on the *Sagittarius* had matched the glyphs on this structure to those detected a year earlier by the crew of the *Enterprise,* on a smaller but otherwise identical structure on a Class-M world threatened by an asteroid strike. The *Enterprise*'s crew had eventually learned that the structure was made by a culture that referred to itself as the Preservers. That "obelisk," as Kirk and his crew had mischaracterized their discovery, had turned out to be an asteroid-deflection system put in place to protect the planet and its transplanted human inhabitants—an amalgam of various early North American cultures.

She craned her head back and gazed up at the structure the Preservers had left behind for the benefit of the Tomol. Why was it so much larger? Could a Changed individual actually pose a more potent threat than an asteroid strike?

Regardless, she knew there was little point in tainting the Tomol's mythology by trying to explain that the Shepherds were actually the Preservers, or that the Tomol had likely evolved on a completely different world orbiting a distant star. Disrupting their worldview in such a manner was not merely prohibited by the Prime Directive; it would, in Theriault's opinion, at best serve no purpose, or, at worst, do more harm than good.

She handed the tricorder back to Hesh. "Can you use this to find a way to activate this thing? Help Seta make it do what it's supposed to do to protect the Tomol?"

"I think I can. Are those your orders?"

"Yes. Get on it." She left Hesh to work and put a reassuring hand on Seta's shoulder. "My friend might be able to help you figure out the last part of your wordstone and stop Nimur. Will you accept our help?"

"If it will protect my people, yes."

"Okay. We'll do what we can. Just give us some time to figure out these glyphs."

Dastin beckoned Theriault with a sly tilt of his head. They stepped off to one side and down a few steps on the pyramid to confer in private. The scout sounded concerned. "Sir, what if this gizmo doesn't work anymore? If we're counting on this old hunk of junk to save our asses, we could be setting up ourselves—and her—for a *big* disappointment."

"I had the same thought." Theriault took out her communicator and flipped it open. "Which means it's time to make sure we have reinforcements standing by." She opened a channel and increased the gain to cut through the interference from the hill's mineral compounds. "Theriault to *Sagittarius*." Seconds passed without a reply. She set her communicator's transmission strength to maximum. "Theriault to *Sagittarius*. Do you read me?" The channel remained silent. She turned toward Hesh. "Is your link to the ship still active?"

He checked his tricorder and frowned. "No. The channel went dead twenty seconds ago."

Theriault closed her communicator and tucked it back into its pocket on her jumpsuit. "So much for calling in the cavalry."

14

Framed by the dull red glow of the bridge's working lights, the main viewscreen of the Klingon battle cruiser *Voh'tahk* served as a window to the cold black reaches of space. Against that span of darkness peppered with stars, a single orb grew larger and brighter by the moment.

Early charts of this sector had designated this galactic backwater the Gujol system, which would have made its second planet Gujol-2. However, having learned from the recon teams that the natives called their world Arethusa, the Klingon High Command had changed the planet's name accordingly in the Imperial Master Catalog. The rationale was that respecting the original name of a planet made its *jeghpu'wI'* more receptive to Klingon control after the Empire conquered them and planted its banner atop a mountain of their dead.

That was reason enough for Kang, son of K'naiah.

His helmsman, Ortok, rotated his seat almost completely around to look up at him. "Captain, we are ready to begin our approach to the planet."

"Good." Looking down from his command chair's elevated dais, Kang swiveled toward his communications officer. "Kyris, tell the *Homghor* to assume an antipodal orbit to ours."

She nodded once. "Yes, Captain."

Kang checked the ship's chronometer. Barring complications, he reasoned his crew could help the recon team exfiltrate within the hour, and then they would be on their way back to Qo'noS with a great prize locked away in the biostasis chamber secured in the *Voh'tahk*'s hold.

His inner cynic gnawed at him. *Since when does any mission go without complication?*

Then the senior weapons officer, Mahzh, silenced a warning on his console. Kang turned toward the man, expecting a report. Instead, Mahzh stared in silence at his display, keying in commands one after another. Kang grew restless. "Mahzh! Report."

"There was a momentary sensor contact. It registered at first as a ship, but then it vanished." He looked back at his screen, as if hoping to find a definitive answer where none had been a moment earlier. "It might have been random cosmic noise, or a glitch in the sensors."

That was not what Kang considered a satisfactory report. "Check it again."

"I did, Captain. No contact."

"Do it a third time." He rotated his chair away from Mahzh and called for his first officer, who also happened to be his science officer—and his wife. "Mara!"

The trim woman—who, like Kang himself, was a *Quch'Ha*, afflicted with the weak, humanized physiognomy produced by the century-old genetic calamity known as the Augment Virus—left the port side console and leaned close to receive her orders. "Captain?"

"Have the gunners make regular sensor sweeps of this system while we orbit Arethusa. If they detect anything out of the ordinary, I want them to blow it to bits."

She bowed her chin. "Understood."

Kang fixed his eyes on the world that swelled to fill the main viewscreen. Somewhere on that planet's surface was a bioweapon that could make the Klingon Empire the predominant power in this quadrant, perhaps even the entire galaxy.

His orders were clear and left no room for interpretation. He was either to capture that weapon for the glory of the Empire, or he was to make certain it never fell into the hands of the Empire's enemies—by blasting this world into a sphere of molten, radioactive glass.

Either outcome had been deemed acceptable by the High Command.

He smiled. Today was a good day to die . . . but it would be an even better day to kill.

Despite all the times Clark Terrell had experienced silent-running operations aboard a starship, he continued to find them eerie and a touch irrational. The practice, like many Starfleet protocols, traced its origins to a bygone era of sea-based naval warfare. Submersible ships seeking to evade sonic detection systems used by surface vessels would halt all onboard activity. Most of a ship's internal machinery would be turned off, propulsion would cease, and shipboard conversations were hushed. Even a single stray sound could betray a submarine's position and doom it to destruction by depth charges, timed explosives dropped from the surface.

In the era of starship operations, silent running typically entailed reducing a ship's ambient energy profile, strictly limiting communications, and switching off the running lights. The first part was the most essential. Ceasing active sensor scans was one of the most effective means of masking a starship's presence; another was throttling back the matter/antimatter mix in the warp core to the minimum level required to maintain the reaction. It also helped to power down all but one segment of the main computer, to minimize the Cochrane distortion produced by a bank of faster-than-light processor cores running in parallel.

What Terrell couldn't figure out was why Starfleet's silent running procedure called for reducing the life-support settings to minimum; its effect on the ship's energy profile was inconsequential, and it wasn't as if the hum of the ventilation system was going to carry through a vacuum. Between the rapid drop in the *Sagittarius*'s internal temperature and the stale air quality, he was giving serious consideration to the notion of saying to hell with stealth, hailing the Klingons with a barrage of vulgar invective, and coming out shooting.

Then he took a fresh look at the Klingon cruiser *Voh'tahk* on the main viewscreen. He recalled the brutal beating the *Sagittarius* had suffered the last time it challenged a similar foe, and he took into account the presence of a second hostile vessel, a fast-moving bird-of-prey.

He rubbed his palms together for warmth. *A little cold never hurt anybody.*

"Helm. How's our anchor holding up?"

Ensign Nizsk answered while reviewing the readings on the forward console. "Steady, Captain. We remain securely tethered to the asteroid." The insectoid helmsman and navigator toggled some settings on her panel. "Ancillary systems remain stable in standby mode."

"Good." Terrell looked over his shoulder at Sorak. "How's our camouflage working?"

"Satisfactorily—for the moment." The old Vulcan turned a look of grudging approval in Taryl's direction. "As the ensign predicted, the mineral compounds in this asteroid are masking our residual energy signature from the Klingons' sensors." The Orion field scout tried and failed to suppress a small but prideful smirk—which faded quickly when Sorak continued. "However, as I warned, because we can't raise our shields without giving away our position, the same radiation that conceals us is also slowly cooking us from the inside out."

Taryl took the criticism in stride. "Already on top of it, Captain. I've coordinated with Doctor Babitz. She's making the rounds with prophylactic anti-radiation meds. As soon as she's dosed the engineers, she'll swing by and get the rest of us squared away."

"Well done, Ensign." Terrell stood and regarded the changing perspective on the main viewscreen. Because the asteroid on which his ship had hitched a ride was tumbling slowly as it drifted toward a close pass with Nereus II, their vantage on the planet and the pair of Klingon ships in orbit was in constant motion. The computer was able to compensate to a small degree, but it was still jarring when the passive visual sensors handed off from the forward angle to the aft and back again. "Mister Sorak, this is making me dizzy. Switch to a tactical grid, please."

"Aye, sir." Sorak swapped out the image on the viewscreen with a computer-generated schematic showing the position of the *Sagittarius* and the Klingon ships relative to the planet.

"That's better." Terrell eyed the Klingons' positions. "Antipodal orbits?" He considered the relative advantages and disadvantages of such a deployment. Without line-of-sight, the two vessels would be unable to render immediate tactical support to each other in a firefight, and they would be unable to transfer personnel via their transporters because of interference from the powerful magnetic field generated by Nereus II's molten-iron core. Terrell could think of only one reason for the two ships to have placed themselves opposite each other on either side of the planet. "They're looking for us. They've spread out to maximize sensor coverage."

Sorak nodded. "A logical deduction."

Ensign Taryl called up a scroll of data on the screen above the sensor console. "If they are, they're not looking very hard. The Klingons haven't made any active scans of this asteroid."

"Yet," Terrell noted, hoping to ward off the jinx Taryl's boast had unwittingly invited.

The bridge door opened with a low hush. Doctor Lisa Babitz walked in, a hypospray in each hand. "Who's first?" Nizsk ignored the doctor's invitation, since her carapace protected her from the asteroid's low-level radiation.

Terrell raised his hand. "Captain's prerogative."

Babitz walked over and pressed one hypo against Terrell's carotid artery. The injection was delivered with a soft hiss and a fleeting sting. "Whatever happened to the captain going down with his ship?"

"I wasn't aware we were sinking."

"Matter of opinion." The tall physician headed aft. "Mister Sorak, you're next."

The Vulcan tilted his head to afford Babitz easier access to his neck. "Once again demonstrating that rank has its privileges."

"Whoever said it doesn't?" She pivoted away from the Vulcan and looked first at Taryl, then at Razka, who was seated on the opposite side of the compartment. "Next?"

Razka pointed at Taryl. "The ensign has rank."

Taryl pointed back at Razka. "The chief has seniority."

Babitz lobbed one hypospray to the Orion woman and the other to the Saurian. "Inject yourselves. I don't have time for this." While they administered their own anti-radiation meds, the chief medical officer looked around, her countenance apprehensive.

Terrell knew that face all too well. "You're fantasizing about disinfecting again."

"No, just wondering how long it's been since anyone sanitized this bridge."

"As if a germ would stand a fighting chance on this ship."

"You just keep telling yourself that." The hyposprays returned to Babitz just as they'd left her—by slow, casual lobs. She caught both of them, one in each hand. "But don't come crying to me the next time you wake up with the Zircolian flu."

"Wouldn't dream of it." He rubbed the sore spot on his neck. "How long will this last?"

"About a day." Babitz turned to show the captain the back of her blond bob as she muttered, "Assuming we all live that long."

Terrell watched his high-strung ship's surgeon leave the bridge, and then he returned to his command chair.

Outside his ship, nothing had changed. Inside, he and his crew had bought themselves a day-long reprieve from the worst effects of their improvised cover. But somewhere down on the planet's surface, his landing party was on their own against odds that had suddenly turned against them—and he had no way of warning them.

For the moment, Terrell had no better option than to engage in a protracted game of hide-and-seek with his Klingon counterparts—and to do whatever he could to keep his ship and crew in play until their own reinforcements arrived to level the playing field.

15

"Don't you see what you're doing to us? To me? To yourself?"

Kerlo had stabbed at Nimur with pointed words, but she was impervious to his appeals. "You speak as if I'm the one who's blind, Kerlo. But I'm the one whose eyes are finally open. I can see everything that's been hidden from us for so long. All our lives we've been told lies, one after another, and any time we dared to ask questions, we were told to trust the Shepherds."

"Why shouldn't we?"

"Because they ask us to go to our deaths just as we mature into our greatest power!" Her mate's willful blindness drove Nimur to distraction. "I have seen people very different from us, people who have lived much longer lives. Why should we cut ours short? Because of some shapes on a piece of stone? How do we know the priestesses haven't been lying to us for ages? Keeping us weak, keeping us fearful and stupid, so they could control us?"

"That makes no sense, Nimur. How would it benefit the priestesses? When their times come, they go to their Cleansings, just as we all do. They live no longer than any of us; they keep their children no longer than anyone else. If this is a plot, what is their reason?"

The village square was packed with fretful witnesses to Nimur and Kerlo's argument. Most of the observers remained well behind the ring of Wardens who surrounded the couple, but a few strained against the defensive cordon, eager to see what a fully Changed person looked like in the flesh. Nimur did not resent their curiosity; it was only natural. What she resented was Kerlo's purposefully obtuse attitude. "Why must you defend those who would walk us to our deaths? Are you that beaten-down? Are you that weak-willed?"

Anger put an edge on Kerlo's voice. "I'm no weakling, Nimur. Neither am I a fool. You talk as if you alone possess the truth—but all I hear from you are delusions, wild fantasies that all make you sound like a hero and the rest of us like idiots."

"What's delusional about not wanting to die an empty death?"

"Nothing. But our sacrifices for the Cleansing aren't empty, Nimur. Each of us knows that if we cling too long to the flesh, we'll become something terrible—an abomination. Our surrender to the fire is our final act of bravery, the moment when we put the good of the people ahead of our own interests. It is our redemption from the evil that lives within us all."

His platitudes filled her with revulsion. "Words. Nothing but words. The same holy gibberish we've been force-fed all our lives. Stop parroting the priestesses and try thinking for yourself!" She turned away from Kerlo and escalated her argument to include everyone within range of her voice. "All of you! Learn to use your minds! Open them to the possibility that the priestesses are wrong! That the Shepherds were wrong! Accept the possibility of your own greatness!" The Wardens tensed as Nimur prowled in a circle, working the crowd. "The Change is a gift! It's our birthright, one that—"

"It's a curse!" Kerlo was furious. "Look at her! Her clothes are stained in blood, but she has no wounds! Whose blood is she wearing?" He thrust an accusatory finger at her. "You killed the priestess and her Wardens, didn't you? Admit it!"

"I deny nothing." Shocked silence fell over the throng. Nimur met their silent reproach with contempt. "Ysan had no right to command me, and she paid the price for her arrogance. As did her so-called defenders." She turned in a slow circle, training her cold stare on each of the Wardens facing her. "I would just as soon rid us of all these hooded monsters, these tools of oppression. What good have any of them ever done us? What other role do they serve but to force us into the fire? Why should I spare any of them? Why should any of you?"

Kerlo stepped into her path. "Because none of us have appointed ourselves their judges."

"Maybe it's time you did." The vacancy in his stare made clear to her that he did not understand what she was implying. Pivoting to drink in the rapt attention of her former friends and neighbors, Nimur saw that none of them grasped what she was revealing to them. As much as it pained her to do so, she would have to spell it out for them. "Within each of you lies the seed of fire that will enable you to become as I am now."

The mere suggestion horrified Kerlo. "Why would we want that?"

"Why?" His stupidity enraged her. "Why do you want to remain an insect when you can become a giant? The hotter my fire burns, the more clearly I see, Kerlo! This universe is but a machine for the creation of gods. It's our purpose, our duty—our *destiny* to ascend."

None of them saw what she did.

Their auras were dull like fading embers, waiting for a divine breath to reinvigorate them. Even as their energies shrank in fear, Nimur saw her own expand. She was the kindling fire that could spark the others. The younger Tomol were not yet ready, but most of those who had been born within a few moon-turns of Nimur stood poised on the threshold of the Change. And now that Nimur saw how their psychic emanations were reacting with her own, she knew that with focus and effort, she could ignite her people into a bonfire of power. With such allies at her side, she could shape this world to her will. In time, all of creation would bend to her demands.

But it was critical, she knew, to be sure that those whose sparks she fanned were ready to be her allies in that new world. They would need to embrace their inner fires willingly.

"None of us wants to die. I am here to tell you that you don't have to. My power can be yours, if you're willing to accept it. Each of you is a flower waiting to bloom, a seed on the verge of breaking its sheath and rising to meet the sun. We were meant for more than this. Let me stoke the fire that dwells within you, and together we will make this world give us what we deserve."

No one spoke, but Nimur knew she had struck a chord. The auras of many Tomol in the crowd became more responsive to her radiated will. The connection was still too weak for her to push them fully into the arms of the Change—but it was close and would come soon enough.

She turned toward Kerlo and gave her former mate an ultimatum.

"I have risen, Kerlo, and soon others will ascend with me. Change with us . . . or die."

Theriault was all but mesmerized as she watched her tricorder translate the glyphs on the side of the metal structure into a string of phonemes and precisely pitched tones. "If this actually works, remind me to write a thank-you letter to Commander Spock."

"Such gratitude would seem premature, sir." Hesh stood beside Theriault, conducting his own tricorder analysis of the one panel of glyphs that Seta had been unable to translate for them. "Commander Spock's discovery that these symbols constitute a system of musical notation gives us a foundation for the study of their meaning and function, but learning the phonetics of a language does not necessarily grant any insight with regard to its syntax."

"First we learn to talk the talk, Hesh. We can learn to walk the walk later."

He furrowed his brow. "Begging your pardon, Commander?"

"Never mind." She turned and called down the steps to their hostess. "Seta!"

The teen bounded up the stone staircase to join Hesh and Theriault. "Yes?"

"I know you weren't taught the translation for this side

of the wordstone," Theriault said. "But did Ysan ever tell you what this side was about? Any clue to its meaning might help us."

Seta looked fearful of the broad panel of alien symbols. "This side of the stone was only taught to disciples who were considered ready to become the new priestess. Ysan said it tells of how to use the wordstone to defend the people from the Changed in times of great danger."

Hesh, intrigued by Seta's statement, lowered his tricorder. "How can the wordstone be used to stop the Changed?"

"I don't know, not exactly. Whenever Ysan mentioned it, she spoke in riddles. It meant 'turning the stone,' she would say. She also spoke of summoning the 'Burning Eye,' which had the power to turn flesh to stone. It could petrify anyone—even one of the Changed."

Dastin, who stood beside the pyramid platform and kept an eye on the cavern's entrance, remarked, "Sounds like something we could use right about now."

Theriault pointed at the glyphs. "Seta, are you saying this thing's an instruction manual for a *doomsday weapon*?" She regarded the towering structure with renewed awe. "Cool."

Tan Bao paced around the pseudo-obelisk. "Now all we need to do is figure out how to turn it on." He let his fingertips slip across the raised symbols on its surface.

His remark vexed Seta. "When the time comes, I alone must be the one who activates the wordstone." Her bravado faltered when she noted the landing party's stern collective reaction, but then she recovered her hauteur. "Please don't misunderstand. I am grateful for your help, but I have a duty to defend not just the lives of my people but the sanctity of our traditions and our holy places—and the Shepherds say only a priestess may command the wordstone."

Theriault recalled reading of a similar custom among the tribe Captain Kirk and his crew encountered after discovering the previous Preserver structure. In the end, the injunction against letting outsiders tamper with the device proved to be an empty one, most likely a rule instituted to limit the degree to which the power of these artifacts could be abused. Regardless, if Seta could do what needed to be done, Theriault saw no reason to disrespect the Tomol's customs. "You have our word: We'll help you learn the wordstone's secrets, and we'll let you control it."

Her promise was enough to placate Seta, who stepped back to let them continue their work. Hesh sidled over to Theriault and spoke in a quiet voice. "The report filed by the *Enterprise* crew indicated that a particular set of sonic tones and syllables opened a hatch to a control area hidden inside the base of the structure. Perhaps we should emulate their actions."

That made sense to Theriault. "Okay. What did they do to open the hatch?"

"The commanding officer opened his communicator and said, 'Kirk to *Enterprise*.'"

"I'm not gonna walk around this thing repeating 'Kirk to *Enterprise*' over an open comm channel. For one thing, if there's a Klingon ship in orbit, I'd be giving away not just our presence but our position. For another, if the captain hears me, he'll think I've gone crazy."

Dastin looked up at Theriault and took out his own

communicator. It emitted a soft electronic chirp as he snapped open its grille with a flick of his wrist. "No one says you have to open a channel. Maybe this oversized *Dom-jot* trophy just likes the noise our gear makes."

Hesh tilted his head as he considered that. "He makes a reasonable point."

"This is a conspiracy, isn't it?"

Tan Bao took out his communicator. "Fine, I'll do it." He flipped open the grille. "Kirk to *Enterprise*." Nothing happened, so he circled ninety degrees around the structure to the next side of glyphs and repeated the phrase, with the same negative result. He performed the same action and spoke the same words on the other two sides of the structure's platform. There was no evidence of any change in the structure or its base. "So much for that," Tan Bao said.

Theriault felt as if they were close to unraveling this mystery, if only she could decipher the clues that were staring her in the face. She paced around the pseudo-obelisk.

"It makes sense the same phrase wouldn't open a different structure," she said. "We need to figure out the 'open sesame' phrase for this one." She considered the variables. "Hesh, assume these are musical notations like the ones on the other object. Commander Spock parsed the tonal vocabulary of the first object, right?"

"For the most part, yes."

"At the time, he didn't know what phrase Kirk had used to open the hatch. Can we use that knowledge to map that sequence of tones to their corresponding glyphs on the first object?"

The Arkenite nodded. "Maybe. Let me try." He worked at his tricorder for a moment. "It appears Commander Spock already made that connection, as well. He identified the glyphs that constitute the hatch's access sequence."

"Okay. Now I want you to examine where those glyphs are on the first object, and what glyphs are adjacent to them—and then look for corresponding relationships and positions among the glyphs on this object."

"You want me to hack its syntax."

"Precisely."

He was excited. "I will try." His tricorder hummed and whirred as it processed the data through its cryptographic analysis software. After a minute had passed, Hesh looked up with an abashed shrug. "This would go much more quickly if I could interface with the ship's computer."

"Just do your best," Theriault said.

"Yeah, take your time," Dastin quipped. "It's not as if the rest of us have jobs to do."

Theriault pointed at the Trill. That and her glare were enough to silence him.

A chime issued from Hesh's tricorder. He showed the display to Theriault. "I think we have something, Commander. A seventy-two point six percent likely access sequence."

"Translate that into an audio playback and let Seta listen to it through the speaker."

Hesh cued up the playback, then ducked out from under the tricorder's strap and handed it to Seta. He coached her with a few gestures to hold it close to her ear, and then he pressed a button on the device to start a looped playback. Seta listened to several repetitions, and then she handed the tricorder back to Hesh, her eyes wide with admiration for the versatile device.

Theriault caught Seta's eye. "Did those sounds make sense to you?"

"Yes. I can remember them." She turned and faced the structure. "You all need to step down, off the platform, for your own safety."

The landing party heeded Seta's advice and regrouped at the bottom of the pyramid's nearest flight of stairs. Alone atop the pyramid, Seta lifted her arms, and her voice resounded in the vast underground space that surrounded the structure.

"Torqilia ngovu ya moto, na kuwata dhibur waovu'oko!"

Her words vanished into echoes that swiftly faded.

Then came a low moan from deep within the bedrock—followed by a deep rumbling that showered the landing party with rocks and dust from high overhead. The quaking grew stronger and became a steady pulse, a bone-shaking low-frequency sonic assault that traveled up through Theriault's feet, followed her spine to her head, and rattled her teeth.

On top of the platform, the massive double-arrowhead structure began to turn. The glyphs on its broad base flared white, and lightning cloaked it on all sides. Seta retreated down the steps and huddled with the landing party, who stared up at the spectacle with fear and wonder.

Hesh tapped Theriault's shoulder. She turned. Behind them, the chalky pools bubbled, and plumes of superheated vapor jetted from countless cracks in the cavern floor. The pseudo-obelisk finished its slow rotation when it had turned one-hundred-eighty degrees.

The chthonic pulsing underfoot grew louder and more ominous.

Dastin grasped Theriault's shoulder. "With all respect to the chain of command, RUN!"

She shouted to the others, "You heard the man! Haul ass!"

Sheltering Seta in their midst, the landing party dashed out the cavern's entrance, raced past the well in the chamber outside, and kept on running, back the way they had come.

Between gasping breaths, Hesh shouted, "Where are we going?"

Theriault sprinted past him. "Anywhere but here! Keep running till you see daylight!"

"Then what?"

"Keep running!"

Ten minutes after scrambling at a breakneck pace out of the cave entrance and down the slope into the jungle, Seta and the landing party staggered to a halt. Everyone was winded, but Hesh was the only one doubled over and fighting for breath. He had never run so far or so fast in all his life, and now he felt sick. He sank into a panting heap on the ground.

Dastin nudged him with his foot. "No time to nap, buddy. We have to keep moving."

In his imagination, Hesh concocted the perfect retort:

No, thank you. After careful consideration I have decided to let myself expire here in peaceful repose. In the flesh, the only reply he could force out of his parched mouth was, "Can't."

Theriault leaned forward, hands on her knees, and let her perspiration-matted red hair hang like a curtain in front of her face. "Dastin. Knock it off. We all need a second."

The Trill scout sat down on the trail and palmed the sweat from his brow. Behind him, Tan Bao fished a hypospray from his satchel and loaded a fresh ampoule of medicine. He injected himself first, with a quick dose to his carotid artery. Within seconds, his breathing slowed, and Hesh could see that the nurse was more relaxed and was perspiring less. Then Tan Bao kneeled beside Hesh and held up the hypospray. "This is tri-ox compound. It'll help your blood bind more oxygen and make it easier for you to breathe."

Hesh nodded, and Tan Bao injected him with the tri-ox. Its effects were just as swift in Hesh's system as they had been in Tan Bao's. Within a few seconds he felt refreshed, and his struggle to draw breath abated. He sat up and nodded. "Better. Thank you."

"All part of the service."

Tan Bao administered the next shot to Theriault. When he turned to offer one to Dastin, the Trill waved him off. "I'm fine," Dastin said. "Save the last few doses for the others." Tan Bao took the scout at his word and turned toward Seta. When the young woman declined with a nervous shake of her head, Tan Bao tucked the hypospray back inside his satchel.

Theriault stood and dusted herself off. "Are we all good to go?" Tired nods confirmed the group was ready to travel. "We're going back to the village. Nimur talked like she has a score to settle, so my bet is that's where she'll go to do it." She looked at Dastin. "Take point."

"Actually, sir, I'd like to bring up the rear for a while. If you don't mind."

Hesh noted a peculiar vibe between the scout and the first officer. They had a few seconds of intense eye contact, as if they were locked in a battle of wills, and then Theriault blinked. "Fine, I'll walk point. Hesh, Tan Bao, flank Seta. Dastin has the rear guard. Move out."

She set off down the trail that led back to the Tomol village. Tan Bao and Hesh took up their positions on either side of Seta, waiting a few seconds to let Theriault get far enough ahead to provide a buffer between her and the team in case of hostile contact.

Dastin tapped Hesh on the shoulder. "Can I use your tricorder for a second?"

"Of course." Hesh lifted the tricorder's strap over his head and passed the device to Dastin. The scout made a brief sensor sweep of the surrounding area. Even viewing the display upside-down, Hesh could see the tricorder had detected nothing out of the ordinary.

Dastin turned off the device and handed it back. "Thanks."

Hesh slung the tricorder strap back over his head and across his torso. "You're welcome."

Seta started walking, and Tan Bao and Hesh kept pace with her. Almost as soon as they were moving, Hesh noticed that Seta seemed fixated on Tan Bao. The young priestess stared at the human man without shame. Her curiosity was like a hunger. "How old are you?"

Tan Bao pretended not to find the intensity of her attention awkward. "Thirty-five."

"Is that old where you come from?"

"Old? I'm not old!" He calmed himself. "I'm still young for . . . for one of my people."

"How long do your people live?"

"It depends. Some longer than others. But if I'm lucky, I might live to be a hundred and twenty. Maybe even a hundred and thirty."

His answer made Seta's jaw go slack with wonder. "A hundred and twenty . . . !" She composed herself. "At what age do your people choose a mate?"

Tan Bao quickened his pace, moved ahead of Seta on the trail, and cast a fast look back at Hesh. "I'll stay ahead of her, you fall back and watch her six."

"Understood." Hesh smiled at Seta and tried to include himself in the conversation she had begun with Tan Bao. "My people can live to be almost two hundred years old."

"That's nice," the teen said, her manner one of utter boredom.

The trail twisted its way through the turquoise foliage of the jungle, down the shallow grade of the hill, and back toward the valley. Overhead a merciless sun beat down and cooked the jungle's ambient moisture into stifling vapor. Shrill caws and whooping shrieks filtered down from the canopy between broken spears of daylight, and distant growls served as a constant reminder to Hesh that this wilderness was not one that would forgive careless blundering.

He looked back, seeking to elicit some measure of bland reassurance from Dastin, even if it came in the form of sarcastic needling. Instead, he saw nothing behind him except an empty path bordered by impenetrable walls of green leaves, brown vines, and fiery-hued fruit blossoms. Hesh slowed his pace, hoping that Dastin had simply fallen back farther than usual and would quickly catch up. Several seconds passed, and the trail behind him remained empty.

Fearful of raising his voice but needing to signal the others, he croaked in a strained faux whisper, "Lieutenant Tan Bao!"

Tan Bao heard him, looked back, and immediately intuited the problem. He halted, stopping Seta, and then he whistled once to alert Theriault.

She stopped, turned around, took stock of the situation, and held out her empty hands. "Where the hell is Dastin?"

From somewhere close by came a throaty roar, a sound of primal hunger.

Hesh swallowed to choke back a yelp of fear. "I am not sure we want to know."

A very fine line separated the tracking of a retreating enemy and the act of fleeing for one's life. Tormog had to concede to his conscience that it was entirely possible he had crossed that line while following the Starfleeters and their pet *novpu'* during their flight from the caves.

Let the High Command call it cowardice, if they choose. Dead men can't file reports.

The Federation landing party and their *novpu'* companion had scurried from the caves like vermin at the first sign of danger. As much as Tormog had wanted to see what they had roused in the hidden cavern, his duty had compelled him to continue his surveillance of their activity on the planet's surface. They apparently were aware of the transformation experienced by the Tomol, but their interest in it seemed to be more abstract. Whereas his orders were to acquire a live Tomol subject for study so that their innate powers could be duplicated and weaponized, the Starfleet team had no clear agenda that he could discern.

Their mad escape had carried them out of the caves and back into the sultry arms of the jungle. Tormog was grateful for the additional cover the tropical environment offered. He could follow the main trail as long as he stayed sufficiently far behind them and used his portable scanner to generate a sensor-blocking field to mask his life-signs. The disadvantage to that strategy was that it prevented him from using his scanner to track the enemy, but since they were hewing strictly to the beaten path, it made little difference. Even a barely trained tracker such as Tormog—who had always preferred the less glorious occupations of genetic sequencing and chemical engineering—could follow the crisp, fresh boot prints in the half-dried mud.

It was one of the Empire's dirty secrets: As much as it venerated its warrior culture—though Tormog had long thought a more appropriate description of the Empire's attitude would be to say that it fetishized its martial roots—it needed a much broader spectrum of ability and experience not only to thrive but even to survive. What good was a warrior without the farmer who provided the food that fed him? Or the chefs who could turn base ingredients into meals worthy of song? What use was a soldier without an engineer to design his marvelous starships, craft his fearsome energy weapons, or architect the integrated sensor and communication systems that made his majestic victories possible? What was the purpose of expanding an empire without a plan for disseminating its profits? How could a warrior learn the inspiring words of Kahless without first learning *tlhIngan'Hol* from a skilled teacher?

No one would ever admit the truth, to themselves or to offworlders. Far more Klingons performed roles that had nothing to do with battle than those who did. All the glory, all the hype, all the power went to those who mastered the art of swinging a *bat'leth,* commanding a space fleet, or grinding a world full of *jeghpu'wI* beneath their booted heels. Little praise ever reached the ears of those like Tormog, whose imaginations were the secret engine shaping the destiny of the Klingon Empire. Bitterness welled up, unbidden, from the deep dark place in his heart. *The only ones for whom the Empire has less love than scientists are the diplomats.*

A change in the tracks he was following jolted him from his idle musings. An entire set of footprints abruptly ceased in mid-stride. All the others continued, winding their way around a bend in the trail and vanishing into the viridescent shadows. But the clearest set of prints, the ones Tormog had been most closely tracking, simply ended in mid-step, as if the person who had been making them had evaporated without warning—or else had been lifted upward by something striking without warning from above.

He halted and slowly tilted his head back. Above him he saw only the interlocking boughs of the jungle's canopy, leafy fingers folded together in a dome above the forest. An emerald glow betrayed the promise of sunlight above the trees, but at this turn in the trail there was none to be seen on the ground. Having studied many arboreal predators on various worlds of the Empire, Tormog searched between the branches for any sign of webs, nests, or lurking fauna.

An unstoppable force from his left slammed into him and knocked him off the trail into the undergrowth. He was on the ground and being punched in the face before he knew he'd been tackled by one of the Starfleeters.

Tormog punched back, knocking his attacker off-balance. He rolled free and drew his *d'k tahg*. The grip of the ceremonial dagger was a reassuring presence in his fist, and green light glinted off its double-edged blade as he rolled to his feet.

The man with spots was already up and facing him, empty-handed but full of confidence. Tormog twisted the dagger back and forth, hoping to intimidate the taller, broader-shouldered man with a warning of what to expect if he pressed his assault.

Spot-man feinted to one side and then led with a jabbing punch. Tormog sidestepped clear, then lunged, thrusting his *d'k tahg* ahead of him. The Starfleeter dodged the stab with a nimble turn, seized Tormog's arm in a fierce lock, and twisted it behind Tormog's back. His *d'k tahg* tumbled from his hand and vanished into the fronds at his feet.

The scientist's survival training kicked in, and he leaped up and backward, pinning his foe hard against a nearby tree and breaking the man's grip on his wrist. Tormog fell forward, somersaulted to his feet, and spun to face his opponent.

That was when he realized the Starfleeter had picked up his *d'k tahg*.

Tormog reached for his disruptor, then remembered he had lost it in the caves. *Damn.*

The next thing he felt was the bite of his own blade tearing through his shoulder. It hit him with such force that it knocked him onto his back. By the time he realized where he was and what had happened, the man with spots was kneeling on top of his chest, covering his mouth with one hand, and using the other to turn the dagger inside the wound, sending white-hot waves of pain through Tormog's entire body.

"Hi, there." The Starfleeter grinned. "I'm Lieutenant Dastin. And you are?"

"Not going to tell you anything."

"Yes you are. It's not a matter of *if,* friend—only of *when.*"

The landing party stood in a circle around the kneeling Klingon whom Dastin had just captured. The prisoner was a smooth-headed *Quch'Ha,* and the relative absence of weapons found on his person, combined with the sophistication of his handheld scanning device, had led Theriault to suspect the man was most likely a scientist or an engineer rather than a run-of-the-mill soldier.

His head was drooped, his hands were bound behind his back, and he swayed slowly as his body reacted to the truth serum Tan Bao had injected into him. The twilight-consciousness effects of the sedative would wear off soon enough, so Theriault wasted no time in lifting the Klingon's head so he could look at her when she asked him questions.

"Identify yourself."

"Doctor Tormog. Lieutenant, Klingon Defense Forces."

"What's your professional specialty, Tormog?"

He slurred out his answer. "Xenobiologist."

The drug seemed to be working. That was a relief to Theriault, because Tan Bao had cautioned her that he had no idea how effective this particular serum formula might be against a Klingon. So far, however, it appeared sufficiently effectual. "What ship do you serve on?"

"The *Voh'tahk*. Seventh Fleet, out of Somraw." His eyes fluttered shut.

Theriault patted his cheek until he reopened his eyes, which struggled to focus on her. "What are you doing on this planet?"

"Recon and research."

"For what purpose?"

Tormog flashed a broad, toothy grin. "Pure knowledge."

That struck Theriault as unlikely. "Anything else?"

"Galactic domination, of course." He chortled and snorted softly, pleased with himself.

"Why did you and your team help Nimur escape from the ritual?" She waited a few seconds for him to answer, but her question was met with silence. She sharpened her tone. "Why are you and your team interested in the Tomol?"

He huffed once, as if in disgust. As he replied, a thin line of drool spilled from the corner of his mouth and stretched toward the muddy ground. "Looking for link. To the Shedai."

The mere mention of the Shedai sent a pang of fear through Theriault's gut. Hundreds of millennia earlier, the Shedai had ruled over the region of space Starfleet called the Taurus Reach. The Shedai had been as powerful, both culturally and individually, as they were hostile to those who had resisted them. They had been able to transmit themselves in the form of disembodied consciousness—which they called "the subtle body"—across vast interstellar distances and control multiple physical bodies at the same time. There also was compelling evidence the Shedai had unwittingly uplifted the Tholian race to sentience. Though the catastrophic ending of Operation Vanguard had given Starfleet every reason to think the Shedai were now extinct, the ancient tyrants' legacy still haunted the Taurus Reach. If there was even the slightest risk of the Shedai rising again, Theriault knew they had to be stopped, at any cost.

The overflow of spittle from Tormog's mouth was increasing. It was time to get down to specifics, while he could still talk. "What were your orders if you found such a link?"

"Capture a Tomol. Put it in stasis. Take it back to Qo'noS."

"And you saw your chance when Nimur made a run for it at the ceremony." The Klingon nodded, so Theriault pressed onward. "This link between the Tomol and the Shedai—it has to do with the Change, doesn't it?" Another sloppy bobbing of Tormog's head. "And if you had gotten her back to Qo'noS? Then what?"

"Map her genome. Weaponize it. Crush the Federation."

Tan Bao chuckled. "Science at its best."

Theriault shushed the nurse, then resumed her questioning of the Klingon. "We know Nimur turned your team into tartare before she got away. What's your plan now?"

"Keep her alive. Tag her. Hail the ship."

"Tag her?"

Dastin stepped up beside Theriault. "I think he means with a subspace transponder."

Hesh nodded. "For transport. Yes, of course. Tagging her to make certain the correct subject is beamed up is most sensible. Otherwise, even in her Changed state, sensors from orbit might not be able to distinguish her from other Tomol."

Theriault picked through the small pile of equipment Dastin had confiscated from Tormog. She picked up a silvery gray cylindrical device approximately twenty centimeters long and one centimeter in diameter. "Is this what you use to plant the transponder?" Tormog nodded, his movements exaggerated and clumsy. A glance at the controls left Theriault mystified as to their intended functions. "What's the range on this thing?" She prayed he didn't say *point blank*.

"Ten *qam*s. Red to fire. White to track." He blinked at Theriault, then smirked. "You're holding it backward."

She reversed her hold on the device. "Thanks for the tip." She nodded at Tan Bao, who gave Tormog another hypospray injection. This one knocked the Klingon unconscious; he fell face-first to the ground and lay there with his left cheek pressed into the fetid muck.

The landing party huddled over Tormog. Dastin frowned at the Klingon. "What do we do with him? Tie him to something heavy and move on?"

"Too many wild animals out here," Theriault said. "We'll have to bring him with us."

Tan Bao checked his satchel. "I'm running short on chemical tricks. If we want to keep him under control for much longer, we'll have to do it without sedatives."

"That's fine," Dastin said. "I'd rather have him up and moving than across my back as dead weight." He looked at Theriault. "So, what's our next move?"

"Find Nimur and make sure the Klingons don't tag her. And, if they do, we have to find a way to jam that transponder's signal so they can't beam her up. The last thing we need is Nimur running amok on a starship." That imperative received nods of agreement all around.

Hesh remained troubled. "Assuming we find Nimur first, what then is our objective? Are we taking on the Tomol's burden as our own? Are we prepared to condemn Nimur to die?"

"Hell if I know. Let's just find her, okay?" Her shipmates reacted with wary, wide-eyed stares of disbelief.

She held up her hands in symbolic surrender. "Cut me some slack here. I'm making this up as I go."

Dastin cast a weary look down at Tormog, then mustered a cynical smile for Hesh and Tan Bao. "*Now* she tells us."

16

All was quiet on the bridge of the *Sagittarius,* and for that small mercy Clark Terrell was thankful; he and his crew had so far evaded detection by the Klingon starships in orbit. There was no telling how long their good fortune might last, so Terrell spent this rare break from his routine thinking. He contemplated responses in case they were found by the Klingons, while at the same time he was trying to imagine a way to warn his landing party of what was happening; neither avenue of reflection was yielding any helpful insights.

The door behind him sighed open, and he looked over his shoulder to see Doctor Babitz walk onto the bridge. Her eyes were fixed upon the data slate in her left hand, and she gnawed lightly on the tip of the stylus in her right hand as she approached Terrell's command chair. As she drew near, Terrell was sure he heard the blond surgeon muttering to herself.

"Something on your mind, Doctor?"

Babitz stopped and did a startled double take at the captain. "Hm? Oh, the slate. Yes." She tapped at it with the stylus, then turned it toward Terrell. "I've been reviewing the data the landing party sent up—the scans of the Tomol who are starting to experience the Change."

Terrell waited a few seconds in vain for Babitz to elaborate, and then he realized she would need a measure of verbal coaxing. "And? What have you found?"

"Hm? Oh. Not as much as I'd have liked, to be honest. All of the Tomol exhibit unusually high degrees of cell mutation during their growth cycles." She pointed out a line of figures on the slate. "I've never seen a species whose DNA has this kind of time bomb."

"You say their cells are mutating? Could there be an environmental factor involved?"

"I don't think so." She switched to a different screen of data on the slate. "No unusual radiation on the planet's surface. No known mutagens in the air, water, soil, flora, or fauna." She gave the scan analysis another look. "I'd say this is a genetic predisposition. I just wish I could figure out what its trigger is. If it's something simple, like a protein sequence, or a hormonal shift brought on by the end of adolescence, maybe we can develop a treatment of some kind."

Her enthusiastic speculation attracted Sorak's reproach. The old Vulcan stood and moved to join her and Terrell. "That would be inadvisable, Doctor. Deliberate interference in the natural evolution of the Tomol would be a blatant violation of the Prime Directive."

"You can't expect me to do nothing and condemn an entire species to die."

Terrell cut in. "We might not have a choice, Doctor. Sorak's right. If this is the Tomol's natural state, we have no right to tamper with it, no matter how tragic that might seem."

"Not even if they ask for our help?"

Sorak's voice was as dry as his logic. "How can they? They have no understanding of genomic medicine. That ignorance renders them unable to make an informed request for aid."

Babitz hardened her countenance. "Oh, really? And if this Change is *not* a natural part of their evolution? If it's an externally inflicted mutation? What then?"

The certainty in her voice snared Terrell's attention. "Are you speaking hypothetically, Doctor? Or did you find something to suggest that might be the case?"

She switched to the last screen of tricorder data sent up by the landing party, called up a detailed scan of the Tomol's DNA, and isolated several long sections. "I found these anomalous enzymes embedded in their genome. They're as alien to the Tomol as the Tomol are to Nereus Two. Long story short, Captain, I've seen this before. Those are genetic markers used by the Shedai."

Terrell froze at the mention of the sector's former interstellar tyrants. "Are you sure?"

"I'm positive. Starfleet may have erased all the Operation Vanguard–related files from our memory banks, but I remember what the Meta-Genome looks like. And as far as I can tell, these sequences were spliced into the Tomol's DNA, probably hundreds of generations ago, if not earlier. And I'll bet you all my dessert-ration cards that those spliced sequences are what trigger the Change." She handed the data slate and its stylus to Sorak, then crossed her arms as she faced the captain. "So, I'm going to ask you again, sir. If the Change is something that was done to the Tomol, are we still required to stand aside and do nothing while they go extinct?"

Terrell suspected that if one asked that question of a Starfleet JAG officer, in the context of requesting authority to intervene, one would be advised to stand down and avoid the risk of aggravating an already bad situation.

Consequently, he decided not to ask their permission. He ignored Sorak's gloomy frown of disapproval and looked at Babitz with a hint of mischief in his eyes. "Tell me, Doctor: Can you unravel the Shedai Meta-Genome from the Tomol's DNA? Or maybe suppress it? And if you did, could you stop or reverse the Change?"

"I'm not sure. But I'd damned well like to give it a try. Sir."

"Take your best shot. But do it fast—the Klingons won't waste time, so neither can we."

"All right, I'm on it." Babitz hurried off the bridge. Sorak remained beside the command chair. Terrell looked at the image of Nereus II on the viewscreen and rubbed his chin; then, noticing his anxiety-driven affectation, he forced his hand back to his side. "If the Shedai had any part in creating this situation, that would explain why the Klingons are here."

Sorak nodded. "It would also mean the landing party is in greater danger than expected."

Terrell cast a curious look at the Vulcan. "Do you think Hesh or Theriault would have noticed the Shedai Meta-Genome in their scans of the Tomol?"

"Doubtful," the Vulcan said. "With the pattern expunged from our computers and all our devices, they would have no means of automatically detecting it. If not for the doctor's exceptional memory, we ourselves might still be unaware of the Meta-Genome's presence."

Vexed by the two Klingon warships orbiting the planet between him and his landing party, Terrell thumped the side of his fist on his chair's armrest. "We need to warn them."

"That would be tactically unwise, Captain."

"They deserve to know."

"It might be *beneficial* for them to know, but it might also prove irrelevant. It's also my duty to remind you that any attempt to hail the landing party runs the risk of revealing our presence—and theirs—to the Klingons."

Ensign Taryl turned her chair from her console to interrupt Terrell and Sorak. "Sirs? I was reviewing our last contacts with the landing party before we went radio-silent. I think you'll want to see what files they were accessing before we closed the channel."

Terrell stood and walked over to Taryl. Sorak followed him, and they hovered over the Orion woman's shoulders to peruse the data on her screen. It was an image of a metallic sculpture whose base was covered with glyphs. The captain squinted at it. "What *is* that?"

"An artifact of a culture known as the Preservers," Taryl said. "These images were recorded last year by the crew of the *Enterprise*." She switched the image to show a larger but very similar structure. Standing off to one side of the towering obelisk was Lieutenant Dastin. "Ensign Hesh recorded this shortly before we lost contact, in a cavern deep below the largest hill on the big island."

"Taryl, I want a full report about that object, and the one that Kirk and his crew found, and at least some kind of working hypothesis as to what in the hell is going on here."

"Aye, sir." She returned to work on her console.

Terrell returned to his chair and sat down. Sorak followed him and stood awaiting new orders. He didn't wait long. "Work with Ensigns Taryl and Nizsk, and find a way to reach the landing party without painting a target on our back for the Klingons."

"Yes, sir." Sorak lowered his voice. "But I wish to note for the log that I still object."

"Noted. But we're making a stand, Sorak—so find a way to make it work."

Orbs of green lightning hovered above Nimur's open, outstretched hands. As the orbs' brightness intensified, so did the panic that spread through the crowd in the square. The villagers were running for cover, for the jungle, anywhere they thought they could hide.

The Wardens who surrounded her advanced in slow steps, their lances level and pointed at her, and there was nothing Kerlo could do to stop them. He grabbed hold of the nearest Warden's arm. "Senjin! Stop! There's been too much killing already!"

Senjin elbowed Kerlo in the jaw and knocked him to the ground. "Get back!"

Kerlo turned his desperate gaze toward Nimur. "Don't do this."

She sneered. "I pity you. Poised at the threshold of greatness, staring at the face of true power, you still don't understand. What I've set in motion can never be stopped."

Her words wounded Kerlo more deeply than he had ever thought possible.

Battle cries split the air. The Wardens fired beams of light from the heads of their lances. Blasts struck Nimur from all sides and cocooned her in cold fire. She became a pale silhouette inside the tiny sun whose heat singed Kerlo's hair and filled his nose with its bitter, burnt stench. Even as the fireball raged and grew hotter, the Wardens marched inward, until they pressed their attack to within arm's reach of Nimur, who seemed to have vanished inside the miniature blue sun.

Then the fire dissipated. The glow faded. And Nimur stood unscathed, her eyes blazing. A manic gleam lit her face. "Rejoice, my friends! Only hours ago, I would have crushed you like bugs for no better reason than spite. Now, I'll reward you instead."

She raised her arms, and all the Wardens around her rose from the ground and lingered there, suspended in slow motion as if they were floating in the depths of the sea. Their weapons fell from their hands and clattered together on the ground below their dangling feet.

Nimur's eyes flared with eerie light. "Feel the fire that burns within us all. Fight it, and it will destroy you. Welcome it, and you will become the lords of creation."

Two of the Wardens convulsed and struggled as if they were choking. One of them arched his back in agony and then burst into green flames that consumed him from within. As his empty headdress crashed to the ground and his ashes fluttered away on a warm breeze, the second struggling Warden suffered the same fate.

The other Wardens twitched for a few seconds, and then they were still. Nimur lowered her arms. The Wardens were returned with gentle care to solid ground. A few at a time, they removed their ceremonial headdresses and cast them aside, next to those of their fallen comrades.

All that Kerlo could do was watch in mute horror as ten former defenders of the people turned slowly toward him. Lying on the ground, looking up at them, he wanted to scream, to weep, to run—but all he could do was cower, half-paralyzed with fear.

All ten had eyes ablaze with the fire of the Change.

Senjin's voice was flat and merciless as he looked back at Kerlo but spoke to Nimur. "What should we do with this one? Kill him quickly? Or make him suffer?"

Nimur stepped through the Changed Wardens' ranks and took her place in front of them. "Leave him. There's nothing he can do to harm us—and soon enough, he'll take his place at our side." She led her new myrmidons out of the village square. "They *all* will."

Theriault watched, agape, from behind the corner of a large hut. Several dozen meters away in the village's square, Nimur manipulated a dozen armed Wardens as if they were cheap puppets. The rest of the landing party huddled beside her, staring in shocked silence, while behind her the priestess Seta stood a seething watch over the bound and still groggy prisoner Tormog. Theriault tilted her head toward Tan Bao. "Are you seeing what I'm seeing?"

"I sure hope not. What I'm seeing has me scared shitless."

"That makes two of us." Theriault winced as one of the Wardens erupted from within, releasing a brilliant flash of emerald flames that rendered his body into smoke and ashes. She ducked back behind the corner, pulled Hesh with her, and snapped him out of his horrified trance with a harsh whisper. "Hesh! What the hell was that?"

The Arkenite fumbled with his tricorder, which had been running since they had returned to the village. "I . . . I'm sorry, sir. I, um, can't explain this data. Bio-electric readings from Nimur are far beyond anything I've ever seen. Similar readings are emerging in the Wardens."

Dastin continued his discreet observation of Nimur. "She's building an army." He reached toward his belt and rested his hand on his phaser. "We need to stop her. Now."

Theriault put her hand on top of Dastin's. "No."

The scout looked at her. "Sir, Nimur can already kill anything she can see—and probably a fair number of things she *can't* see. We can't let her get any stronger."

Seta took hold of Theriault's free arm. "Your friend is right. Nimur must be stopped."

"We're not your assassins," Theriault said to the young priestess. Then she turned her baleful glare on Dastin. "And this isn't our fight."

Seta was desperate. "How can you say that? You've seen what she can do. Not even the Wardens can stop her now. We need your help!"

Theriault felt sympathy for Seta and the other Tomol, but she had to remember her duty as a Starfleet officer. "I'm sorry," she told the frightened teen, "but my friends and I all swore an oath a long time ago not to interfere in the lives of others."

Her declaration made Seta shake with anger. She pointed at Tormog. "You've *already* interfered! When he and the others helped Nimur escape! Without them, the

Wardens could've caught her and brought her back to finish the Cleansing while there was still time!"

"We're not responsible for what the Klingons do," Theriault said.

Tan Bao sounded doubtful. "I don't know, sir. We could have stopped the Klingons from helping Nimur, but we let them get away. I think that makes us at least a little bit responsible." He shrank back and swallowed as Theriault slowly turned a withering look in his direction.

Hesh's expression turned from concerned to alarmed as he watched his tricorder's display. "Actually, it might be too late for us to intervene at this stage. If one considers that four phasers set on heavy stun were not enough to subdue Nimur in the cave, and then extrapolates the escalation of her power from the increased levels in her bioelectric and neuroelectric fields, it would seem that no offensive power we possess at this time will be sufficient to stop her."

Dastin scrunched his face at the science officer's report. "Are you kidding? Do you really expect me to believe that a phaser set on full power can't bring her down?"

"At this stage, I would rate its likelihood of success as 'minimal.' Such an assault might prove effective against the Tomol in whom she has only just now triggered the Change, but against Nimur herself, I fear such an effort would be futile at best."

"A concerted attack, then. All four of us, firing on full power—"

"Would have only a nine percent chance of killing Nimur," Hesh interrupted.

The Trill wasn't ready to give up. "All right, so side-arms can't get the job done. But we could use a tricorder to pinpoint her position, relay her coordinates to the *Sagittarius,* and they can take her out using the ship's phasers."

Theriault couldn't believe what she was hearing. "Over-kill much?"

"Sir, this bitch ripped five Klingon warriors limb from limb using *only her mind,* and she left a cave painted with their guts. Now she has ten friends just as crazy and dangerous as she is. If anything, I'd call a precision strike from orbit a proportional response."

Tormog slurred, "S'what I'd do."

Theriault gave Tormog a punitive kick. "No one asked you." She turned and confronted Dastin. "What if she and her friends are powerful enough to sense the *Sagittarius*? Right now they don't know about space travel or starships, so they might not think to look for the ship. But if phaser beams start shooting down from the sky, the Changed might expand their new senses to figure out where those attacks are coming from."

"All the more reason to dust them now and be done with this," Dastin said.

Hesh shut off his tricorder and stepped between Theriault and Dastin. "Sir, we are presently out of contact with the ship, so soliciting their aid is a non-issue. Furthermore, we have another option. While four phasers set on kill might not possess sufficient firepower to stop Nimur and her Changed allies, those same phasers set for simultaneous overload and used as a localized demolition charge could release enough energy to destroy the Changed."

Tan Bao held up a hand in a cautionary gesture. "Whoa. It's a nice idea—in theory. But to make it work, you'd need Nimur and all her new friends in the same place. I mean, *really* close together. Even with four phasers bundled into one improvised explosive, the instant-kill radius won't exceed eighteen meters. Against creatures *this* powerful, I'd expect the effective radius to be as little as ten meters. If they split up, this plan is toast."

Dastin stole another look around the corner, then ducked back behind cover. "What if we grabbed a few of those lances the Wardens dropped? We could add those to a phaser barrage."

Theriault shook her head. "Forget it. They hit Nimur with twelve of those things, and she didn't bat an eye. Those might be useful against someone who's still early in the Change, but once a subject starts to exhibit real power, those glorified stun-sticks are basically useless."

A dejected silence settled upon the landing party. Seta grew visibly agitated watching the Starfleet team contemplating their doomed navels. "So, that's it? You lie down and die?"

Theriault resisted the urge to slap the brash young teen. After all, the girl's entire world was teetering on the verge of collapse. Who wouldn't lapse into hysteria under those conditions? Instead, she decided to do what she thought was best for her team, the ship, and the Tomol.

"Okay, new plan. Step one: Gag the Klingon. Step two: We hide."

17

Sickbay's door slid open at Captain Terrell's approach, and he stepped forward—face-first into a tangled web of duotronic cables and optronic wiring. "What in the hell—?"

"Sorry, Captain," shouted Crewman Torvin from the other side of the wall of data fibers. Terrell couldn't see the shaved-headed young Tiburonian, he could only hear him. "Had to open up a few junctions to run some bypasses, and, um, putting them back is, um—"

"Complicated?"

"Yes, sir."

"Time is a factor, Tor."

"I understand, sir. Hang on." From behind the veil of duotronic webbing came the scrape of shuffling feet, the harsh spit of raw power dancing off live wires, and the low curses of an enlisted man in over his head while keenly aware of his commanding officer's waning patience. After nearly half a minute of indeterminate sounds, the spaghetti junction of cables and wires parted to reveal Torvin's flushed and anxious face. "Almost done, sir."

He unraveled the Gordian knot of optronics that obstructed Terrell's path and then pulled aside one half of the cable curtain to grant the captain ingress to sickbay. Terrell ducked through the narrow, temporary gap and looked around, bewildered by the chaos that greeted him.

Sickbay had, as far as Terrell could see, been ripped open on all sides, and its duotronic viscera spilled across its bulkheads and deck, as if the ship's sole medical facility had been gutted by force. Seated in the middle of all that chaos, hands pressed against the sides of her head and hunched over a small computer terminal wrapped in twisted metal, was Doctor Babitz.

"Do my eyes deceive me, Doctor, or has sickbay committed *seppuku*?"

Babitz pointed at Torvin. "His fault."

Terrell turned to face Torvin, whose face was stretched taut by a nervous grin. "I know this looks bad, sir, but I can explain, really."

"Don't let me stop you, Crewman. I would *love* to hear this."

Torvin tugged one of his fin-shaped, outrageously large earlobes. "Well, I heard sickbay's computer activate ten minutes ago. Thing is, we're on a silent-running protocol—"

Terrell held up a hand to stop Torvin because he understood. "Which restricts computer operations to minimize our energy signature."

The enlisted engineer nodded. "But then Doctor Babitz said she had priority orders to work on a medical emergency—"

"And she needs the computer to do it," Terrell cut in. He hung his head in shame; this was his fault. Despite having ordered the ship into silent running, he had directed Doctor Babitz to conduct vital medical research. He was able to guess what had happened next. "So you isolated the sickbay computer from the main core and contained its energy signature."

"Yes, sir. Well, I mean, I'm doing my best. It's a work in progress."

"I trust you'll be able to put this all back together later, yes?"

"Probably."

"Carry on, Crewman."

"Aye, sir. Thank you, sir." Torvin hurried away, opened another panel on the overhead, and freed a bundle of optronic cables that spilled over him like the entrails of a gutted beast. The young man stumbled, struggled under their weight, and then set to work on a new bypass.

Terrell sidled over to stand beside Babitz's computer terminal, which was surrounded on five of six sides by a hastily assembled metal framework. The captain flicked his index finger against the crudely assembled encasement. "Dare I ask?"

Babitz shrugged. "It's based on something called a 'Faraday cage.' Tor's expanding the concept to encompass all of sickbay so I can use the rest of the systems later, if necessary."

"Looks like a mess. But if it works, I'm all for it."

Torvin looked across the compartment at Terrell. "It'll work, sir."

The captain marveled again at how sensitive Torvin's hearing was. "Tell me something, Tor. If you're right, why don't we design our ships this way to begin with?"

"Because as long as this signal-blocking grid remains in place, sickbay can't access the ship's main computer core, and it becomes a blind spot to our internal sensors."

"Good to know." Terrell turned back toward Babitz. "What have you got?"

"Nothing good, I'm afraid." She beckoned Terrell to stand behind her, so he moved to look over her shoulder as she continued. "The challenge isn't suppressing the She-dai Meta-Genome segments in the Tomol DNA, or even removing them. I could accomplish either with a retro-viral gene therapy. The problem is, suppressing or excising those sequences would constitute a fatal alteration to the Tomol's DNA. It would kill them almost instantly."

Every new piece of the puzzle magnified Terrell's concerns. "Why?"

"Because the Meta-Genome sequences appear to have replaced original strings of the Tomol's DNA. Strings that were essential to their nervous and endocrine systems. Without a map of what those original portions of their genome looked like, we can't replace them."

Terrell tensed with frustration. They were close to an answer, he could feel it—he just couldn't *see* it. "What about obstructing just part of the Shedai tampering? Shutting down only one or a few of the inserted sequences?"

"I explored that option. Some combinations are just as fatal as removing all the Shedai material. Some partial extractions or suppressions would have no effect. A few might make the Changed even more dangerous, by triggering sequences I think are related to telepathy and other high-level psionic abilities. And at least one would spark spontaneous combustion."

"Would this apply only to the Tomol who have begun the Change?"

"No. It's species-wide. I can't see any way to stop the Change before it starts, or reverse it after it's begun, without killing the subject."

"Quite an effective bit of genomic sabotage the Shedai wrought here."

Babitz's shoulders slumped. "You're telling me." She stared at the genetic riddle on her computer screen. "If the Tomol's mutation is so unstable, why do the Klingons want it?"

"Why do the Klingons want anything? Because they think it'll add to their power." He crossed his arms and thought for a moment. There was something about the Tomol's dilemma that didn't add up for him. He thought about the data that the landing party had linked to the obelisk under the hill on the planet's surface. "What I can't figure out is why a culture like the Preservers would save a species like this. The first human settlers they had rescued from Earth's North American continent lived in harmony with nature and were generally peaceful."

"So are the Tomol, according to Hesh's preliminary report."

"True. But if every one of them has the potential to turn into a bloodthirsty monster—"

"I'd say that makes them about average," Babitz said.

Her cynical observation drew a grim nod from Terrell. "Sadly, yes."

Silence was a bad sign. A Klingon warship was a place for hearty laughter, roaring songs, and heated arguments. A quiet warship was one on which something was wrong. Kang was sure of it.

He watched Mara from across the bridge until he caught her eye. She acknowledged his unspoken summons with a rise of her chin, then she parted from tactical officer Mahzh with a curt order and returned to Kang's side. "Yes, Captain?"

"Have we made contact with the recon team?"

"Not yet, sir. Kyris hailed them on all frequencies, but she reports no response."

Kang's vague disquiet was hardening into suspicion. "Have we detected any other communications? On the planet or in this system?"

"None." Mara stole a glance at the image of the ringed planet on the viewscreen. "You think there is someone else here." Her eyes narrowed. "Starfleet, perhaps?"

"I don't know. But it is possible."

Mahzh looked up from the weapons console. "Captain, we're picking up unusual activity on the planet's surface. An energy wave unlike any we've encountered before."

With a sideways nod, Kang sent Mara to check out Mahzh's report. She stepped around the dais that supported Kang's command chair and nudged Mahzh aside so she could look at the sensor readouts. "Most unusual." She adjusted a few controls. "Mahzh is correct. Our memory banks hold no match for this energy waveform."

"Analysis?"

Mara stepped aside to let Mahzh resume his duties. The weapons officer hunched over the sensor readout, which painted his face with red light. "Very powerful, strongly ordered. Definitely artificial." He applied some filters and submitted the scans to the computer. "Power source is underground, beneath a large hill on the planet's only populated island."

Kang felt a prickling of alarm at the nape of his neck.

"The same hill that's honeycombed with caves?" He looked at Mara. "The recon team was using those caves as a base."

She looked away, toward the deck, as she often did when she was concentrating. "This sector is riddled with ancient artifacts. Could they have found one and triggered it by mistake?"

Kang had read reports of entire worlds throughout the Gonmog Sector being laid waste or shattered without warning by the fearsome technology of the now-extinct Shedai. Was this another doomsday weapon, left behind to punish the unwary? He wanted to know more about the threat before he settled on a plan of attack. "Get me a detailed scan of that power source."

Mahzh struggled with the sensor controls, then gave up. "I can't, sir. There are sensor-blocking mineral compounds in the hill. We can detect the excess energy that escapes from the surface, but we can't penetrate the bedrock to identify the cause."

"So be it. Could those compounds be blocking communications with the recon team?"

"No, but the energy field might be." Mahzh pressed a few keys at his station, then let out a low growl of satisfaction. "I will try to design a signal-canceling frequency that will negate the energy field's interference. If that is what is obstructing our comms, this will correct it."

"Good. Tell me when you're ready."

Mara returned to Kang's side. "There could be another reason the recon team has not made contact." Her ominous tone had made her implicit message clear: *They might be dead.*

Kang considered his options. "If we've lost the recon team, we'll need to finish their mission. Put together a landing party, heavily armed. Make sure they know what to look for. If they meet any resistance, they can shoot to kill. We only need to take one test subject alive."

"Yes, Captain. I can have them on the surface in ten minutes."

He held up a hand. "No, keep them on standby. If Kyris can raise the recon team after Mahzh cancels the interference, we'll let them finish their mission, as planned. But if Tobar and his men remain missing in action after the channel is clear, we'll send in a recovery team."

"Understood, Captain."

Mara stepped away to supervise the preparation of the landing party, and Kang returned his attention to the main viewscreen—only to notice that the *Voh'tahk*'s orbit was shifting. "Helm! Why are we deviating from standard orbit?"

Ortok answered while monitoring readouts on his console. "Emergency course change, sir. Sensors detected an asteroid on a close approach vector. I've compensated by increasing orbital range by six thousand *qellqams* and adjusting orbital latitude one point nine degrees toward the equator. The asteroid will clear our standard orbital path within the hour."

The helmsman's reaction to the threat of an asteroid collision had been in perfect accord with Imperial procedures, but Kang distrusted any new wrinkle in their mission. "Put it on-screen." Ortok punched in the command. The viewscreen switched to show the asteroid, heading in a slow tumble toward them and the planet. It was a nondescript hunk of rock. Kang regarded it with a wary stare. "Just how large is that thing?"

Ortok read the statistics off a screen. "Approximate diameter: point nine three *qelIqam*s. Composition: silicon, carbon, iron, nickel, fistrium, traces of kelbonite. Velocity, twenty-one point four *qelIqam*s per second."

"Is that on any of our navigational charts?"

"No, sir. But that's not unusual. Most of the systems in this sector have barely been charted. Minor objects like this were deemed too small to merit tracking."

Kang swiveled his chair toward Mahzh. "Any chance that rock will hit the planet?"

Mahzh switched his sensors to study the asteroid. "None, sir. Just a close shave."

That was good news, at least. A passing notion made Kang crack a mischievous smile. "Maybe you'd like to use it for target practice?"

The weapons officer shook his head. "Not this close to the planet, sir. An hour ago, I would have. But any detonation while the asteroid is inside our orbital track would pose a high risk of bombarding the planet with debris. Given the asteroid's mass, the damage would be substantial enough to threaten the success of our mission."

"Pity. Reset the viewer." Kang reclined in his command chair as the screen reverted to the image of Arethusa. "Mahzh, tell Kyris when you've canceled that interference. We'll give Tobar and his recon team one more chance to reply. After that, we'll finish this ourselves."

• • •

For the sake of morale, Terrell did his best to mask his mounting anxiety. He took a deep breath to steady his voice before he spoke. "Sorak? Any sign the Klingons are onto us?"

The Vulcan was calm as he monitored his console. "Negative. They've adjusted their orbit to avoid colliding with the asteroid, but their shields and weapon systems remain inactive."

Terrell studied the tactical readout on the main viewscreen. "What about the bird-of-prey? Any risk they'll see us as they round the planet?"

There was a note of pride in Ensign Nizsk's reply. "No, sir. I have adjusted the attitude of the asteroid along its longest axis to obstruct the bird-of-prey's vantage at all times. Both it and the cruiser should have obstructed lines of sight once we are in position to transmit."

"Well done." Terrell had never harbored any serious doubts about Nizsk's competence as a helm officer; it was simply that he had found it hard to believe that the young Kaferian—or anyone else, for that matter—could ever live up to the tradition of daredevil excellence set by her predecessor, the late Andorian *zhen* Celerasayna zh'Firro. Nizsk had proved him wrong.

The two ensigns on the bridge—Nizsk and Taryl—had teamed up to devise a truly cunning means of putting the *Sagittarius* in a position to contact its landing party while staying hidden from the two Klingon ships in orbit. Using only the maneuvering thrusters and one-tenth impulse power, Nizsk had forced upon the asteroid a series of precision trajectory and velocity adjustments designed by Taryl, while at the same time stabilizing its erratic three-axis spin into a single-axis slow roll. Most remarkable of all, she had done it with a minimal power expenditure, ensuring that they didn't exceed the sensor-blocking properties of their natural camouflage.

His only qualm had been Taryl's insistence on setting the asteroid upon a potential collision course with the Klingon cruiser. That had felt to him like too brazen a tactic, but after a brief review of known Klingon starship protocols, Sorak had assured Terrell the maneuver was a logical one, in that it had the highest likelihood of forcing the Klingons to alter their orbital position, ensuring that the *Sagittarius* would have the best chance to send a subspace radio signal to the landing party without being detected or intercepted.

Seconds passed like cold molasses through a jug with a narrow mouth, and Terrell's patience ebbed. "How long until we're ready to hail the landing party?"

"Fifteen seconds," Nizsk replied.

Terrell knew the window for communications would be brief—no more than two minutes. He didn't plan on wasting even a moment of that precious time. "Sorak, open a channel to the landing party in ten seconds. Hail them as soon as we're in position."

"Aye, sir."

"And everyone? Good work. My log will include commendations all around." He saw a subtle smile of gratitude from Taryl, but Sorak, *Kolinahr* master that he was, evinced no reaction, and Terrell had no idea how to read the emotions of insectoid Kaferians like Nizsk.

From the helm, Nizsk announced, "We're directly above the largest island."

"Channel open," Sorak said. "Hailing the landing party." He waited for a response, his hand pressed gently to the transceiver tucked into his elegantly curved and pointed ear. Then he looked up at Terrell. "Captain, I have Commander Theriault."

"On speakers," Terrell said. "Vanessa? Are you all right?"

"Yes, sir. Scrapes and bruises, but we're all accounted for."

Terrell breathed a short sigh of relief. "Glad to hear it. Listen, we don't have much time. There are two Klingon ships in orbit, and we're using up the last of our tricks for this chat. What's your mission status?"

"We've gone from one superpowered homicidal maniac to eleven. Plus, we have a Klingon prisoner, the sole survivor of a recon unit. He says his team planned to tag one of these Changed aliens with a transponder for beam-up. If you ask me, I'd advise against it."

"How dangerous are these transformed natives?"

"They can turn us inside-out just by thinking about it, and the stronger they get, the less effect our phasers have. Also, it looks like the leader can now transform others at will. Orders?"

"Fall back and lie low, if you can. *Endeavour's* en route, ETA twenty minutes."

"Any chance you could beam us up?"

"Sorry, not right now. Using that much power would tip off the Klingons for sure. Besides, we'd have to beam you up one at a time, and we'd have to abandon the rover, which I'm pretty sure would be a Prime Directive violation."

"I figured, but I had to ask. One more thing: We discovered a structure under the largest hill on the big island. We matched it to a Preserver obelisk—"

"—found by the *Enterprise* crew. I know; Taryl showed me your search query."

"We also matched its energy emissions to the ones detected by our long-range probe."

"Yes, we noted that, too."

"One more thing: We might have . . . sort of, kind of . . . switched it on."

"Come again? You did what?"

"We translated its glyphs using the Enterprise's *research and synthesized the activation tones for this planet's obelisk. And now it's building up to . . . well, to something."*

"Could you be more specific?"

"Believe me, I wish I could." After an awkward silence, Theriault asked, *"Orders?"*

Taryl turned from her console to interrupt the conversation. "Captain? The bird-of-prey is adjusting its orbit. They'll be in position to intercept our signal in thirty seconds."

Terrell never liked having his back to the wall, but when it was, he recalled his Academy years as a champion boxer and came out punching. "We'll do what we can up here to make sure the Klingons don't beam any Tomol off the planet. But if the Klingons get past us, do whatever you have to down there to stop them from tagging any of the Changed for beam-up."

"Sir? Are you sure that's a good idea? If you challenge those Klingon ships, you'll be outnumbered and outgunned for at least the next twenty minutes."

"Don't remind me, Commander. You have your orders. Do your best, and stay safe. *Sagittarius* out." He looked at Sorak and pulled his thumb in a slashing motion across his throat. The Vulcan confirmed with a curt nod that the comm channel was closed. Nizsk and Taryl both turned and looked to the captain for new orders. He thumbed a button on his armrest to open an internal comm channel to the engineering deck. "Master Chief?"

"Yo."

"We're done with silent running. Give me full power, on the double."

"Comin' online now."

Terrell turned his attention to the tactical schematic on the main viewscreen. "Taryl, switch the main screen to a forward angle, normal magnification. Nizsk, release our tether to the asteroid and set a course to obstruct the Klingon cruiser's line of sight to the big island. Sorak, raise shields, charge phasers, and sound Red Alert." The klaxon whooped twice, in synchronicity with the flashing crimson panels on the bulkheads. The starfield on the viewscreen stopped spinning and settled into a view of the planet. Terrell steeled himself for the coming fray.

"Hang on to your hats, people. This ride's about to get rough."

Kang accepted the data tablet from Mara and looked over the list of personnel she had selected for the landing party. All of them were warriors of impeccable honor. "Status?"

"All are gathered in the transporter room. Ready to beam down on your order."

"Good." He handed her the data tablet and snapped at Mahzh. "Scan the surface! Find an isolated concentration of Tomol and relay those coordinates to the transporter room." Mahzh appeared distracted as he keyed commands into the *Voh'tahk*'s sensor console. After several seconds passed without him acknowledging Kang's order, the captain bellowed, "Mahzh! Scan the surface! I want target coordinates for the landing party!"

Mahzh peered into the ruby glow of his display, and then he looked back at Kang, his teeth bared in a show of alarm. "Federation battle cruiser closing on our position at warp nine!"

That was the last news Kang wanted to hear. "Time to intercept?"

The weapons officer checked his readings. "Just under twenty minutes."

An irrational hope preoccupied Kang. Could it be the *Enterprise*? Its commanding officer, James Kirk, had repeatedly proved himself a thorn in the side of the Klingon people. From Kirk's role in the Organia debacle, to the tribble fiasco he had inflicted upon Koloth, and, of course, Kang's own ill-fated run-in with a non-corporeal entity that had delighted in using him and the Starfleet captain as puppets for its amusement in a perpetual bloodsport, the human captain and his vessel had quickly become notorious among soldiers of the Empire.

Kang's blood ran hot at the prospect of facing Kirk once more. "What ship is it?"

It took a few seconds for Mahzh to compare his sensor readings to information in the *Voh'tahk*'s memory banks.

"Energy signature is a match for the battle cruiser *Endeavour*."

Fek'lhr *laughs at me from the flames of* Gre'thor. An unexpected encounter with a heavily armed Federation starship was always an opportunity to seize glory, but part of Kang yearned for the special renown that would come from being the one to defeat Kirk.

Someday, he vowed to himself. *Someday.* "Tactical to my monitor." He swiveled his chair left toward his command panel, which included a small screen on which he could review a variety of data, such as battle diagrams, or receive audio-visual subspace communications. He noted the *Endeavour*'s course and speed. "They are in quite a rush, aren't they?"

Mara leaned in close beside him to steal a look at his screen. "I wonder why."

It was a reasonable question—one that left Kang searching for a satisfactory answer. "Why, indeed? There's no Federation colony here. They have no shipping lanes in this sector, let alone this system. And this world seems to have none of the things Starfleet values: No dilithium. Little arable surface. No advanced culture to seduce into their pathetic Federation."

"And yet," Mara said, lightly tapping one sharpened fingernail against his command screen, "the *Endeavour* charges into a burning house, and dares us to do battle in the flames."

She was right. Starfleet vessels rarely risked armed confrontation without provocation. So why was the *Endeavour* racing toward Arethusa at high warp?

Then Mahzh raised his voice, and Kang had his answer.

"New sensor contact, bearing one-seven-nine mark nine-four!" The weapons officer changed the viewscreen to show an aft-facing angle. A familiar shape emerged from behind the asteroid that was passing through Arethusa's prime orbital plane. "Starfleet vessel, *Archer*-class. Energy signature confirmed. It's the scout ship *Sagittarius*." He looked up from his sensor panel. "Her shields are up, phasers charged—and she is placing herself between us and the big island."

Mara reasoned out the Starfleet ship's purpose at a glance. "They're trying to prevent us from beaming down our landing party."

Kang smiled. "Well, this is a turn for the unexpected." He wondered what the scout ship's commander was thinking. Was he foolish enough to think his tiny ship was a match for the *Voh'tahk*? Or was this some kind of feint, a ruse to distract Kang from his mission? Regardless of the answer, he admired the Starfleet commander's audacity if not his tactics—but he knew better than to take victory for granted, or to leave important matters to chance.

"Mahzh, get those beam-down coordinates to the transporter room, *now*. Kyris, hail the *Homghor* and tell them to regroup with us. This pest is their size—let them swat it away so we can maneuver clear and beam down our landing party. Mara, raise shields and arm all weapons." The bridge crew set to work quickly and quietly, their focus as keen as a *bat'leth*'s killing edge. Kang pressed a switch on his armrest to snap the overhead lights from soothing red to harsh white, and to open a ship-wide PA channel.

"All hands, this is Captain Kang. Two Federation warships are converging upon our position. They mean to thwart our mission and rob us of our glory. We're going to make sure they fail. Today is a good day to die—as long as our enemies die first. Battle stations!"

18

Adrenaline coursed through Theriault's lithe form as she darted from one hut to the next, using the ramshackle structures for cover as she and the landing party followed Nimur and her gang of corrupted Wardens across the Tomol's village. Sprinting and then crouching, over and over, the youthful Martian-born woman became keenly aware of the aching in her calves and the fleeting jabs of pain between her ribs as she forced herself to draw deeper, slower breaths.

Dastin scrambled after Theriault. All the way across the village, he had never been more than a second behind her, except in a few moments when he'd had to hang back to avoid being seen by Nimur or her new disciples. He arrived at Theriault's side, ducked low, and peeked around the next corner. "Looks like the villagers are making a run for the fire pit."

Theriault stole a look around the corner and saw the panicked crowd of Tomol fleeing down a long trail, running from Nimur and the other Changed. Hearing the villagers' high-pitched shrieks of terror, and seeing their tiny, slender shapes retreating into the jungle, she was reminded of the cruel fact that the entire village was populated by children—all of whom were in danger of suffering grisly fates unless someone put an end to the rampage of the Changed.

She checked the charge on her phaser. "Nimur and the others don't seem to be in a hurry to catch up to them. Maybe they figure time's on their side, so why waste effort running?"

The Trill drew his phaser and handed it to Theriault. "Whatever they're thinking, this might be our best chance to take them out with minimal collateral damage." He risked another furtive glance at the Changed. "I can grab a Warden's lance and use it to draw their attention."

"I'm not sure that's a good idea."

"Why? What could go wrong? I mean, other than everything." He hooked a thumb toward the Tomol. "At the very least, we might buy the Tomol time to find a place to hide."

It was a good argument, as rationales for suicide went. Theriault decided to act while she still had options. "All right, but you don't get to be the bait. That's my job." She handed back his phaser, looked toward the rest of their group, and signaled Hesh and Tan Bao to join them. Seta drew her ceremonial dagger, put it to Tormog's throat, and nodded her assurance to Tan Bao that she would be all right guarding the Klingon, who remained drugged, bound, and gagged.

The two men ran to Theriault and Dastin. She held out her hand. "Phasers. Let's have 'em." The nurse and science officer surrendered their weapons to Theriault, who handed them to Dastin. "Tan Bao, take Seta and Tormog back the way we came and hide in the jungle. Dastin, make those phasers into an explosive by linking their charging coils and setting them for a high-speed synchronous overload. Hesh, jury-rig a trigger for the explosive that you can remotely activate with your tricorder. As soon as the charge is ready, hide it beneath some piece of loose debris in the street just around that corner over there, then regroup with Tan Bao and the others."

Dastin telegraphed his doubts with a single arched eyebrow. "And where will you be?"

"If I'm lucky? Right behind you."

Tan Bao asked, "And if you're not?"

"Then I'll be all around you, in the form of free radicals."

Hesh frowned. "I do not care for this plan, Commander."

"Good thing I don't have to ask your permission." She pointed Tan Bao toward the trees. "Get moving." The nurse hurried away and led Seta and Tormog to cover in the jungle. Theriault faced Hesh and Dastin. "Get that charge rigged and placed on the double. I'm not sure how long I'll be able to harass Nimur and her brood before I'll have to make a run for it."

The scout started pulling apart the three phasers, one at a time. "You know that I can't make this work like a shaped charge, right? This thing's gonna vaporize everything inside its blast radius—so you'd better not be inside it when Hesh pulls the trigger."

"Don't worry." Theriault stood, tightened her grip on her phaser, and turned the corner moving in bold strides toward the Changed. "I've got my running shoes on."

And a death wish, apparently.

She marched toward Nimur and her company of Changed, who all were facing away from her as they walked in slow pursuit of their escaping Tomol brethren.

None of them seemed to take any notice of her, not even when she had narrowed the gap between them to less than ten meters. She decided to grab their attention in the most direct way possible.

The blinding, full-power beam that screeched from her phaser was powerful enough to blast apart boulders or vaporize a small shuttlecraft. It slammed into the back of one transformed Warden and knocked him forward, onto his hands and knees. As he lingered, stunned, on all fours, the other Changed stopped, turned in fearsome unison, and trained their cold glares upon Theriault. Nimur stepped between her companions, and then in front of them, to confront her.

"Ah, yes—your version of the Warden's lance." She looked down at her humbled follower. "I see it has even more of a kick than the one I felt in the cave."

Theriault mustered her bravado. "It had enough juice to make you run."

Tendrils of electricity began to crawl over the hands and arms of the Changed, and a nimbus of pale violet light formed around Nimur's hands and head. She cracked a sinister, taunting smile. "Four of them at once did. Care to test your luck alone?"

Eleven versus one would be atrocious odds even in a so-called fair fight, and Theriault knew this melee promised to be anything but equitable. Her only hope of survival rested in her observation that, so far, Nimur's ability to attack appeared to be limited to what she could see.

The young Starfleet officer slowly lowered her phaser, as if to surrender.

As soon as it was pointed at the ground beneath

Nimur's feet, Theriault fired. A shriek split the sultry jungle air, and the first meter of earth beneath the Changed flared and vanished; the next two meters beneath that became molten rock and sand, and the Changed plunged into it feet-first and vanished beneath its surface, immersed in white-hot liquid glass.

Theriault didn't wait around to see what happened next; she knew her dirty trick would only make the Changed angry and slow them down for a few seconds. As Nimur and the others arose, howling with rage as they clawed their way from the impromptu slag pit, Theriault was already running for her life and firing random shots at the ground behind her, filling the air with superheated dust. Through the smoky amber veil, she heard Nimur roar, "Destroy that one!"

And away we go.

Shock waves hammered through the village all around her. Each psionic pulse splintered several empty huts and scattered their broken thatch walls and roofs like shrapnel. Theriault felt the concussive force of each wave that leveled the structures around her. A storm of shattered pottery erupted into the street and peppered her with stinging shards. An impact knocked her to the ground half a second before another fearsome invisible force tore past above her, sending ripples through the curtains of dust and smoke that had separated into discrete layers.

She rolled supine, pointed the phaser back the way she had come, and fired several short blasts through the impenetrable haze. Her effort was rewarded by cries of pain and fury from the Changed. She snapped off two more shots for good measure as she got back up and resumed running for the ambush position. She plucked her communicator from her hip pocket and flipped it open on the fly. "Theriault to Dastin! Ready?"

"Ready! But you'd better haul ass, they're right on you!"

Theriault saved her breath for the run to cover and flipped her communicator shut. She hurdled over assorted debris littering the trail between rows of huts, which were being swept away en masse by unseen waves of force, and fired a few more shots behind her to maintain what little cover smoke and dust could offer her. Then she made the turn down a short path that dead-ended at the tree line and forced herself to ignore the sensation that acid was pumping in her veins and her muscles were tying themselves into knots from the exertion of her mad dash.

A thundercrack and blistering white flash from behind her launched her through the wall of low brush and foliage, into the jungle, and into the arms of her landing party.

When the dark spots began to fade from her vision and the dull silence in her ears gave way to the painful ringing of tinnitus, Theriault blinked and got her bearings. Seta stood a couple of meters away, looking nervous as she turned back and forth between the village and Tormog. Dastin and Hesh were on Theriault's right. They watched Tan Bao, who kneeled at Theriault's left and scanned her with a medical tricorder. His voice sounded as if he were speaking through several heavy blankets. "No permanent damage. I can fix her up once we get back to the ship."

She reached up and seized the front of Dastin's jumpsuit. "Did it work?"

"We hit 'em." He looked over his shoulder and grimaced. "And boy are they *pissed*."

"So, that would be a *no*."

"Pretty much." Dastin took Theriault's left arm and nodded at Tan Bao. "Help her up. We gotta go." He noted the confusion on Theriault's face and added, "They're still coming."

She pressed her phaser into Dastin's free hand. "Just in case."

"Got it." He waved Hesh, Tormog, and Seta into motion. "Let's motor."

Seta refused to be moved. "To where?"

"The beach," Dastin said. "We're getting off this island."

The teen backed away. "I won't abandon my people."

Dastin's temper frayed. "Look, kid, I don't have time to argue with you. Come with us and live, or stay here and die. Your call."

She was unmoved by his tough talk. "I wish you well, and I hope you all make it home. Good-bye." Without waiting for anyone to respond, she scurried away and vanished into the jungle's verdant embrace, on a heading that would take her around the edge of the village.

Tan Bao raised his chin at Tormog as he asked Dastin, "Where are we gonna put *him*?"

"We'll stuff him in the cargo box." He tossed the phaser to Tan Bao. "Watch him."

Hesh silenced an alert from his tricorder. "The Changed are closing on our position."

"Move out," Theriault said, her voice reduced to a pained groan. "Stay off the trails."

The landing party retreated single file through the trees, with Dastin in the lead and Tan Bao bringing up the rear, prodding the stumbling Tormog forward at phaser-point. Behind them, sharp cracks and heavy crashes reverberated through the jungle. Theriault chanced a look over her shoulder, and she glimpsed enormous trees toppling in various directions, as if the landing party were being pursued by a demolition machine.

So much for avoiding the trails, she realized. *The Changed are just making a new one.*

"Hesh," she said between labored gasps, "how many are chasing us?"

"All of them."

That put a smile on her face. *Good. Mission accomplished.*

Now all the landing party had to do was reach its amphibious rover, pull the vehicle out of its hiding place, pack the Klingon prisoner like cheap luggage, climb inside, and escape into the sea before Nimur and her murderous band of freshly minted demigods caught up to them.

Piece of cake, as long as nothing else goes—

A stunning force, like a giant fist of steel, hit Theriault in the back.

She was airborne, tumbling and off-balance. On all sides the jungle blurred past, its details spinning by too quickly for her impact-purpled vision to discern. Around her, the others rolled or traced shallow arcs through a low-hanging cloud layer of tiny insects. Then she struck something immovable that knocked the air from her chest. She collapsed in a heap to the ground. Curled up in her own agony against the gnarled trunk of an ancient tree, she felt several trickles of warm blood trace random designs down the side of her face. Somewhere close by, hidden beneath the jungle's dense carpet of fronds and flowering brush, she heard Dastin groan.

Theriault rolled onto her stomach and looked around in vain for any sign of the Klingon prisoner. Then she heard footsteps drawing near.

She was clinging to consciousness when Nimur and three of her minions surrounded her. They looked down at her with eyes afire. There was no pity in their gaze, no compassion, only contempt. "Outsiders," Nimur sneered. "You should never have come here."

"Actually? We were just leaving."

"You will leave here in pieces, as a warning to all who would violate my domain."

Nimur's eyes blazed brighter—and then a nearby wash of white noise accompanied by a shimmering of light turned her head. She and all the Changed spun to confront a new threat.

As the transporter beam faded, Theriault savored the irony as she realized this was the first time in her life she had ever been happy to see a Klingon landing party.

It had galled Tormog to play the part of an invalid while in the Starfleet team's custody, but his fleeting humiliation proved worthwhile as soon as the natives' attack left his captors stunned.

Nimur and the corrupted Wardens were not yet on top of the fallen Starfleeters by the time Tormog regained his feet. His mouth remained gagged and his hands were bound behind his back, but he was up and able to run, and for the moment that was enough. He made a hard sprint through a tangle of low-drooping vines thick with broad leaves, and he didn't stop until he heard the familiar sing-song whine of an Imperial transporter beam.

He turned back, paralyzed by conflicting desires. He wanted to be free of his bonds, and to get off this miserable planet-sized ball of mud, but he knew that what little honor he still retained as a lowly scientist would be stripped from him if it became known that he had been taken prisoner. *A warrior would not ask for help,* he decided. *He would free himself.*

He crouched in the undergrowth and blindly searched the ground behind his back for a sharp-edged rock. All he found were half-buried roots, rotting vegetation, and what he suspected were desiccated animal feces. *Damn this useless planet! It denies me even this simple gift!*

A root caught his foot and tripped him onto his back. Seconds later, the angry whine of disruptor blasts resounded through the jungle, and several wild shots ripped through the foliage above him, cutting smoldering paths through the greenery. Suddenly, flat on the ground seemed to Tormog like an ideal place to be.

Proud, defiant Klingon battle cries gave way within seconds to primal howls of pain. Lying on his back, all but hidden in the leafy cover of the jungle floor, Tormog found a jagged shard of bone nestled among the festering slime that coated the ground. His fingers seized on that splinter and turned its sharpest edge against the knotted vines the Starfleeters had used to bind his hands. As he sawed through his bonds with patient precision, the sounds of battle lost their stridency, and the shrieks of disruptor fire became less frequent. The last sinews of vine gave way, and his hands broke free. He pulled the gag from his mouth and rolled to a low crouch.

He had run quite a ways from the Starfleeters, none of whom were anywhere to be found. All he saw were Nimur and her Wardens using their telekinetic powers to sadistically twist and break Klingon warriors who Tormog could tell, even from a distance, were already dead.

Lurking behind a thick-trunked tree, the last Klingon warrior standing primed his tagging device. Tormog wanted to signal the man, to warn him not to bother with such a hopeless and futile gesture, but the scientist's overactive instinct for self-preservation left him mute.

The warrior pivoted around the tree, aimed at Nimur, and fired a transponder at her.

At first, Nimur showed no response. Then she and the other Changed released their holds on the Klingon bodies they had been levitating and tormenting post-mortem. The broken corpses fell limp to the ground. Nimur turned and fixed her stare upon the warrior.

In a blur, the Klingon's head spun completely around, and the crack of his snapping cervical vertebrae echoed between the trees. His lifeless eyes seemed to stare at Tormog as he collapsed and disappeared into a hip-deep miniature forest of dark-green fronds. Tormog ducked and crabwalked to cover behind a tree while he eavesdropped on Nimur and her cohorts.

"The others are running for the beach," Nimur said.

A Warden with a scar on the left side of his neck pointed in the opposite direction. "We should return to the village and finish what has begun."

Nimur continued to look away in the direction of the shore. "Not yet. I sensed something in the ones who escaped. If we don't stop them, they could pose a danger to us."

Another Warden, one with a bald stripe shaved down the middle of his silver-haired head, sounded unconvinced. "If they are such a threat, why do they fly like frightened songbirds?"

"I don't know. It's just a feeling. They run from us—but only to strike from a distance."

The Wardens traded glances, and then Neck-Scar spoke for them. "Then they must die."

"Follow me," Nimur said. She led the other Changed away from the village. As they advanced through the jungle, they uprooted and knocked aside the dense sea of trees in their path with their fearsome telekinetic assault. Great cracks of splintering wood, like the breaking of a titan's bones, drowned out all the other sounds of the jungle and sent multitudes of small animals skittering and flying away in panicked retreat. Where the Changed had passed, searing hot sunlight beat down through newly torn wounds in the forest canopy.

Tormog remained behind cover, not daring to move for fear of bringing Nimur's wrath back upon himself. He had only narrowly evaded her in the caves; he had no desire to face her again out in the open, where he had so few places to seek shelter.

The air was heavy with the odor of fresh-spilled blood and the stench of ruptured viscera. It would not be long before the jungle's natural scavengers and carrion-eaters came to feast on the Klingon dead. Tormog knew it would be best if he were gone before that came to pass. But where was he to go? In pursuit of the Starfleeters, who had the murderous Changed following them? Back to the caves, to await his next confrontation with Nimur? Or into the forsaken vale beyond the great hill, the barren rocky sprawl filled with graven figures of men and women frozen for eternity in poses of torment and horror?

He was still weighing his meager options when he heard, from somewhere close by, the low beep of an Imperial communicator receiving an incoming signal.

You fool! You're surrounded by everything you need! He rushed across the killing field and waded through the greenery, moving from one corpse to the next, searching for the one whose communicator was beeping. Along the way he grabbed a disruptor from one corkscrew-twisted body and jammed it into the empty holster strapped to his thigh, and from another slain warrior he snatched up a *d'k tahg* and tucked it under his belt.

His ears led him to the source of the insistent beeping. He yanked the communicator from the dead lieutenant's belt and flipped it open. "This is Doctor Tormog."

A woman answered. *"This is the* Voh'tahk. *Where is Lieutenant Kurz?"*

"I can tell you where his legs are. The rest of him? I'm not so sure."

"What is your status?"

"Ready to beam up."

"Has the target been tagged?"

Tormog was unsure how to answer. He had seen the horrors Nimur could wreak with a thought. Unleashing such a monster aboard an Imperial starship would be a disaster. But if he confirmed that Nimur had been shot with a transponder, he had no doubt the ambitious but shortsighted officers commanding the ships in orbit would insist on beaming up the homicidal alien. He decided that a lie was in everyone's best interest. "Negative."

"Then why are we receiving a transponder signal? Who was tagged, Doctor?"

"No one. Ignore it. Just beam me up."

Muffled murmurs over the comm channel were followed by a deep, gruff voice that Tormog knew all too well. *"This is Captain Kang. Why are you lying to us, Doctor?"*

"It's a long story, Captain. Beam me up and I'll explain."

"I'll hear your explanation now, Doctor. And unless I find it extremely persuasive, you're going to spend the rest of your miserable life on that planet. Do I make myself clear?"

"Abundantly, sir."

"Good. Start talking."

"The short version is this: If you beam up any of these *novpu'*, we're all going to die."

19

Terrell watched the Klingon cruiser grow larger on the *Sagittarius*'s main viewscreen. He put on a brave face and wiped the sweat from his palms on the legs of his jumpsuit. "Keep hailing them, Chief. Hail them until someone answers us." *Or until they blast us into dust.*

Razka kept quiet as he re-sent Terrell's message to the Klingon vessel's commander. While the Saurian noncom waited for a reply, Terrell swiveled his chair so he could look aft toward Sorak. "Any luck pinpointing their landing party's beam-down coordinates?"

The white-haired Vulcan shook his head. "Not yet, sir. All I can say for certain is they beamed down near the natives' village on the big island."

From the sensor console, Taryl raised a note of alarm. "The cruiser has raised shields and is locking disruptors and charging its forward torpedo launchers. The bird-of-prey is coming up fast on our aft starboard quarter. Its shields are also up, and its disruptors are coming online."

That was bad news that Terrell wasn't ready to deal with, not yet. He looked away from Taryl, toward Razka. "Any response?"

"No, sir. But I'm picking up encrypted signals between the cruiser and the surface."

"Send out a wide-band jamming signal. I want that conversation cut short."

"Aye, sir." Razka set to work on the scrambling the Klingons' comms.

Sorak left the aft console and leaned close to Terrell to offer discreet counsel. "Sir, a wide-band jamming frequency will also interfere with our ability to contact *our* landing party."

"I'm aware of that, Commander. But right now I have to play the ball as it lies."

The Vulcan cocked one eyebrow. If Terrell's use of a uniquely human idiom had confused him, he kept it to himself. "Understood, sir."

Taryl's large, dark eyes were fixed upon the sensor display. "The bird-of-prey has locked disruptors and is charging its torpedo tube."

Terrell was in no mood to humor the Klingons' usual posturing. "Helm, increase orbital range to sixteen thousand kilometers and roll us thirty degrees to port. Taryl, lock phasers on the bird-of-prey. Target her engines and command deck." He thumbed open a channel to the engineering deck. "Master Chief, ready one torpedo."

"We're on it, Skipper. Tor! Cahow! Lock 'n' load!"

Reassured he would have at least one photon torpedo at his disposal, Terrell looked back at Taryl. "Lock that onto the cruiser. Aim for effect."

"Aye, sir." The Orion entered targeting solutions into her console.

It would take only seconds for the Klingons' sensors to confirm the *Sagittarius* was just as committed to its combat preparations as their ships were. Terrell hoped that would mean that whoever was in charge of their mission would see fit to answer his thrice-repeated hail.

Razka's bulbous reptilian eyes widened in response to a change in the status of the communications panel. "Captain, I have the Klingon commander on Channel One."

"Put him on-screen, Chief."

Terrell stood and took a step forward because he hoped it would make him appear larger and more intimidating to his Klingon counterpart. Then the main viewscreen switched to show a swarthy, goateed visage with thick, dramatically upswept black eyebrows. He had seen this man's face before, in briefings from Starfleet Command. This was no ordinary Klingon starship commander. This man was nefarious, as respected as he was feared.

He glowered at Terrell. *"I am Captain Kang, commanding the battle cruiser* Voh'tahk.*"*

There was no point echoing Kang's contemptuous tone, so Terrell focused on keeping his voice low and steady. "I am Captain Clark Terrell, commanding the Starfleet vessel *Sagittarius.*"

"Why are you interfering in our mission of exploration?"

"We weren't aware you were engaged in exploration of this system."

"A lie. Your team on the surface abducted one of our scientists. Why?"

For the sake of diplomacy, Terrell chose to err on the side of euphemism. "My people didn't abduct anyone, Captain. If they had any contact with your scientist, it was to render aid."

"By drugging him? Interrogating him? Binding his hands and gagging him? Is this how Starfleet defines 'rendering aid'? If so, I pity those foolish enough to seek your help."

Terrell had no desire to defend the losing side of a debate. "Let's put that aside for the moment, Captain. My crew and I just want to help you avoid making a terrible mistake."

"How generous of you. And what is this grave error we're about to commit?"

"You beamed down a landing party a few minutes ago. You need to beam them back."

"Too late. They're dead."

"I'm sorry to hear that."

"Don't be. They died to complete their mission. No more could I ask of true warriors."

"What was their mission, Captain?"

Kang's eyes narrowed. *"That is no concern of yours."*

"I'm afraid it is. My team has been studying the natives of this planet, and it is absolutely imperative that you not try to beam any of them up to your ships."

"Thank you for your concern, Captain. But my crew and I don't need your help, or your advice. Do not interfere with our mission—any obstruction will be considered a hostile act, and will be dealt with accordingly. This is the only warning you will receive. Voh'tahk out."

The transmission ended, and the main viewscreen switched back to an image of the Klingon cruiser looming large between the *Sagittarius* and the planet.

Terrell returned to his command chair. "Nizsk, stand by for evasive maneuvers. Chief, keep their comms scrambled as long as you can. Taryl, if the Klingons fire on us, you're to return fire at will." He looked to Sorak, hoping for good news. "What's the *Endeavour*'s ETA?"

"Fifteen minutes."

Taryl tensed and clutched the edge of her sensor console. "Incoming!"

A disruptor blast rocked the scout ship, and Terrell gripped the arms of his chair. Behind him, Sorak stumbled half a step before recovering his balance.

On the viewscreen, the two Klingon ships diverged, beginning a maneuver that Terrell knew was intended to diminish his ship's offensive strength by forcing it to split its attacks between two foes spread far apart, rather than allowing him to cluster phaser blasts and torpedo attacks for maximum effect. It was a judicious tactical decision on Kang's part, albeit an entirely unnecessary one; there was little chance the *Archer*-class scout ship could hope to inflict any significant damage against a cruiser as imposing as the *Voh'tahk*. But it served to remind Terrell that even when all the odds were in Kang's favor, he remained a shrewd and disciplined soldier.

And now we have to survive fifteen minutes toe-to-toe with him.

He was planning his next counterpunch as he leaned forward. "Helm, evasive maneuvers, full impulse. Everyone else, hang on to something heavy."

The Starfleet scout vessel on the *Homghor*'s viewscreen taunted Captain Durak. It was fast and agile enough to evade Captain Kang's battle cruiser, and its human commander was wise enough to use hit-and-run tactics that kept him at the edge of the *Homghor*'s weapons range.

That would not be enough to save him, not if Durak had any say in the matter. "Helm, set attack pattern *pach*.

Cut them off on their next pass." The helm officer, Zuras, engaged the new course as Durak snapped at his weapons officer, "Volcha! Show those *petaQpu'* on the *Voh'tahk* how to shoot! I want us to be the ones who bring that Starfleet ship down!"

Durak had never made a secret of his ambitions. He had climbed through the ranks in a very short time, making best use of his highborn status, his House's wealth, and his family's lofty connections—and all the perquisites those advantages offered to a young officer. After less than a decade in the Defense Forces he had taken command of the *Homghor*, but he considered the bird-of-prey little more than a stepping stone to a grander destiny that awaited him. Destroying the Starfleet scout ship would be Durak's next stride forward on his road to glory.

Phaser blasts from the enemy scout ship rocked the *Homghor* and momentarily scrambled its main viewscreen and duty station monitors. Over the fading rumble of the attack, Durak's first officer, Commander Magron, called out, "Three hits, shields holding."

The *Sagittarius* reappeared on the viewscreen as Zuras adjusted the *Homghor*'s course. Volcha manually adjusted the ship's targeting systems. "Disruptors locked!"

"Fire!" Crimson pulses lashed out through the void and caromed off the Starfleet vessel's shields. Half a second later, the scout ship made an abrupt course change and accelerated out of view. Durak clenched his fist, as if that would prevent this opportunity from slipping away.

Magron moved to the sensor console and called up a tactical report. "The Starfleet ship is making another run at the *Voh'tahk*. Both ships are firing—minor shield damage to both. And the Starfleet ship is breaking off, making another dash for the planet's debris ring."

"Clever," Durak muttered. He realized Magron was looking at him, awaiting an explanation. Durak pointed at the planet's rings. "The Starfleet commander wants to separate us from the *Voh'tahk* by luring us onto opposite sides of the rings. If we split up, only one of us can engage him at a time. If we stay together, he can lurk on the far side of the rings for cover between attacks, and we'll be forced to defend ourselves while he sets the pace."

The first officer nodded. "Cunning, for a human." He looked at Durak. "Orders?"

"Give him no rest. Helm, all ahead flank, direct pursuit course. Put us on their aft quarter and keep us there. Weapons, use harassing fire to limit their maneuvers until we're at point-blank range, then destroy their warp nacelles. Magron, angle all our shields forward. Let them bloody our noses if they like, that won't put a stop to the chase. By *Fek'lhr*'s beard, we *will* have them!"

His crew snapped into action, energized by the promise of battle—and then Kazron, the communications officer, answered an incoming hail. He straightened his back as he looked up and turned from his station to face Durak. "Captain. The *Voh'tahk* has broken through the Starfleet interference. Captain Kang demands to speak with you."

Ambition could trump many things—caution and common sense being the two most obvious—but one thing it couldn't overcome was the privilege of rank. Durak erased all semblance of emotion from his face and straightened his own posture. "On-screen."

Kang's face filled the main viewscreen. *"Captain, my crew is sending you the frequency for a transponder they tagged onto our research target. Break off your pursuit of the scout ship, locate that target, and beam it up as soon as possible. And if Doctor Tormog asks you to beam him up, tell him I said to leave him right where he is."*

"What about the scout ship? It will try to block our transporter beam."

"Ignore them. They pose no threat. They just want to impede our mission."

"Understood, Captain."

"Report in as soon as you have the subject aboard. Kang out."

The image on the main screen switched back to a view of the *Sagittarius* racing through the planet's rings, heading back toward the *Voh'tahk*. It galled Durak to let them go, but he had his orders. "Helm, break off pursuit, return to low orbit. Volcha, scan for the transponder and relay its coordinates to the transporter room. Magron, tell that oaf Lessig to power up the transporter. Let's get this done so we can get back in the hunt."

There was nothing for Durak to do while his crew worked but stew in his resentment of Kang, who no doubt would steal for himself the glory of capturing the Starfleet vessel.

Kazron looked up again from the communications panel. "Captain, we're being hailed from the surface by Doctor Tormog."

Durak knew better than to unleash his bitter rage on Kang, but no one would hold him to account for exorcising his fury on an infamous worm like Tormog. "Put him on speakers." He paused until Kazron nodded, signaling that the channel was open. "This is Durak."

"Captain Durak, I monitored your communication with Captain Kang. You must not carry out his order to beam up the tagged subject."

Incredulous stares were exchanged among the *Homghor*'s bridge crew. Durak had no idea why Tormog wanted to dig his own grave, but he was happy to let him. "Why not, Doctor?"

"The Tomol transform into something monstrous. They can kill with a thought! The one we were following, the one Kang's people just tagged—she tore apart the rest of the recon team with nothing but her mind. Energy weapons don't seem to affect her, and she—"

"Sounds like you've been hitting the bloodwine again, eh, Doctor?"

Tormog turned defensive. *"Mock me if you want, but do not beam that thing up."*

"Explain something to me, Doctor. You say she killed the rest of the recon team with just her mind. If that's true, how did you survive?" When his question was met with silence, Durak was certain he had intuited the answer. "Might it be that you ran like a frightened *petaQ*?" Throaty laughter filled the *Homghor*'s bridge. Over the comm there was only wounded silence.

Durak motioned for his men to subdue themselves. When order was restored, he put an end to his conversation with the coward. "Thank you for your sage counsel, Doctor Tormog, but my warriors and I are more than capable of subduing a single primitive."

"If you beam her up, you're all going to die."

"Find a warm place to hide, Doctor. My men and I have work to do. *Homghor* out." Kazron closed the channel, and Durak resigned himself to finishing this mission as Kang's glorified courier. "Volcha, locate that transponder. It's time we tamed the doctor's runaway pet."

Thorny vines slashed at Theriault's bloodied and dust-masked face as she ran. To her left, Dastin raced ahead of her. She and the Trill had inched ahead of each other a couple of times during their mad run toward the beach. Hesh and Tan Bao trailed them by a few paces. Their running strides generated an alarmingly loud white noise of rustled greenery and snapping twigs—not that they could hear much of it over the incessant clamor of their pursuers, who were clearing a path through the jungle by means of brute-force telekinesis.

A two-meter-wide tree trunk on Theriault's right cracked from roots to boughs, splitting the air with a jarring bang that knocked her and the others off-balance. Hesh tripped and landed hard on his face. Before he had time to call out in pain, Tan Bao pulled him back into motion and gestured for Theriault and Dastin to forge ahead. "Go! We're okay!"

There was no debate—everyone kept running.

Daylight flashed between the trees ahead of them—they were near the beach, no more than twenty meters, close enough to hear the roar of breaking waves on the sand.

Dastin raised his phaser and fired a wide-angle, full-power beam that disintegrated a huge swath of jungle ahead of him. He beckoned with a broad overhead swing of his arm. "This way!"

Theriault and the others detoured left into the trail Dastin had just cut for them. Liberated from the need to weave between trees or power through thorny veils of low-hanging vines, they broke into a flat run. Propelled by adrenaline and a keen desire to get off the island alive, they raced across the long stretch of burnt and smoking ground dotted with low blackened stumps.

The Trill cleared away the last few meters of jungle growth ahead of them with another phaser blast, and then his weapon emitted a pathetic-sounding tone that meant its power cell was drained. He hurdled over the last row of charred stumps onto the beach, then looked back as he barreled toward the rover's hiding place. "C'mon!"

Ponderous cracks of breaking wood, from trees striking one another and crashing together to the ground, turned Theriault's head. She looked over her shoulder and saw the jungle's canopy collapsing in a straight line, heading directly toward them. She waved Tan Bao and Hesh ahead of her, then fell in behind them.

They hit the sand running and rushed to catch up to Dastin, who was a dozen meters down the beach, tearing away the camouflage he had draped in front of Vixen. As soon as the curtain of leaves was cast aside, he clambered over the rover's hood and slipped through its barely open driver's-side door. By the time Theriault and the others reached the rover's hiding spot, Dastin had pulled it forward and opened all its doors. "In! We gotta go!"

Rather than waste time circling the vehicle to get in from the passenger's side, Hesh grabbed the edge of the roof and swung himself feet-first through the rear hatch. He landed in the rear passenger-side seat just in time for Tan Bao to jump into the seat behind Dastin.

At the same time, Theriault vaulted across the rover's hood, sliding on her hip and landing on the far side in one graceful leap, and then she held on to the rover's chassis with one hand as she pivoted into the front passenger's seat. "Punch it!"

Sand spit from the rover's wide spinning tires as its hatches fell shut.

Nimur and the Changed emerged from the smoky jungle clearing Dastin had created. Looking past Dastin, Theriault saw Nimur point at the rover. "Faster!"

Dastin swerved away from the Changed. "This is as fast as it—"

Telekinetic force hammered the rover from behind and sent it tumbling through the air. Everything outside the windows was a blur of beige and green—and then they slammed nose-first into the water. Violent deceleration threw all of them forward, pushing Hesh and Tan Bao against the backs of the front seats, pinning Theriault against the forward console, and trapping Dastin against the steering controls. Half a second later the inertial dampeners kicked in, and they were able to sit back and steal a breath.

Dastin accelerated the rover and set it on a shallow dive toward open water. Theriault reached for her safety harness and locked it shut around her torso. "Strap in. That's an order." Hesh and Tan Bao complied immediately, but Dastin kept his hands on the rover's controls. Theriault was about to chastise him when she saw the tactical display on the forward console. There were multiple signals in the water, pursuing them. She looked back at Tan Bao. "Help me get Dastin strapped in." Together, the two of them secured Dastin into his safety harness without interrupting his control of the rover.

Meanwhile, Hesh took his own look at the tactical screen, and then he powered up his tricorder. "Commander? This is most intriguing. Nimur and the other Changed appear to be pursuing us even though we have submerged more than twenty meters beneath the surface."

"Thanks, Hesh, but we already know that."

"Do you also know that they've experienced a reversion mutation, to an amphibious life-form? One that has been dormant in their genome since early in their species' evolution?"

"No. I didn't know that."

Dastin scowled at the Arkenite. "Is that information supposed to be useful?"

"Not in the general sense. But it might interest you to—"

"Hang on." Ahead of the rover loomed an opaque wall of vegetation. Dastin yawed the rover several degrees to starboard and patched in the vehicle's auxiliary power supply. Seconds later, the kelp forest swallowed the craft, which bladed its way through the aquatic jungle. Keeping his eyes on the path ahead, Dastin prompted Hesh, "You were saying?"

Hesh held up his tricorder. "I was about to say, my scans of their altered physiology suggest that they will be far more maneuverable inside the kelp forests than we

will, so I would advise keeping to open water in the hope
that we can outrun them at greater depths."

The rover jerked to a sudden stop and listed hard to
port. Dastin opened the throttle, and the purring of the
MHD grew loud enough to hear and high-pitched enough
to hurt.

On the tactical display, the eleven blips were closing in
faster by the moment. Theriault knew what the next words
out of Dastin's mouth would be. She glared at him. "Don't
say it."

"I think we're snagged on the kelp."

"I told you not to say it."

Tan Bao covered his eyes with one hand and massaged
his temples. "I hate irony."

Dastin struggled with the controls. "Let me try putting
it in reverse, see if we break free."

Hesh adjusted his tricorder. "Perhaps I can use this to
create a subsonic pulse that, when propagated through the
aquatic medium, will disorientate them long enough for
us to escape."

Theriault couldn't take her eyes off the tactical display.
"Five seconds to intercept! If someone's gonna do something, now would be the time."

They all looked up and around at one another. No one
had anything to say.

Everything was quiet for several seconds. And then for
several more.

Tan Bao looked up and around. "Oh-kay . . ."

Dastin glanced left, then right, perplexed. "What happened?"

Hesh stared numbly at his tricorder. "I think someone

beamed up Nimur and the Wardens." He adjusted the device. "Based on the specific residual ionization in the water, I think it was the Klingons."

His news drew a cynical laugh from Dastin. "That's twice today they've saved us by mistake." The scout nudged Theriault. "Maybe we ought to thank them."

"If we get off this rock alive, I'll send them a basket of tribbles. Now break us free and get us moving, before something else down here decides to eat us."

20

"Transporter room! Answer! What is your status?" Durak wanted results, but all he was getting from the *Homghor*'s transporter room was intermittent static punctuated by deep thuds. No one had answered his first two demands for information, and now the third was being ignored, as well. He skewered Magron with a look. "Find out what's going on down there."

His first officer snapped to attention. "I've confirmed the transport sequence was completed. Because of interference with the signal lock, multiple subjects were beamed aboard."

"Don't just repeat what the computer tells you! I could have a trained *puQat* do that. Take that *petaQ* Tegras and go secure the prisoners. Move!" He chased Magron off the bridge with his hateful glare, then turned his eyes back toward the enemy ship on the viewscreen. "Zuras! Hard about. Set attack pattern *jav'negh*, full speed. Volcha! Target the Starfleet vessel's engineering deck. Disruptors at half power—Captain Kang wants them alive."

Grunts of acknowledgment came back to Durak, and that was enough to satisfy him that his orders had been understood. Digits on his command screen counted down the dwindling *qelIqam*s that separated the *Homghor* from the Starfleet scout ship. Victory was within reach, Durak was sure of it. He would strike the decisive blow against the interlopers, and then even Captain Kang would have to recognize him as a warrior worthy of honor and advancement.

"Twenty seconds to firing range," Volcha said. "Locking—" He did a double take at his console. "Target has changed course and speed. Attempting to reacquire weapons lock."

Durak watched the nimble little Starfleet ship twist and dart through the planet's rings. Behind it, Kang's cruiser pursued like a lumbering brute, blasting the rings with torpedoes.

"Helm, break to starboard! Keep us out of the *Voh'tahk*'s firing solution!"

Low curses fell from Durak's lips. He had underestimated the Federation ship and its crew. Even though he had heard of how fast and maneuverable the *Archer*-class scout ships were, until now he had never faced one in action. The tiny ship exceeded its lofty reputation.

We're never going to catch it if all we do is trace its movements. We need to get a step ahead of it and let it come to us. "Helm, hard climb. Take us through the rings and put us into a reverse orbit. I want to go nose-to-nose with the Starfleeters on the other side of the planet."

"Executing hard climb," Zuras confirmed. The planet's rings dominated the viewscreen for several seconds as the *Homghor* shot through them. Once clear on the other side, instead of orbiting in the direction of the planet's rotation, which was standard operating procedure, the bird-of-prey banked in the opposite direction and orbited against the planet's movement.

It was a tactic whose chief advantage was also its greatest risk: surprise. It was unlikely the Starfleet ship would expect to see the *Homghor* rushing into a head-to-head confrontation; however, putting the entire planet between himself and his prey meant that Durak was flying blind into battle. He wouldn't know his opponent's position, attitude, or speed until the moment of engagement. This gambit could be either his triumph or his undoing.

Anticipating glory, he grinned. *War holds no honor for the timid*.

Volcha's eyes were wedded to his display. "Estimate target intercept in ninety seconds."

"Look sharp, my friend. We'll have the advantage, but only for a moment. You'll need to take a snap shot as soon as we have sensor contact. Make it one worthy of a song."

The weapons officer nodded. His finger hovered over the firing switch. "I will."

Durak thumbed open a channel to the transporter room. "Magron! Report!" His demand was once again met by silence. He opened an intraship PA channel. "Bridge to Magron!"

There was no response. *What in the name of* Fek'lhr *is going on down there?*

Behind him, the hatch to the port-side corridor slid open. Magron—bloody and battered almost beyond recognition—staggered through it and fell face-first to the deck. Somewhere far aft, hidden in the ruddy shadows, Klingon warriors screamed in agony. Everyone on the bridge turned to face this new threat from within. Durak leaped from his command chair to Magron's side and pulled the first officer over the threshold onto the bridge. "Report!"

Magenta spittle dribbled from Magron's split lips. "They're coming."

"Who? The *novpu'*?"

Magron shuddered and coughed up a mouthful of blood. "The *mIgh'Qugh*." As soon as he'd forced out the words, Magron expired with a long, rasping rattle of weak breath.

Durak dropped the empty husk of what had once been a warrior. "Secure the bridge and seal all interior hatches. Zuras, Volcha, continue with the attack." He pointed at the communications officer. "Kazron, get over here and help me guard the entrances."

"Shouldn't we hail Captain Kang?"

"We'll hail Kang when I say so, not before. Our first duty is to defend this ship. Now draw your disruptor and defend the starboard hatch."

"Yes, sir." Kazron stood and moved aft to stand on Durak's left. The two Klingons drew their disruptor side-arms and stood facing the sealed hatches, waiting to open fire on anything that dared to breach them that wasn't a Klingon.

Echoes of pandemonium resounded through the hull from beyond the locked duranium barriers. Durak had heard such blood-curdling clamor only once before, as a junior officer on a cruiser whose hull had been breached in combat. It was the sound of bulkheads rupturing under strain, hatches being torn from their frames, a starship's guts being torn out by a force of nature.

By the time Durak began to suspect that Doctor Tormog's warning had not been an exaggeration, the hatches to the bridge were buckling inward, one ear-splitting impact at a time, as if the long-dead gods of Klingon antiquity had risen with a vengeance. Sparks flew from both doors' magnetic control systems, and then with a final booming roar the hatches flew inward. The starboard hatch slammed into Kazron and pinned him to the deck. Durak dodged the port-side hatch by a whisker and fired a wild barrage of disruptor blasts down the corridor.

He watched, horrified and enthralled, as a female *novpu'* walked with preternatural calm onto the *Homghor*'s bridge. Long silvery tresses framed her aqua face, whose sides were marked by golden spots that continued down her neck and underneath her primitive garments. She seemed oblivious of the fusillade of disruptor pulses Durak fired at her. They all seemed to be absorbed into her without inflicting any damage to her or her clothing. By the time she confronted Durak, he had ceased firing. All he could do was stare at her, awed and agape.

Her voice was rich and melodious. "I am Nimur. What is this place?"

Durak stammered, "It's—it's the *I.K.S. Homghor.*"

"I do not understand. Explain."

"It's a ship."

Several other *novpu'* from the planet followed Nimur onto the bridge as she stepped past Durak. She stared, bewildered, at the main viewscreen, which showed the darkened side of her planet. Then she turned back to face Durak. "What is that?"

"That's your world." Her reaction revealed she didn't understand. "As seen from space."

"From what?"

"From very high above."

She looked around the bridge. "How can a ship travel where there's no water?"

He remembered she was a primitive. "It travels in the darkness between the stars."

Comprehension dawned quickly in Nimur's eyes. "Incredible." She looked around at the remaining bridge crew. "You will make this vessel obey my commands now."

Volcha rested his hand on the grip of his disruptor. "We don't take orders from *you*. We are sworn to obey Captain Durak—and no one else."

Nimur was skeptical. "Are you all so loyal as this one?" She studied the rest of the crew's reactions. Slow nods were accompanied by more hands moving toward sidearms. "Very well."

A grotesque wet cracking noise filled the bridge. Durak winced for only a fraction of second—and when he opened his eyes, he saw that every one of his officers' heads had been twisted around until their necks had snapped like brittle twigs. Only he remained standing.

Then an invisible hand gripped his throat and lifted him off the deck.

Nimur stepped in front of him, as calm as she was malevolent. "They would not obey me, Durak. You will—or else you'll experience agonies more horrible than any you've ever imagined. Now . . . tell me how to use this ship. Tell me *everything*."

It was all but impossible for Kang to see the *Sagittarius* through the storm of broken rocks and ice blurring past on the *Voh'tahk*'s main viewscreen. He was losing patience with his crew's fumbling hunt of the Starfleet scout ship. "Mahzh, *anticipate* your target, don't follow it. You're just wasting torpedoes." He keyed in a new dispersal pattern on his command screen and relayed it to the weapons console. "Box them in! Then finish them with disruptors!"

"Yes, Captain." Mahzh set to work entering the new firing solution.

Their tiny prey darted through Arethusa's rings like a prize fish that refused to be reeled in. In open space, it would be no match for the *Voh'tahk,* but in an environment rich with natural obstacles, it was proving more than elusive. If not for the impending arrival of a more pressing threat, he might have been content to pass the hours matching wits with the scout ship's commander. To his regret, that was for the moment a luxury he could not afford. Keeping his eyes on the *Sagittarius,* he called out to his wife. "Mara, how long until the *Endeavour* arrives?"

Her own attention was steady on the sensor display. "Twelve minutes."

There were too many variables in play for Kang's liking. He needed to know if the *Homghor* had recovered the *novpu'* targets from the planet's surface. If Captain Durak—a consummate striver, if ever Kang had met one—had followed orders, both the *Voh'tahk* and its bird-of-prey escort could declare this mission completed and break orbit without risking an unnecessary confrontation with Starfleet. Kang knew some might question his honor for seeking to avoid a potential combat situation, but bitter experience had taught him the high price of war. He was in no mood to court its wrath without good reason.

He swiveled toward the communications officer. "Kyris. Any word from the *Homghor*?"

She shook her head. "Not yet, Captain."

"Hail them. Tell Captain Durak I want an update right now."

"The *Homghor* is currently out of contact, sir." She noted Kang's pointed stare of inquiry and elaborated. "They're on the far side of Arethusa. We can restore contact in fifteen seconds."

Kang was about to curse Durak, but then he reasoned out the younger warrior's tactics. *He's trying to head off our prey and catch them in his own snare.* The captain nodded to himself. *He's not as clumsy as I'd feared.* Kang could only hope that Durak had been able to keep his infamous ambition in check long enough to obey orders and beam up the *novpu'* before he'd committed his crew to his daring maneuver against the *Sagittarius*.

"Helm, move us above the rings and accelerate to full impulse."

Mahzh looked up from the weapons console. "If we stay above the rings, the *Sagittarius* will just stay beneath them."

"That's what I want them to do," Kang said. "And I suspect it's what Captain Durak wants them to do, as well. Maintain harassing fire. Keep the scout ship's attention on us."

"Understood, Captain."

Kyris turned from the communications panel. "Captain? I've hailed the *Homghor*, but it's not answering."

"Are you sure they're receiving?"

"Positive. But they do not acknowledge."

An intuition of danger stirred in Kang's gut. "Mahzh, scan the *Homghor*."

"For what?"

"Life-forms. Anomalies. *Anything*."

Mahzh trained the *Voh'tahk*'s sensors on the bird-of-prey with a few simple commands. Then he shook his head. "Their shields are raised."

His meaning was implicit: The *Voh'tahk*'s sensors could not penetrate the *Homghor*'s shields. They had no way of knowing what was transpiring aboard their escort ship. Kang stroked his goatee. "Is the *Homghor* on an attack vector?"

"Negative." Mahzh switched to a tactical analysis screen. "They should have the Starfleet ship on their sensors, but they are not moving to engage."

Something was wrong on the bird-of-prey; Kang was certain of it. But was it something that would sort itself out given time? Or was it a catastrophe in the making? He had a hunch he knew the answer—but if he was wrong, loyal soldiers of the Empire might die at his hands.

Unfortunately, if he was right, those loyal soldiers were dead already.

No one had laid a hand on Durak, but he was pinned to the deck as if he had been run through and staked down by half a dozen spears through his torso. Excruciating sharp jabs twisted in his gut, and he heard his ribs crack under his skin as they surrendered to the constant, overwhelming pressure from a vise he couldn't see. He wanted to roar

out his pain and fury, but he couldn't draw enough breath
to make a sound.

Nimur and her cadre had surrounded him. Their sea-
green faces gazed down at him as he squirmed at their
feet, helpless before their telekinetic assault. To the
Klingon's jaded eye they looked like scrawny children
who would flee in tears from the least aggression, and
here he was, humbled by them, writhing in agony and utterly helpless.

His pulse thudded in his ears, and the pressure in his
temples made him delirious. He was sure that at any moment his heart would burst, or his lungs would collapse, or
the *novpu'* would tire of killing him by degrees, and he
could finally give up his hold on his broken flesh and
begin his journey to *Sto-Vo-Kor*. Death in battle would be
a fitting end to his life's pursuits, he decided; it would let
him face his ancestors without shame. His only regret
would be that he had failed to slay any of these filthy
Ha'DIbaHpu' in the bargain.

The pressure abated. Nimur made a lifting motion with
her hand, as if she were a puppeteer pulling invisible
strings that controlled Durak's body. His limp and abused
form levitated off the deck and hovered before the woman-
child with eyes of fire. "We have shown you only a small
taste of the horrors we can inflict upon you, Captain. How
do we use this ship to make you and your kind leave us
alone?"

Durak struggled to draw a breath. As soon as he had
filled his lungs with air, he used it all to spit a mouthful of
blood into Nimur's face. He grinned and laughed, and
then he coughed hard enough to send fresh blades of pain

through his flailed chest. He couldn't help but be her prisoner, but he was determined not to become her pawn.

She wiped his spittle from her cheeks and forehead, then smeared her hand dry across the front of his uniform. "I admire your spirit. You do not grovel like your kinsmen on the planet."

Before he could ask what she meant, the fingers on his left hand bent sharply backward at each knuckle, one by one. By the time his thumb splintered in two easy snaps, Durak was howling loudly enough to shake the *Homghor*'s bulkheads. His reddened vision cleared after seconds that felt like a lifetime, and he looked down at the mangled atrocity of his hand. It felt unreal, as if he were looking at something far removed from himself; he was going numb.

Not numb, he corrected himself. *Into shock. Stay in the moment. Take the pain.* He tried to follow his own advice, but it was too much to overcome. He couldn't breathe.

Nimur made a circular gesture with her index finger, and Durak's body slowly spun around to face the main viewscreen. A tactical schematic had been superimposed over the image of the planet. Automatic threat-detection software built into the ship's sensor apparatus was tracking the Starfleet ship, which was coming into range, and standard-issue IFF—identify friend or foe—systems had flagged the *Voh'tahk* as an allied Klingon vessel.

The Tomol female's breath caressed his ear as she asked in a whisper, "What is that?"

Durak was determined to remain silent, no matter how many of his bones she crushed. Then he felt a sickening pressure in his groin, coupled with a half-twist of his *loD'HIch,* and his courage failed. "Our ship can sense when others are near. The one circled in red is our ally. The one marked by a white triangle is an enemy."

"Can your ship destroy its enemies?"

"If properly commanded."

"Show us how."

He coughed out another mouthful of blood. "It would take too long. My men trained for years to run this ship, and they were born warriors. I can't teach you what they knew." The congestion in his chest worsened. Each hacking cough grew wetter and rougher. He felt fluids pooling in his lungs. It would be only a matter of time before he drowned in his own blood.

One of the male *novpu'* whispered something to Nimur. She listened until he finished, and then she turned a skeptical stare toward Durak. "You could pilot this ship alone."

"Not for long." He lifted his forearm to block his next coughing jag and spluttered a spray of blood across his sleeve. "Without my engineers, the ship will break down, and I won't be able to fix her. Without my crew, I'd—" He stopped himself from revealing the functions of the ship's autopilot, but not before he had teased its secret. He cursed his loose, foolish tongue.

Nimur turned him around again to face her. "Without them, you would what?"

"Die."

"You'll die anyway, Captain. The only question is how soon, and in how much pain. I know that's not what you were going to say. Tell me how to control this ship with no crew."

He lifted his chin and forced out a rasping growl of defiance.

His right foot spun backward. The wet crack of his ankle breaking in half a dozen places was drowned out by his primal roar of outraged pain.

The alien witch smirked at him. "There's no point in lying to me, Captain. I can see the colors of your mind change when you speak. I've learned the hues of truth and deception." She lowered her voice to a whisper that was hot against his face. "I will ask you again, and for your own sake, I urge you to tell me the truth. How do I control this ship without a crew?"

"You don't. You go down in flames, shrieking like the *be'yIntagh* you are."

Durak's left arm jerked down and separated from his shoulder socket with a crunch and a pop. Then the pressure in his groin went from uncomfortable to horrific. Half of what he had hoped might be spared was crushed beyond recovery. Waves of nausea pushed through him, and he vomited all he had eaten in the last half day onto the deck between himself and Nimur.

His last ounce of strength was spent. His will to resist had collapsed.

Nimur lifted his drooping head and looked into his half-open eyes with her orbs of flame. "I am not without mercy. Give me what I want, and I will consider letting you go back to your people alive, and with all your broken pieces still attached. But if you defy me again, I will take you apart, one tiny piece at a time, and make you dine on your own flesh. Now, Captain"—she pinned him against the forward bulkhead—"show me how to control this ship!"

• • •

The landing party's news was even worse than Terrell had feared. "You're sure it was a transporter effect? Is it possible they just broke off pursuit?"

Theriault's reply left little room for doubt. *"Hesh is positive, sir. It showed all the telltale signs of a Klingon transporter effect. And to be honest, I don't think there's anything else on this planet that would have made them stop chasing us except for that."*

"All right. Check in when you reach the rendezvous point. We'll pick you up as soon as we're clear. *Sagittarius* out." He signaled Chief Razka to close the channel, then just as quickly added, "Hail the *Voh'tahk* again. Tell Captain Kang it's urgent."

The Saurian slow-blinked, a behavior Terrell had come to recognize as the reptilian's equivalent to a long-suffering sigh. "Aye, sir. Hailing the *Voh'tahk*. Again."

"Taryl, where's Kang's ship now?"

The Orion woman updated the sensor readout. "Holding position above the rings."

"And the bird-of-prey?"

"Dead ahead below the rings, sir. She circled the planet on an intercept course."

Terrell beckoned Sorak away from the aft console to stand at his side. "We were scrambling the cruiser, so the bird-of-prey must have beamed up the Tomol from the surface."

The Vulcan gave a slight nod. "Yes, sir. That stands to reason."

Several worst-case scenarios were unfolding in Terrell's imagination. "If they're all developing powers like Nimur's, we can't risk them leaving the planet."

"I would be forced to agree, sir. Extreme measures might be called for."

"How long until the *Endeavour* gets here?"

Sorak knew the answer without checking the chronometer. "Eight minutes, ten seconds."

It didn't sound like long, but Terrell knew that a lot could happen in far less time than that. "As of now, our top priority changes from hindering the cruiser to containing the bird-of-prey. Helm, set a pursuit course. Taryl, let me know as soon as we're in weapons range."

Razka reacted to a change on the communications panel. "Sir, I have Captain Kang."

"On-screen." Terrell stood from his command chair as the image on the main viewscreen switched to show the imposing, swarthy visage of the Klingon starship commander.

Kang's words were laced with condescension and disgust. *"What do you want?"*

"I have reason to suspect your escort has beamed up some very dangerous passengers."

"They are trained to deal with such threats. Your concern is unnecessary."

Terrell took half a step forward. "Actually, Captain, I think it's more than warranted."

"And why do you think that?"

"My scout team reports that the natives undergo some kind of transformation, one that—"

"You have a scout team on the surface?"

Terrell bristled at being interrupted. "Yes. As I was saying—"

"The Klingon Empire has claimed this world as a protectorate."

"If so, you forgot to tell anyone else, which is the same as not doing it at all." The captain took a breath to calm himself, lest he aggravate the already tense situation. "Regardless, we've observed an alarming change that occurs in members of the native population when—"

"We are aware of this biological phenomenon. What of it?"

Could the Klingon be this obtuse? Or was he just being an obstructionist because it amused him? Terrell wondered if there was any way to make Kang see reason. "Captain, my team tells me your bird-of-prey beamed up nearly a dozen of those transformed aliens."

Kang's eyes widened at that news. *"Did you say nearly a dozen?"*

"Yes, Captain. And correct me if I'm wrong, but isn't the complement on a bird-of-prey approximately two dozen officers and crew? Do you think your escort's crew is up to this fight?"

The Klingon simmered but refused to concede rhetorical defeat. *"We have the situation in hand, Captain. You're to treat this as an internal Klingon matter and stand down."*

Taryl interrupted the commanders' conversation. "Sir? The bird-of-prey is increasing speed to full impulse and changing course."

"Prepare for evasive maneuvers and—"

"Sir, they aren't attacking—they appear to be breaking orbit."

Terrell threw an accusatory look at Kang. "Is that part of your grand strategy, Captain?" Kang turned away from the conversation to snap orders under his breath to his officers. Rather than wait for the Klingon's reply, Terrell decided it was time to act. "Helm, pursuit course, full impulse. We need to corral that ship back to the planet and force them down, right now. Taryl, target their shield generators, then their engines."

Sorak sidled up to Terrell. "Captain, if we break away from the rings, we'll be—"

"I'm aware of the risks. But we can't let the Changed escape with a starship."

"Understood, sir." The old Vulcan stepped away to assist Taryl.

On-screen, Kang's anger took a turn for the volcanic. *"Captain! Cease your pursuit!"*

"Can't do that, Captain. I think you know as well as I do that you've lost control of one of your ships. Since you won't rein it in, you leave me no choice but to do it myself."

The Klingon's mien took on a diabolical cast as he stepped forward, making his face fill the entire screen. *"This is your last warning! If you fire on a Klingon ship, I will destroy you!"*

"You're welcome to try. *Sagittarius* out." A slashing motion of Terrell's thumb cued Razka to close the channel. Terrell returned to his command chair and sat down. "Here we go."

Moments later the hull rumbled from the first salvo of disruptor blasts fired by the *Voh'tahk*. Taryl clutched the sensor console and answered with forced calm, "Shields holding."

"That was a warning shot," Terrell said. "The next one won't be. Lock phasers."

Taryl keyed in the command and tensed for battle. "Locked."

Terrell had committed his crew to a sacrifice play, and he knew there would be no turning back. He could only hope they would still be standing in seven minutes when help arrived. Until then, he would do what had to be done.

"Ensign: Fire at will."

21

"Keep trying to raise the *Homghor*," Kang snapped at Kyris.

The communications officer wisely avoided eye contact with Kang and kept her focus on her console and displays. "Still no response, Captain."

A cat-and-mouse game played out on the viewscreen. The bird-of-prey veered away from the planet, as if it meant to leave orbit; the *Sagittarius* emerged from the debris rings and pursued the *Homghor,* which responded with evasive maneuvers. That was proof enough for Kang that Captain Durak and his crew were no longer in control of their ship. "Helm! After them! All ahead full. Mahzh, charge all weapons. Target both vessels and fire at will."

The weapons officer turned his lanky frame toward Kang. "Captain?"

"You heard me. Destroy them both." His repetition of the unusual order prompted wary looks from his senior officers. He was not in the habit of explaining himself or justifying his orders to his subordinates, but given their predicament, he made an exception. "Durak is a blowhard, but he would never run from a battle. The *Homghor* has been captured, probably by those *novpu'* it beamed up. We can't let them escape with an Imperial starship."

Mara moved quickly to his side. "Are you sure that's

the only option? We could send over a boarding party to retake the ship."

He scowled at the image of the fleeing vessel. "Mahzh said it himself—their shields are up. Until they drop, we can't beam over, and we can't take remote control of their computer."

Mahzh remained unsettled. "Captain, what if the *Homghor*'s crew is still alive?"

"If they are, they're either prisoners or traitors. Either way, death is their reward."

Doubts plagued the weapons officer. "But if we knock out its shields, we can access its computer. I could run a command override and trigger the ship's intruder counter-measures."

"And if these *novpu'* are immune to nerve gas? Then what?"

His debate with Mahzh seemed to kindle a spark of hope in Mara. She rested her hand on Kang's arm, a gesture more in keeping with her role as his wife than as his first officer. "We could vent the *Homghor*'s atmosphere into space. I don't care how powerful these creatures are—the last time we checked, they still needed to breathe *something.*"

"We don't have time to pull our punches, Mara. The Federation battle cruiser is only minutes away. I want this dealt with before they arrive." He noted with satisfaction that Ortok had carried out his orders and accelerated into a pursuit course. The *Voh'tahk* was only moments from optimal firing range on both the *Sagittarius* and the *Homghor.* Now all Kang needed was for the rest of his officers to perform their jobs as well as the helmsman had done.

Mahzh sat down and scanned the *Voh'tahk*'s two targets. "The *Sagittarius* is opening fire on the *Homghor*," he reported. "The bird-of-prey is continuing evasive maneuvers."

Kang watched Mara, whose keen eyes observed the battle between the two smaller ships. Had she witnessed the same telltale clue he had just noticed? "What do you see?"

"Those aren't the maneuvers of a skilled helmsman." Her gaze narrowed. "That's the work of the autopilot system." Her mood darkened. "You're right. They've lost their ship."

Being right about the fate of the *Homghor* gave Kang no pleasure. "The *novpu'* robbed Durak and his crew of honor. We will give it back to them." He smiled as he watched the scout ship pepper the *Homghor*'s shields with another volley of phaser fire. "Best of all, the Starfleeters will take the blame. As long as we keep their battle cruiser in check, we might yet coax a victory from this wretched day. Mahzh! Do you have a targeting lock yet?"

"Negative. Both ships are moving too quickly for a hard lock."

Kang took a few seconds to study the smaller vessels' flight pattern. Both ships were pushing their impulse engines into overdrive, accelerating them to more than half the speed of light. He could only imagine the strain being inflicted on their inertial-dampening systems. He called up a tactical profile on his command monitor and relayed it to Mahzh's station. "Set the torpedoes for spread pattern *Qib'HoH* and use the disruptors to limit their maneuvering options."

"Yes, Captain." Mahzh armed the *Voh'tahk*'s disruptors and torpedoes. Moments later, the first salvo launched from the nose of the battle cruiser, followed moments later by several sweeping blasts from its twin disruptor cannons. Searing flashes of light erupted on the main viewscreen as Mahzh declared, "No direct hits. Minor damage to both ships."

"Lock and fire again. Spread pattern *Qaw'Hoch*, disruptors for flank coverage."

Another barrage of torpedoes sped away from the *Voh'tahk* as crimson streaks on the viewscreen. The dense red cluster scattered into far-flung ruddy sparks as viridescent pulses from the cruiser's disruptor cannons arced through the emptiness around them. Then came another blinding matter-antimatter supernova that washed out the viewscreen for a fraction of a second.

Kang winced but forced his eyes to stay open and fixed upon his prey, even though the two ships were little more than grayish blurs darting in and out of sight. "Mahzh, report."

"Both ships slowing. *Homghor* is venting coolant from its impulse system. *Sagittarius* is leaking plasma from its port warp nacelle." He reacted to a sensor update. "They're changing course—orbiting the planet. *Sagittarius* is closing on the *Homghor* and locking weapons." Another alert buzzed on his console until he silenced it with a swat of his hand. "The *Endeavour* is six minutes out and scanning the system."

A channel light blinked on the communications panel. Kyris pressed her hand to her earpiece to block out ambient noise from the bridge while she listened. "The *En-*

deavour is hailing us, Captain. Its commander orders us to cease our pursuit and break orbit."

"It'll be a bright day in *Gre'thor* before I take orders from a Starfleet captain. Tell the *Endeavour* its scout fired on the *Homghor,* and we are responding in kind. End of message."

On the viewscreen, the *Sagittarius* chased the bird-of-prey once more through the planet's multicolored rings of ice-crusted rocky debris. Both vessels left slowly dissipating vapor trails—one a bluish twist of expanding coolant, the other a dusky streak of ionized plasma.

As the *Homghor* pushed itself through a hard turn, slowed, and made a shallow dive into Arethusa's atmosphere with the *Sagittarius* mere seconds behind it, Kang saw the moment he'd been waiting for. "Mahzh! Spread pattern *yay'joq*—directly ahead of the *Homghor!*"

"Locked!"

Now the *novpu'* and the Starfleeters would both learn the price one paid for being an enemy of the Klingon Empire.

"Fire!"

The unearthly, minor-key wailing of the *Sagittarius*'s engines grew louder and pitched farther up the tonal scale with each passing moment. Terrell clung to the command chair's armrests as he shouted to be heard over the fusion-powered din. "Port yaw, ten degrees! Lock phasers!"

Each roll and hard turn of the scout ship overloaded the inertial dampeners, and the turbulence had become far worse now that they had penetrated the planet's mesosphere. Terrell was certain he heard the hull plates shuddering against one another, and he felt the temperature rising from the intense friction of atmosphere against the ship's duranium skin.

Sorak's stately voice cut through the clamor: "Incoming! Brace for impact!"

"Pull up!" Terrell needed to stop the bird-of-prey, but not enough to let his ship go down with it, not if there was any other path to victory. "Evasive, starboard!"

White light burst from the viewscreen as a deafening concussion rocked the ship. For one heart-stopping moment, Terrell thought his ship had been shot out from under him—then the glare on the screen faded to gray static, and the eardrum-punishing thunder dwindled to a steady rumbling—revealing the sudden downward pitch of the engines' whine.

He thumbed open a channel to engineering. "Damage report!"

Ilucci hollered over a nightmare of hissing, grinding, and shrieking mechanical noise. *"We took that one on the nose, Skip! Starboard nacelle's ruptured, warp core's down!"*

Terrell watched the image on the viewscreen switch to a head-on angle of the planet's surface—which meant the ship was plunging nose-first toward the sea. "What about impulse?"

"We were hopin' you wouldn't ask." A low boom over the comm coincided with a frightening tremor that shot through the deck and dimmed the overhead lights. Over the comm, frantic shouts full of jargon and curses were muffled by crackles and pops. Ilucci coughed. *"Just lost the fusion core. Main power's toast. We're on batteries."*

No main power. That meant no phasers, no torpedoes, no shields. Whether Terrell liked it or not, his battle with the bird of-prey was over. It was time to salvage his own ship, if it was still possible. "Helm! Can you maneuver on thrusters?"

Nizsk struggled with four of her six limbs to lift the scout ship out of its dive. "Negative, sir. Insufficient power. We need the impulse engine! Even one-tenth power would be enough."

The roar of atmosphere against the hull grew louder by the second. Overhead, the main lights stuttered and went dark, leaving the bridge crew illuminated only by faint spills of light from their consoles and the flickering video hash of the main viewscreen.

Terrell hoped the channel to engineering was still open. "Master Chief? We can't pull up on just thrusters. Can you run the impulse coil off the batteries?"

"Negative—the lines have been severed!"

"How long to run a patch?"

"Ten minutes."

Nizsk looked back from the helm. "We will hit the surface in four."

Terrell knew Ilucci had heard that. "Master Chief?"

"Roger that, Skipper. One miracle, comin' up. Engineering out!"

A dark streak cut a smoky diagonal line across the viewscreen. Terrell pointed at it. "What was that?"

Sorak slapped his stuttering console until its display stabilized. "That was the *Homghor*, sir. It suffered a direct hit. All its primary systems are offline."

Down in flames and falling like a rock. Terrell

heaved a grim sigh. Watching the bird-of-prey plummet to its doom gave him no sense of accomplishment, no pride of victory. All he could think of was how terrified anyone still alive on that ship must have felt at that moment.

The *Sagittarius* jolted, as if it had been struck by something solid. Then the ship jerked and rocked again as plasma manifolds ruptured in the overhead, showering short-lived sparks across the bridge and everyone on it. Terrell acted by reflex, swearing under his breath as he swatted white-hot phosphors from his head, shoulders, arms, and thighs. "What hit us?"

"Disruptor blasts from the *Voh'tahk*," Sorak said. "It seems Captain Kang plans to make sure we do not recover from our current dilemma."

Taryl vented her disgust. "Kicking us while we're down? So much for Klingon honor."

Terrell almost had to laugh. "Their notion of honor and ours tend to differ, Ensign."

Nizsk gave up trying to make the helm respond to her commands and resigned herself to reading off the countdown until their collective demise. "Three minutes and thirty seconds."

As fervently as Terrell wanted to believe his engineers could work yet another miracle, he had to proceed on the assumption that they couldn't. "Chief Razka, Ensign Taryl. Round up any non-essential personnel and report to the escape pod."

The Saurian and the Orion both were out of their seats before Sorak stopped them. "Belay that order. Our unshielded entry into the atmosphere compounded damage already sustained to the pod's release mechanism. It is jammed and cannot be ejected, not even manually."

The field scouts returned to their stations and sat down. Terrell watched the details of the surface grow sharper through the hazy veil of static on the viewscreen. "Commander, is our subspace antenna still working?"

The Vulcan nodded. "Aye, sir."

"In that case, I think we'd better send out an S.O.S.—while we still can."

Darkness, sickening smoke, and fire surrounded Nimur. Orange flames licked at her flesh but brought little pain. She was pinned against one of the walls inside the ship, held fast by some invisible force even greater than the one she now wielded. It had seized her and her Wardens just after a booming crash had buffeted the vessel and extinguished its lights. The pressure that had snared her was so great she could barely draw breath, and it took every bit of fight she had left to raise her voice above the eerie howling that engulfed the metal sky-ship.

"Senjin! Make the Klingon speak to his ship! Make it stop!"

The Warden grimaced and struggled to reply. "The captain is dead. The fire took him."

Nimur cursed the dead Klingon commander for his weak flesh. "Then we need to make it obey us!" She recalled the phrases they had forced the Klingon to reveal, the ones that had enabled him to control the ship by verbal commands alone. "Computer! Engage override!"

She waited several seconds, but nothing happened; her

desperate order went unheeded. As far as she could tell, it had gone unheard by anyone except her Wardens. Whatever part of the ship had obeyed Durak, it was as dead now as he was.

Cracks cut across the walls. Wind screamed through the spreading fissures. The rush of fresh air fed the flames around Nimur, stoking them into a yellow-white blaze.

The ship lurched and rocked, and the invisible hand holding the Changed against the back wall evaporated. They tumbled forward, slammed against the elevated command chair and its platform, caromed off railings and consoles, and landed in a heap against the opposite wall. Only minutes earlier the central panel on that wall had been like a window on the universe, looking down at their world from high above. Now it was dull and blank, just an empty frame.

Disoriented and stumbling like someone drunk on fermented nectar, Nimur seized Senjin by his shoulders and shook him until he focused on her. "We need to get off this ship!"

"How?"

"The same way we came here, with the portal device."

The Warden shook his head. "We don't know how it works. Or if it even still does."

She pulled him to his feet. "We have to try! Get the others up and follow me." She waited until they were all standing and looking at her. She pointed up, at the back of the ship that was now above them thanks to the ship's surrender to gravity. "We need to get back there."

A Warden protested, "There are no handholds! How are we supposed to climb?"

"We can lift each other! Concentrate! We need to work together!" She closed her eyes for a moment and purged herself of fear. Then she reached out and embraced the Wardens with her power, and a wave of relief washed over her as she felt their mental energies uniting with one another's and with hers. In her mind she divested herself of the burden of weight and willed herself to rise, slipping free of the leaden chains of the world below—and she did.

Her feet rose from the metal wall and she climbed up and away, as free as smoke on a breeze. Behind her followed the Wardens. Senjin had tethered himself to Nimur, and the others followed single-file behind them, each one helping to pull up the next.

They snaked through the ship's empty passageways and through a narrow ladderway to the next deck. Nimur led them by memory alone, retracing the steps from their first rampage through the ship, until they were gathered once more in the room where they all had appeared after being stolen from the sea. She pointed Senjin toward the panel she assumed controlled the Klingons' mysterious portal. "Wake it up! Hurry!"

He tapped at the console, slammed his hands against its sides, and finally punched and kicked it out of sheer frustration. "It's as dead as the rest of this ship!"

Loud booms resounded through the vessel's fracturing hull. Walls and floors buckled. Narrow strips of the hull tore free and broke away, driven by gusts of wind and plumes of fire, revealing slivers of Arethusa's twilight sky streaked with sun-splashed clouds.

Black, acrid smoke filled the small compartment, and tongues of flame licked through the open doorway from the corridor, which transformed within seconds into a roaring conflagration.

The youngest of the Wardens, a sinewy youth named Masul, gave in to panic and shouted like the frightened child he had been only hours earlier. "Nimur! What are we going to do?"

"The only thing we can do," she said, determined to face the inevitable with her pride intact. "We're going into the fire."

Kang watched the *Homghor* and the *Sagittarius* plunge toward the planet's surface, each ship wreathed in flames and trailing grayish-black smoke all the way from the mesosphere to the sea. He had dealt each mortally wounded ship a deathstroke with blasts from the *Voh'tahk*'s disruptor cannons, just to make certain neither vessel returned to haunt him.

"Mahzh. Any sign of them restoring main power?"

The weapons officer gazed at his sensor display. "None."

"Time to impact?"

"Approximately two minutes."

The captain looked at the command monitor beside his chair. The Starfleet battle cruiser would arrive in just under four minutes. Though he would have preferred to observe the final moments of the *Homghor* and the *Sagittarius,* to be certain the deed was accomplished beyond reversal, he couldn't afford to wait that long to confront his next opponent. "Well done, soldiers of the Empire! A battle well-fought! But it's not over—in fact, it's only just begun. Helm! Increase to full impulse. Get us into position to meet the Federation battle cruiser."

The *Voh'tahk*'s engines wailed and its hull groaned as it accelerated far past its rated orbital velocity. It was the sound of a ship's limits being tested—music to Kang's ears.

On the main viewscreen, he perceived the faintest gray dot moving among the stars and ever so slowly growing larger and brighter. At last, he would have an opponent worthy of him.

"Mahzh, as soon as it's in range . . . lock all weapons on the *Endeavour*."

22

"Pull!" Ilucci and Threx lifted another unbolted dura-nium deck plate free of the *Sagittarius*'s spaceframe. As soon as they had it upright, Threx used his formidable muscle mass to heave the cumbersome rectangular slab of metal aside against the bulkhead. Once Ilucci was sure the deck plate was clear of the work area, he waved Cahow into the crawl space beneath the engineering deck. "Hus-tle, Cahow! Hop to!"

The flaxen-haired petty officer adjusted her welding goggles and jumped feetfirst into the crawl space, then limbo-danced her way under a crossbeam and around a perpendicular support strut. As soon as she was past the obstructions, she pulled a plasma torch from a chest pocket on her coveralls and started cutting through the shielding above the impulse coil housing.

Just a meter aft of Cahow, Crewman Torvin was al-ready ensconced in the narrow gap between the main deck and the engineering deck, the blazing light of his own plasma torch reflecting off the black goggles shield-ing his young eyes. He and Cahow were both cutting in clockwise circles relative to the ship's nose; he had started his cut at the nine o'clock position, and she had started at three o'clock. Each would finish where the other had started.

Ilucci waved for Threx to follow him to the warp core.

"Scrounge the high-load cable from the starboard conduit! All you can get! I'll raid port-side!"

"You got it, Master Chief!"

Threx and Ilucci split up at the intermix chamber and each attacked one of the plasma relay conduits, which fed power from the warp core to the nacelles. By the book, it would take over an hour to pull out the relays' high-load power cables. They had sixty seconds.

Ilucci kicked open the deadbolt that kept the conduit's access panel closed during routine operations, then reached inside with both hands and seized the wrapped bundle of high-load cables, whose twisting-ribbed texture he knew as intimately as the scratch of stubble on his chin. He unplugged one end of the bundle from the intermix chamber; that had been the easy part. The hard part would be separating it from the warp nacelle—a process that was sure to leave one end of the cable without a functioning plug interface.

Roaring to summon every bit of his strength, he pulled on the bundle of cables and tore it free of its anchors. The first pull gained him half a meter of slack. He backed up and pulled again, and this time he put his legs and his back into it. A couple more meters came loose.

Almost there. He adjusted his grip and his center of balance, and as he pulled he shouted a string of obscenities he was sure his mother would find bloodcurdling.

Two more meters of quality cable tore free of the conduit. That would be enough. He cut the salvaged cable free. Then he held on to the bundle's end as he sprinted back to the opening he and Threx had made in the middle of the engineering deck. The lanky Denobulan was right beside him, hauling his own length of roughly salvaged power cable.

Down in the crawlspace, Torvin and Cahow were both within centimeters of finishing their cuts. Ilucci's impatience boiled over. "Move it! No extra points for neatness, dammit!" He pointed at the nearby workbench. "Threx, get set to place the mag-handles!"

Threx dropped his length of cable, clambered down into the workspace, and planked himself atop the crossbeam. Ilucci dropped his cable, ran to the workbench, and grabbed two magnetic work handles. He activated the first one and tossed it to Threx, who stuck it onto the part of the shielding plate the engineers were cutting free. Then Threx reached up, and Ilucci passed the second handle down to him. By the time Threx had the second handle affixed to the plate, Torvin and Cahow finished their cuts. Threx lifted the plate and shifted it clear of the opening.

A blast of heat rushed up at the engineers. Beneath the crudely cut, not-quite-circular opening was the ship's impulse coil assembly. It was a hot space to work in under the best of conditions, but the ship's unshielded dive through the planet's atmosphere had heated the compartment to potentially lethal levels.

Ilucci glanced at the chronometer. Fifty-five seconds to disaster. No time to play it safe. He pointed into the furnace-like compartment. "Go! We'll feed the cable down to you!"

On some level, Ilucci expected Torvin and Cahow to balk, even if just for a moment, but they slithered through the gap into the inferno without hesitation, questions, or a single look back. As soon as they were inside, Ilucci passed most of one bundle of cable to Threx, who handed it down, plug-end first, to the junior engineer's mates.

Ilucci held on to the ragged end of the bundle and used an automatic splicer to join it to the raw end of the length of cable he had pulled from the warp drive. The tool fused the cables' ends perfectly in a matter of seconds. Ilucci tested it with a quick tug; the splice was solid. They now had one extra-long cable with a working plug at each end. He shouted over the roar of wind and the groaning of the hull. "Threx! How're they doin'?"

"Almost done! They're patchin' in now! Hook it up!"

Ilucci let his cable bundle unspool behind him as he ran toward the starboard battery panel, which had weathered the fight with the Klingons far better than the portside panel. If this worked, if the splice was as functional as it was tight, if the impulse coil hadn't been damaged, and if there was still the least bit of juice left in the ship's emergency batteries, they might just make it out of this mess alive. He rounded the corner to the battery panel and lifted the plug—

—and jerked to a stop as his cable ran out of slack, just centimeters shy of the panel.

"Threx! More slack!"

"There isn't any!"

Ilucci stared at the plug in his hand and the ten-centimeter gap separating it from the batteries that could save the ship. Then he saw the countdown on the master engineering console: He had twenty seconds to find a fix for this mess, or else they were all about to die.

• • •

Vixen's magnetohydrodynamic drive thrummed a few thousand cycles per minute faster as the amphibious rover pushed its way up the slope toward the beach. Between islands, visibility ahead of the craft had been decent when it wasn't enmeshed in one kelp forest or another, but as it entered the shallows, it was enveloped by clouds of sand churned up by the crashing waves.

Theriault leaned forward, straining against her safety harness, hoping her eyes could pierce the swirling froth and floating dust. "We sure this is the place?"

Her question seemed to offend Dastin. "What're you saying? You think I don't know how to use a navcomp? Or pilot by instruments?"

"No, I'm just saying I can't see a damned thing."

A soft crunch from outside signaled that the rover had made contact with sand. The Trill scout opened the throttle. "Hang on. Next stop, the beach."

A whine from the engine lasted a few seconds, during which the rover's windshield broke through the waves into open air. Another wave broke against the back of the craft and washed over it from rear to front, briefly blurring the forward view. Then the veil of seawater retreated from the hydrophobic coating on the windshield, revealing the deserted beach where they had landed less than twenty-four hours earlier. Deep, hard-edged impressions left by the landing gear of the *Sagittarius* in the sand above the high-tide mark were still clearly visible.

Dastin pulled up onto a level stretch of the beach, far from the breaking surf, and stopped. "Last stop, folks. Welcome to No-Name Island, also known as your exfiltration point." He popped open the driver's door and climbed out, breathing a sigh of relief as he went. Tan Bao got out behind him while Theriault and Hesh exited on the passenger's side of the craft.

They had not been submerged for long, but it felt good to Theriault to be back on land. Something about the literal and figurative pressure of being underwater affected her in a way that her cognizance of the vacuum of space outside a starship didn't. She chalked up the difference to one of simple familiarity; she had been living aboard starships for well over a decade. Despite its myriad perils and unforgiving realities, space had come to feel like home to her.

Hesh drifted to her side. The young Arkenite looked out across the water, toward the island of Suba. "Not much of a first-contact mission, was it, sir?"

"I can think of a few that went worse."

"Did any of them *not* involve genocide or the catastrophic loss of a starship?"

She ran down the list of FUBAR first-contact missions she could remember, some of them nearly a century old. "Well, um . . . there was the, um . . . no." She reached for her communicator. "Maybe we should just focus on getting out of here." A flick of her wrist opened the grille of the communicator, which double-chirped to signal it was ready to transmit. Theriault set it for the ship-to-shore frequency. "Theriault to *Sagittarius*. Do you copy?"

The compact device lay silent in her hand. She increased the gain on her transmission and tried again. "Theriault to *Sagittarius*. Captain Terrell, do you read me? Please respond."

There was no sound but the crashing of waves against the beach and the wind through the trees. Anxiety widened Hesh's already large eyes. "That seems an unfortunate omen, sir."

"I'm aware of that, Lieutenant."

Tan Bao and Dastin walked quickly toward her and Hesh. The Trill called out, "Is that the ship? How long till they get us off this rock?"

"The ship is not responding," Hesh said, trumping Theriault's opportunity to put a positive spin on the unhappy news. "The reason for their lack of response is not yet known."

Theriault cuffed the science officer's shoulder. "He wasn't asking *you*, Lieutenant."

Hesh froze as he realized his faux pas. He said nothing as he avoided eye contact with her and the rest of the landing party, choosing instead to spend the next minute inspecting his boots. Unfortunately, from Theriault's perspective, the damage had been done.

Tan Bao aimed his own nervous stare across the sea toward the big island. "What if those things get beamed back down? What if they come after us?"

Dastin was less optimistic. "Nguyen, are you kidding? Nimur and her gang are the least of our problems. What if the ship left without us? What if we're stranded? I didn't pack more than a day's rations, did you? What if the fruit here tastes like *mugato* shit?"

The nurse squinted at Dastin with mock suspicion. "Do I even want to know why you're familiar with the flavor of *mugato* excrement?"

"Actually," Hesh interrupted, "my scans of the local

environment suggest there is sufficient potable water and consumable food on this island to last us indefinitely. Furthermore, based on the levels of fructose in the native fruits, and their relatively modest levels of various acidic compounds known to produce sour flavors, it seems likely the local produce will prove more than acceptable to our respective palates."

The Arkenite's reward for an attempt at peacemaking was baffled glares from Dastin and Tan Bao, and a scrunched grimace of confusion from Theriault.

Dastin shook his head. "Never let facts derail a good rant, Hesh."

"I do not understand." Hesh thought for a moment, then seemed to have an epiphany. "Wait. You have told me about this. You were 'busting' on each other." Slow, pained nods of confirmation from Tan Bao and Dastin. "My apologies."

"Forget it," Dastin said.

A crackle of static spat from Theriault's still-open communicator. She lifted it, hoping to hear a reply from the ship, but there was nothing on the channel except noise. She set the gain on the transmitter and was about to hail the *Sagittarius* again when she heard a distant scream in the sky. She looked up, more out of reflex than because she expected to see anything. A sick feeling swirled in her gut as she saw a fiery streak slash across the heavens high overhead. The burning trail cut a sharp arc through the purpling dusk and then made a sharp and decisive diving turn.

Watching the fireball descend, Theriault became aware that the landing party had pressed in close behind her, all of them with eyes turned skyward. For the first time that she could recall, there was fear in Dastin's voice.

"Is . . . is that . . . ?"

Hesh lifted his tricorder. Its high-pitched oscillations lasted only a few seconds. "It is too far away for me to make a definitive scan. However, radiation emissions are consistent with a vessel approximately the mass of the *Sagittarius*, and containing a matter-antimatter reactor. Its trajectory will put its crash site on the far eastern shore of the populated island."

The incandescent blaze went into a straight dive and picked up speed as it neared the planet's surface, indicating that it was in the throes of an uncontrolled descent, a slave to gravity. It dipped beneath the dark edge of the horizon and vanished. For several seconds, the only evidence of its passage was the fading streak of ionized gas it had left in the atmosphere.

Then came a harsh white flash from beyond the horizon, followed by a mushroom cloud.

The landing party stood and stared, shocked and silent for nearly half a minute. Then the far-off rumbling of the blast reached them, and Theriault felt a tear form in the corner of her eye.

She wiped it away with the side of her palm and reminded herself she was in command.

"Dastin, help me build us a shelter. Hesh, scrounge up some of that fruit you were talking about. Tan Bao, see if you can find a source of potable water. And let's be quick about it. It's getting dark, and I think we might be here a while."

• • •

"Helm is not responding! Still no main power! Twenty-five seconds to impact!"

Terrell heard Nizsk's frantic reports from the helm, but he had no more orders to give her, no advice that could delay calamity. They had already been robbed of the option to bail out in the escape pod. They were all going down with the ship, captain and crew alike.

Momentum pinned Terrell into his command chair, to which he clung with every sinew in his hands and arms. The sickening sensation of free fall warned him that the ship's inertial dampeners were close to failing. Even if, by some miracle, the *Sagittarius* regained enough power to pull out of this death-spiral into the sea, there was a serious risk the *g*-forces associated with such a maneuver might crush the ship's humanoid crewmembers into pulp.

We should be so lucky as to have that chance.

The main viewscreen had long since turned to dark static-snow, a fact for which Terrell was almost grateful. Watching a planet's surface rush up to meet one could be a hypnotic experience, exactly the sort of thing to make one's mind go numb at what might prove to be a critical— or final—moment in one's life. That was not how Terrell wanted to meet his ending. He was determined to die with his eyes open, to go down fighting with every last ounce of strength he possessed. He refused to die as a mere spectator to his own fate. He would *feel* it.

Time crawled as death beckoned. Terrell took note of every fleeting expression on the faces of his bridge crew. The rigid tension of Razka, who sat poised over the communications panel; the barely contained melancholy and terror of Ensign Taryl; the frantic labors of the otherwise inscrutable insectoid Ensign Nizsk, fighting to make the helm answer her commands; and the preternatural, hard-earned calm of Lieutenant Commander Sorak, whose Vulcan training had given him the tools to control his fear and face the inevitable with eerie *sangfroid*.

Nizsk's high-pitched shriek pulled Terrell back into the moment: "Fifteen seconds!" As if the Kaferian had uttered a magic spell, consoles around the bridge sputtered to life, along with the helm. Nizsk keyed in commands and cried out, "Hang on!"

The impulse engines whined, and the hull creaked and moaned as if the ship were a dying leviathan suffering a final indignity. Some of the consoles that had just been revived stuttered back into their dark slumbers, and the centripetal force of their course change crushed Terrell against his command chair so hard he couldn't breathe.

Images flashed across the main viewscreen, snippets of the view outside the ship. At first it was just a teal wall of static, and then Terrell saw the line of a horizon as his ship turned its nose away from a direct impact with the sea. Gravity's deathgrip relaxed its hold on Terrell as a dark smear on the screen resolved itself into a tiny landmass—an island—and rushed forward to meet them as they skimmed the water's surface at a distressingly low altitude.

"Helm, pull up!"

"Not enough power, sir! We have to set down!"

Terrell hoped he had heard Nizsk incorrectly. "Where, Ensign? There's no clearing!"

"It's there or in the water, sir."

Long years of training at Starfleet Academy had taught Terrell that water landings were often the preferred choice in crash-down scenarios. He looked over his shoulder at his Vulcan second officer. "I'd take water, wouldn't you?"

Sorak was unusually emphatic in his reply. "Given the current state of our hull? *No.*"

There was no time to argue, so Terrell trusted the old Vulcan's wisdom. "If you say so." He raised his voice for Nizsk. "Put us in the weeds, Ensign!"

"Landing gear deployed! Firing braking thrusters!"

The sparkling emerald expanse of the sea blurred past until only the forbidding silhouette of the jungle island remained ahead of the *Sagittarius*. Then they slammed into the wall of trees, and the violent deceleration launched Terrell from his chair. He and the rest of the bridge crew were thrown against the forward bulkhead, which quaked from the constant, excruciatingly loud, bone-jarring cacophony of impacts. The overhead lights went dark, leaving only the dim glow of emergency lighting to trace the outline of the bridge.

A final thud of collision signaled the halt of the ship's uncontrolled skid through the jungle. It took a few moments for Terrell's eyes to adjust to the much dimmer lighting on the bridge. He listened for sounds of breathing or distress. "Everyone, sound off by rank."

"Sorak here, sir."

"I'm okay, sir," Taryl replied.

"Ensign Nizsk, still at my post."

Razka rasped, "Bruised but ready to serve, Captain."

Terrell drew a deep breath, blinked once, and was relieved to be able to distinguish the unique profiles of all his people. "Good flying, Nizsk. Sorak, Razka, get me damage and casualty reports, on the double. Taryl, go outside and scout the area in a half-kilometer radius."

Everyone acknowledged with overlapping muted replies of "Aye, sir," and went to work. Terrell, suddenly aware of a painful twinge in his left knee, limped back to his command chair and slumped into it, grateful to be alive.

That's one wish granted. Now let's see if I can get all my people off this rock in one piece.

Sweat ran in heavy beads from Ilucci's scalp. His thinning hair made his perspiration's descent to his forehead easier each year. Only his unkempt eyebrows had kept him from being blinded during the majority of his working hours.

Above his head dangled the battery panel, to which he had connected the high-load cable that his engineers had risked their asses to patch directly into the impulse coil.

With seconds to spare, he had realized that if there was no more slack to be wrung from the cable, then it would have to come from the panel. And that was when he had recalled that one of the peculiarities of Starfleet design was that starship construction crews rarely cropped the cables behind most utility panels if they could use a standard-issue one-meter cable, coil the excess, and tuck it behind the panel to save time during the final stages of assembly on a ship of the line. Every panel Ilucci had ever serviced aboard the *Sagittarius*—not to mention every other ship he'd ever served on—had embodied that lazy, wasteful practice.

That "wasteful" bit of institutional sloth had just saved the ship.

As the seconds had counted down to disaster, he had torn the battery control panel off the bulkhead, and then he had pulled the input jack for the transfer cable free of its mount. To his relief, it had been backed by a typical excess of nearly thirty centimeters of slack wire.

Ilucci had guffawed like a maniac as he plugged in the high-load cable and then fell to the deck. Then he'd heard the whining of the impulse engines. *What a beautiful sound.*

Next had come the wild percussion of collisions, and the roar of the hull gouging a path across solid ground. Now the ship was silent, full of smoke, and miraculously still intact.

He glanced over his head at the loose panel, which was anchored by nothing except the high-load power cable he had jacked into it. It was in violation of nearly half a dozen Starfleet safety regulations. Technically, he had turned his entire engineering deck into a case for his own court-martial.

He rested his head against the bulkhead and shut his eyes. *If they want to write me up, that's fine by me. But for the next five minutes, I'm taking a nap.*

23

Tensions had been high on the bridge of the *Endeavour* before it had received the mayday from the *Sagittarius*. Now the ship was at Red Alert and on a direct course for danger. Panels on either side of the main turbolift flashed with crimson light, but all of Captain Atish Khatami's attention was on the ominous threat pictured in the center of the main viewscreen—and the troubling fact that, to all appearances, the Klingon cruiser was the only ship in the vicinity.

Her first officer, Lieutenant Commander Katherine Stano, looked up from the hooded sensor display. "The *Voh'tahk* is holding position but coming about to face us."

Khatami recognized the Klingons' maneuver as pure posturing. "They're daring us to make orbit. Helm, steady as she goes. Lieutenant McCormack, arm phasers and torpedoes but don't lock them onto the *Voh'tahk* until I give the order."

"Aye, Captain," replied the freckle-faced young navigator. Her colleague at the helm, the Arcturian pilot Lieutenant Neelakanta, confirmed the order simply by following it.

The pair had served together the past few years at the helm of the *Constitution*-class starship and had gelled into an effective partnership, even if at first glance they might appear mismatched. Young, slight of build, and red-haired,

McCormack looked like an out-of-place farmer's daughter, while Neelakanta resembled—to Khatami's eyes, at least—a half-melted bald man made of dull red wax, his long face defined by its overlapping, drooping layers of flesh.

Stano stared at the Klingon ship as it grew larger on the viewscreen. Khatami put her first officer back to work. "Commander, keep scanning the planet's surface for any sign of the *Sagittarius*. Their S.O.S. might have meant they were making a forced landing."

"Yes, sir." Stano turned back to the sensor display and hunched over it, eyes wide and searching for a reason to hold on to hope.

Watching the younger woman, Khatami at last found a small degree of grudging respect for Stano's choice of a neatly tucked beehive hairstyle. It didn't need to be pushed away from her face when she leaned forward or bent down, so it spared her what had once been a frequent distraction. As utilitarian as the hairdo was, however, Khatami still preferred her own neatly coiffed bob cut—just as she preferred her uniform with trousers, while Stano had elected to adopt Starfleet's miniskirt uniform, for reasons that still eluded Khatami's understanding.

Lieutenant Hector Estrada, the oldest of the ship's senior officers, swiveled away from the communications panel. "Captain, we're being warned by the *Voh'tahk* not to enter orbit."

"Return the favor, Lieutenant. Warn the *Voh'tahk*'s commander not to get in our way."

The mostly bald, mustached Estrada arched his thick eyebrows with momentary alarm before slowly rotating his chair back toward his console. "Aye, sir."

Khatami had no desire to start a shooting war with the Klingons, but she refused to be pushed around by them, either. *The Organians said we'd be friends one day.* She stifled a soft, cynical laugh. *You can't be friends with someone you don't respect. And you can't respect someone who lets you bully them. So we'll just call this my overture to friendship.*

Her ruminations were interrupted by Lieutenant Stephen Klisiewicz, the ship's third-in-command and senior science officer. "Captain? I think you should see this." He handed her a data slate with a report he had just extracted from the ship's library computer.

It was an update from Starfleet Intelligence regarding the *I.K.S. Voh'tahk*. Specifically, an alert concerning who had just been placed in command of the D-7 heavy cruiser. Khatami handed it back to Klisiewicz and lowered her voice. "How recent is that?"

He whispered back, "Confirmed nine days ago by first-hand sources on Somraw."

She regarded the Klingon vessel with a new measure of caution and respect. Not many Klingon commanders had reputations that preceded them, and even fewer had become infamous to the point that their presence would give Khatami pause. Captain Kang fit both descriptions.

"Thank you, Lieutenant. Return to your post." Klisiewicz nodded, and then he climbed the short stairs out of the command well and returned to his regular station on the upper level.

Stano snapped upright and turned toward the captain. "Sir, I've found the *Sagittarius*!"

"Is she intact?"

"Looks like it." Stano keyed commands into her console. "Estrada, I'm sending you their coordinates. Hail them on a coded frequency, see if you can raise them."

Estrada was already at work on the task. "Aye, sir. Transmitting now."

Khatami used the panel on her command chair's armrest to open an internal comm channel to sickbay. "Bridge to Doctor Leone."

The ship's nasal-voiced chief surgeon answered at once. *"Go ahead, Captain."*

"Tony, it looks like the *Sagittarius* went down hard on the planet's surface. We don't know yet how bad they're hurt, but they might need medical help."

"Understood. I'll have Nurse Sikal put together a triage team while I prep sickbay."

"Very good. Commander Stano will let Sikal know when to meet the landing party. Bridge out." She thumbed off the channel to sickbay and opened another to main engineering. "Bridge to Commander Yataro."

The ship's recently assigned new chief engineer, an ambitious Lirin officer, responded after a brief delay. *"Yataro here."*

"Commander, prep a damage control team to beam down to the *Sagittarius*."

"Understood. Anything else, sir?"

"That's all for now. Bridge out." Khatami closed the channel. She had adjusted quickly to the new chief engineer's habit of curt conversations. He seemed to have a keen dislike of small talk, and he preferred his duty-related conversations to be short, direct, and unambiguous. Strangely, he was an excellent problem-solver and unraveler of riddles—byproducts, Khatami suspected, of his deep-seated aversions to uncertainty, chaos, and obfuscation.

Estrada touched his hand to the transceiver nestled in his ear, listened intently for a moment, then shot a hopeful look at the captain. "Sir, I have the *Sagittarius*."

"On speakers." Khatami waited until Estrada signaled her that the channel was open, and then she continued. "*Sagittarius,* this is Captain Khatami on the *Endeavour.* Do you copy?"

Terrell's voice was blanketed in static. *"We read you, Captain."*

"What's your status?"

"Heavy damage across the board, and I think we scuffed the paint something awful. Nothing a week at Starbase Pacifica won't fix."

"Do we have our neighbors to thank for that?"

"Naturally."

"How's your crew holding up?"

"Still counting fingers and toes, but we're all here. Just heard from my landing party, and they're on their way back now."

"All right, Clark. Hang loose and we'll beam down some help—just as soon as we have a little talk with the neighbors."

"Tell them I said hello."

"Oh, I plan to tell them a *lot* more than that. *Endeavour* out." Khatami narrowed her stare at the image of the *Voh'tahk,* which had grown large on the viewscreen. "Hail Captain Kang."

She knew it would take a few moments for Estrada to

establish a real-time vid link to the Klingon commander, so she used the interval to stand from her chair and smooth the front of her green captain's tunic. By the time Kang's visage filled the viewscreen, Khatami had fixed her own countenance into a stern mien that Stano affectionately referred to as a *game face*.

"Captain Kang. Would you care to explain why you fired on a Starfleet vessel?"

The goateed, smooth-foreheaded Klingon mirrored Khatami's dour glare. *"We acted in self-defense. Your scout ship launched an unprovoked attack on our escort vessel."*

"I doubt that, Captain. If the *Sagittarius* fired on a Klingon ship—"

"If? You dare call me a liar? You would mind your tongue if you knew my reputation."

"If you knew mine, your ship would be on the far side of this planet by now. Go ahead, Captain. Have one of your officers look me up. I'm sure the High Command has some kind of file on me and my ship. Pay close attention to our service at the Battle of Vanguard."

A smirk pulled at the corner of Kang's mouth. *"Is that a threat, Captain?"*

"Call it a warning." She stepped forward and stole a fast look at the tactical display on McCormack's console, which confirmed her suspicions. "I see you've locked weapons on us."

He cocked his head at a rakish angle. *"Call it a warning."*

"I know you don't play games, Captain. Neither do I. So I'm giving you a choice. Release your weapons lock without firing in the next ten seconds—or I'll blast your ship into dust within the next thirty. Your call. What'll it be?"

"Do you really think you and your ship are a match for me and mine?"

"I guarantee it."

The standoff stretched on for long, painfully quiet seconds. As one moment after another slipped away, Khatami dreaded having to make good on her threat. What could possibly be so valuable that the Klingons would risk starting a war for it?

Kang turned his head and snapped at his female first officer, *"Stand down."*

McCormack looked over her shoulder at Khatami. "The *Voh'tahk* has released its targeting lock and powered down its weapons."

"Tactical systems to standby, but keep our shields up."

The Klingon commander simmered with resentment. *"What now, Captain?"*

"We need to tend to our people on the planet, and I'd rather not have you breathing down our necks while we do it. Move your ship into an antipodal orbit from here. As long as we keep the planet between us, we can both go about our business. Agreed?"

Disgust twisted Kang's frown. *"For now."* He signaled someone off-screen, and the transmission ended. The main viewscreen reverted to a view of the *Voh'tahk* banking away and making a swift orbit of Nereus II, until it disappeared beyond the planet's equatorial curve.

Stano slipped away from the sensor console to stand beside Khatami. "That was close."

"I'm sure it won't be the last time. Get a landing party together, medics and engineers. We need to get the *Sagittarius* off this rock as fast as we can."

"And if it's irreparable?"

"Evac the crew and phaser the wreck into slag to keep it away from the Klingons. But whatever we do, we'd better do it fast. If I know Kang, he's already looking for some way to seize the advantage and come back at us— and I want to be long gone before that happens."

Kang paced his quarters like a wild animal fresh to a cage and waiting to avenge itself on its keeper. "I will make her pay for this. I will make her pay in blood."

Mara watched him with sullen disapproval. "You will do no such thing." When he shot a lethal stare at her, she was unmoved. "If you had wanted to sacrifice all our lives in a pointless battle, you'd have done so. The matter is decided."

"She should have withdrawn."

"Why? Because you rattled your *bat'leth*? Would Kirk have run from you?"

His wife was right, and that infuriated Kang. "She reminded me of him. Her stare."

"Yes. She has the same intensity."

Kang stopped and opened a low cabinet in which he kept a few choice libations. He chose a bottle of good *warnog*, opened it, and half-filled a pair of metal goblets atop the cabinet. He picked them up and handed one to Mara. "We need to complete our mission without revealing our purposes to the Starfleet crew."

Mara swallowed a long draught of the potent alcohol. She savored its long finish with her eyes closed. When she opened them, they shone with a new clarity. "To satisfy the High Command and the High Council, we'll need to leave here with viable test subjects. I see now the recon team waited too long to select one for removal. We should select natives who show no signs of transformation, and put them into stasis before they start to change."

"I agree. We'll be in orbit above the natives' island within the hour. We can select two at random, beam them up—"

"No, not at random. We can't tell from orbit which ones are within months of the Change and which are years shy of it. We need to send down another team to identify the right subjects."

Kang finished his drink and sleeved the moisture from his lips. "Very well. Make their jobs easier—tell them to find that *petaQ* of a scientist, Tormog. Perhaps it's *not* yet a good day for him to die."

24

It was next to impossible to move quietly through the dense jungle that covered most of the island, not that Tormog had ever possessed a knack for stealth. Though he'd been born into a culture that glorified its relatively small population of warriors out of all proportion to their achievements, and to the grave detriment of the rest of Klingon society, he had dared to become a scientist rather than a soldier, a man of letters rather than a man-at-arms.

No regrets. I've been true to my nature, and used my gifts for the glory of the Empire. They can question my prowess with a blade, but I won't let them tell me I have no honor.

Bitterness and resentment stewed inside him. It had rankled him not just to have his advice ignored, but to have been mocked for trying to save the lives of his fellow Klingons. Why should he have to suffer such indignities for trying to help them avoid a disaster? He had served beside the warrior caste for years, but he doubted he would ever understand them.

He pushed through a tangle of vines and vaulted over the broad trunk of a fallen tree, all while keeping track of the large crowd of Tomol he was following. They were on the trail, moving in small groups. Their conversation was limited to frightened murmurs as they drifted toward whatever had crashed on the island's east side.

None of them seemed to notice Tormog following them. What would they do if they did? They didn't seem prone to violence—at least, not before they transformed. And if Nimur's reaction to the recon team had been any indication, they appeared to be receptive to contact with other intelligent beings, even those that looked significantly different from them. He knew his caution might be unnecessary, but until he had the advantage of backup he could count on, he planned to stay in the shadows.

His communicator buzzed softly against his hip. He flipped it open and lifted it close enough to whisper into it and be heard on the other end of the channel. "What?"

Kang's voice was deep, dry, and droll. *"Making yourself at home, Doctor?"*

"I'm following the natives to the crash site." He swatted his way through a cluster of thorny vines, then caught the faint, far-off scent of smoke. "Dare I ask whose wreck it is?"

"Ours. The Homghor *went down with all hands."*

"I warned them not to beam up the *novpu'*. They should have listened."

The captain let out a disgusted huff. *"But they didn't. What matters now is what comes next. A Starfleet vessel crash-landed on an island near yours, and there is another in orbit, a battle cruiser. We need to act fast if we want to salvage our mission from this blunder."*

Tormog stopped and turned his full attention to the conversation. "Meaning what?"

"We need to replace the subjects we lost in the crash of the Homghor. *Can you select two from the crowd near you? A male and a female?"*

The scientist resumed walking and straining to catch glimpses of the Tomol through the close-packed foliage and the rows of gnarled tree trunks. "Yes. But how do we transport them without sharing the *Homghor*'s fate?"

"We take them before they start to transform."

That made sense to Tormog. "Yes, of course. As long as we sedate them before they begin the Change, that should work."

"But they can't be too young. You'll have to choose subjects who are close to turning."

"I understand." Ahead of him, past the crest of a low hill, the trees thinned, and a distant reddish glow dominated the sky. "How much time do we have?"

"None. Every moment we spend now is one we have to steal."

"Understood. I'll contact you as soon as I've chosen my subjects."

"Good. A landing party will be standing by. Voh'tahk *out."* The channel closed with a barely audible click. Tormog tucked his communicator back into its pocket on his belt.

The cover of the forest gave way within a few strides to an apocalyptic hellscape of smoking ground, scorched trees, and thick drifting curtains of impenetrable black smoke. All at once Tormog realized he was standing in the open, plainly visible to anyone who might chance to turn in his direction. Because of the spectacle that filled the plain beyond the hilltop, however, no one was looking at him. They all faced the nightmarish aftermath of the crash site.

Thousands of small fires burned on the denuded landscape. Huge chunks of starship wreckage littered the blackened-glass slopes of the impact crater. The nadir of the crash site was a pool of what looked like molten obsidian. Scablike patches of crust had formed on the black pool's surface as the slagged rock cooled. Great pillars of smoke climbed skyward from the sprawl of smoldering devastation. It reminded Tormog of the ancient paintings of the mythical horrors of *Gre'thor,* the underworld realm of *Fek'lhr,* who condemned dishonored Klingons to an eternity of torments as sadistic entertainment for their betters, who could look down from *Sto-Vo-Kor* and laugh forever at the well-deserved fates of the damned.

The Tomol spread out along the periphery of the blast area, forming a ring of bodies. Tormog could only wonder what the natives thought they were looking at. Had they ever seen a meteor strike this planet before? Or observed a starship crash? Did they have any sense of what had just happened here? Or had they simply come like insects drawn to a flame?

All questions to be answered some other time. Tormog kneeled behind a large, charred stump and assessed the nearest Tomol, sorting them mentally by age to determine which ones would be best suited for a protracted stasis voyage to the Klingon homeworld.

If it's test subjects Kang wants, then test subjects he shall have.

Everyone in the village had seen the falling star—just as they all had heard Nimur's voice inside their heads. Her inchoate roar of pain and rage had been impossible to block out or ignore. To Kerlo, who had been closer to Nimur than anyone else, it had been unbearable, cleaving his thoughts like a burning blade, forcing him to his knees until all he could do was hold his head and cry out for mercy that refused to come.

Then had come the eruption in the east, the white dome of light that had turned red as it diminished and shrank behind the distant hilltops. Other voices called out, then, in concert with Nimur's. The Wardens she had corrupted—they were with her. But what had happened to them? How had they risen so high? And what had cast them down? Was this the legendary justice of the Shepherds, the retribution the priestesses had long warned would be delivered on those who dared to flee from the Cleansing?

Kerlo needed to know. They all did. And so together they walked toward the new sunset, the one that lingered in the east, a red glow beckoning them to come bear witness.

Standing beside his neighbors and kin on the edge of the great crater, Kerlo felt his heart swell with grief. He had loved Nimur once; and though he had come to fear her after the Change, part of him had hoped she was at least partly still the woman he'd adored, the mother of his child. His most earnest wish now was that she was truly and finally gone, so that the land and the people could be at peace. But even so, he mourned her, and he wept to think that the woman who once had woven such beautiful fabrics with her delicate hands, and had kissed his bruised head with the tenderness of a morning breeze, had driven herself to such a brutal, pointless ending.

• • •

As grateful as Hesh was that the *Sagittarius* had survived its harrowing brush with annihilation, he was ever so slightly vexed that it had crash-landed on a completely different island from the one on which they had set their exfiltration site. Consequently, returning to the ship had proved to be a rather roundabout affair. It had entailed another submerged journey through pitch-dark seas—a journey made navigable only by Hesh's own effort to link his tricorder to the rover's navcomp so that it could detect and plot routes around treacherous kelp forests.

Now, as they surfaced onto a strange new alien shore, Dastin proclaimed, "See! Told you guys I'd get us back to the ship in one piece!"

Hesh left his criticism unspoken: *As if he could have piloted around those kelp forests that his Trill eyes lack the acuity to perceive in the dark.*

The Arkenite suppressed his urge to set Dastin's beard aflame and concentrated instead on making tricorder scans of the area for the good of the group and the mission. "I have detected the *Sagittarius*," he said. "Relaying coordinates to the navcomp. Be advised, there appears to be a great deal of impassable jungle between us and the ship. We might need to proceed on foot."

Dastin checked the ship's position on the navcomp. "On foot? Don't make me laugh." He stepped on the accelerator and swung the wheel to the right. "Hang on, this might get bumpy." The rover fishtailed its way down the beach, charging through the breakers for a few kilometers until Dastin jerked the wheel hard to the left. "There we go."

Lit by the glow of the planet's two moons, the straight and level swath cut by the *Sagittarius* through the jungle was like a smoky canyon with trees and vines for walls. Most of the debris had been knocked aside or driven under the dirt by the small starship's violent passage, leaving an eerie, wide dirt road stubbled with low stumps. A dust cloud in the middle distance promised an imminent end to their odyssey across this increasingly inhospitable planet.

Theriault opened her communicator. "Theriault to *Sagittarius*. We have you in sight."

Captain Terrell answered, *"Roger that. The door's open."*

A couple of minutes later, the rover reached the *Sagittarius,* which was planted nose-first into the ground. The jungle hugged the dented, torn-up scout ship on three sides; only the aft quarter of the primary hull was clear of obstruction, but the ramp to the cargo bay was several centimeters off the ground because the ship's forward landing gear had dug itself into the dirt.

Terrell, Cahow, and Ilucci stood on the ramp, watching the rover's return. The captain lifted his arm and waved in salutation. Dastin flashed the rover's headlights in response.

The vehicle rolled to a gentle stop a few meters from the ramp. Dastin turned off the engine, and Theriault opened her door. "Okay, kids. We're home." She got out, and the rest of the landing party followed her. As soon as Hesh was free of the rover, he did the first thing that came to mind: He ran another tricorder scan of the area. Just to be safe. It was.

As they walked toward the ship, Hesh got his first good

look at the captain, the chief engineer, and Cahow, who were bathed in light from the rover's headlamps. All three of them were scuffed, sweat-soaked, and covered in a fine layer of grime, but Cahow seemed the worst off of the three. Her face was bloodied, bruised, and reddened, and her flaxen hair looked as if it had been assaulted by an open flame that had left it crisped in several spots.

"Good to have you back, all of you," the captain said. He shook Theriault's dusty hand and clapped her shoulder. "Everybody okay?"

"Fine and dandy, sir. How's everybody else?"

"We'll manage."

Dastin surveyed the damage to the ship, glanced back at the rover, and then turned to face Ilucci. "Damn, Master Chief—and you thought I was a menace."

The gentle jibe lit the chief's fuse. "I'm the reason this goddamn ship is *still here*."

"Whoa!" Dastin lifted his hands in a defensive posture. "Sorry, Master Chief."

Terrell pressed his open hand lightly against Ilucci's chest. "Stand down."

Ilucci took a deep breath as he backed off and unclenched his fists. "Sorry, sir."

"S'all right. We've all had a hell of a day. And it ain't over yet."

Theriault stepped onto the ramp and motioned for the others to follow her inside the ship. "Do we have a repair schedule yet, Master Chief?"

Ilucci, Dastin, Tan Bao, and Terrell followed the first officer up the ramp and inside the cargo bay, but Cahow lingered outside and stared into the night, so Hesh stayed behind with her. He wanted to reach out and touch her singed hair, as if that might offer some comfort, but he didn't know enough about human customs in general, or about Cahow in particular, to be sure such an act might not be misinterpreted, so he kept his hands to himself. "Are you all right?"

"I've been better." She sniffled and wiped nascent tears from her eyes. "I bet you wish now you'd never signed up for starship duty, right? Then you could be home with your *sia lenthar* instead of stuck here on a bird with clipped wings."

Hesh took a chance and trusted his instincts. He reached out and held Cahow's hand. "There is nowhere I would rather be than here. When my friends back home hear what a fine *sia lenthar* has welcomed me on the *Sagittarius,* I will be the envy of every soul on Arken."

Her eyes shone with overwhelming emotions, and she released her pent-up tension with a short, self-conscious laugh. "That's great, Hesh." She smiled at him. "We like you, too."

White heat surrounded dark thoughts. Every direction seemed to promise more of the same—nothing but endless fire and boundless pressure, a burden beyond measure, as bright as the sun.

Fleeting memories stitched themselves together in the blinding inferno.

The Klingons' sky-ship had fallen from its heavenly perch and returned to the world cloaked in flames. Its magic window had gone blank, leaving only darkness and fear, the all-consuming dread that came with knowing the end was near but being unable to see it arrive.

Alone in the blackness, huddled around the magical device that refused to awaken, the Changed had united their powers and linked their minds. They had fled the fire only to have it find them. The Cleansing would not be so easily defied.

Wind had screamed through the splintering ship and its metal skin had wailed as it bent and broke apart. Then had come the bone-crushing stop and a flash like a thousand dawns.

All that was had seemed to end. Only the searing light and heat of the crucible remained.

Now thoughts stirred and coalesced; they grew clearer as the Changed surfaced from their blinding slumber. This boiling sea was a pit of molten rock beneath a crust of glass. Beyond that fragile barrier lay the promise of freedom. The Changed siphoned raw energy from the liquid rock and willed themselves toward the darkness above.

The glass cracked and heaved upward at their point of impact. Fractures radiated across its obsidian surface, like strands in a hidden web suddenly revealed.

Another upward surge, another relentless push for liberty—and the Changed exploded through the glassy crust into open air. Once the balmy breezes might have seemed warm to them, but after their immersion in a lake of fire, the sultry night felt blissfully cool.

Emancipated, the Changed separated and strode across the jagged remnants of the crater's glassy crust. With each step they divorced their minds a bit further from one another, until at last Nimur was alone with her own thoughts. She led her Wardens up the slope of the crater, toward the circle of Tomol who had gathered around its perimeter. Every member of the throng projected fear in waves, but none of them ran; they all stood as if paralyzed.

At the top of the slope, Kerlo waited for Nimur. His fearful aura was tinted with sadness as he looked upon her. "What are you going to do to us?"

"I'm going to lift you all up."

It was obvious he did not trust her. "You mean you're going to make us all like you."

"Yes. This is our birthright, the heritage the priestesses denied us. I'm giving it back."

"What if we don't want to be like you?"

She was baffled by his refusal of her generosity. "Don't be a fool, Kerlo. We were born to live as gods. Why choose to live and die as a worm?"

His terror turned to contempt. "I don't see any gods here. Only monsters."

"After I open your eyes, you'll see the truth. Then we can rule this world together, as we were always meant to."

"I would rather be cast into the fire now, as the person I am."

Nimur's temper flared. Like an alien presence in her mind it cried out for violence, for retribution, for the chance to hurt Kerlo until he submitted to her authority. She fought back against the urge, but it was like trying to stop the ocean from crashing against a beach. Her hands clenched into aching fists. "If death is what you crave, Kerlo, keep refusing my kindness. I am offering you a life longer than any you ever dreamed of."

"There are measures of a life more meaningful than its duration."

"What good is a life that fades like a spark from the fire?"

Kerlo gestured toward the smoldering pit. "As opposed to what? Burning out of control and consuming the world? Sooner or later, we all go into the darkness. But I'd rather soar as a spark for an instant than destroy everything beautiful that made life worth having."

"And what of our daughter? Don't you want to see her life?"

"Of course I do. But not if it means she grows up seeing her parents as abominations. Not if it means she has to be twisted into something ugly to survive."

There was no more point in arguing with Kerlo. Nimur could see that her mate's foolish idealism had left him blind to what really mattered. She was offering him the world, but he was too timid to take it—for now. "You will join me, Kerlo. You won't be able to help yourself."

"You think giving me power like yours will make me want what you want? Or make me forgive you? Or follow you, like these puppets who used to be Wardens?" He stepped forward until their noses almost touched. "Give me that power now. Watch what I do with it."

Did he want her to kill him? Was his urge to self-destruction so compelling? Slaying him might serve as an example to the others and preempt future challenges to her authority—or it could alienate the rest of the Tomol and spur them to reject her boon. She knew their resistance could be overcome, but what if Kerlo was able to make good on his threat? What if by Changing all the others, she inadvertently empowered her own enemies?

Right now I have the advantage, Nimur reasoned. *If I'm to keep it, I have to be more careful about whose powers I awaken. I need to be sure those I lift up are loyal to me.*

She stepped aside and gestured with a sweep of her arm toward the crater of molten rock. "Cleanse yourself in the fire, then, if that's your wish. I won't stop you." Kerlo met her taunting gaze with an angry look. He tensed as if to begin his march into the molten stone, but then he paused—and took half a step backward. Nimur laughed at him. "Just as I thought. When your time comes, you'll welcome the Change." Her mate closed his eyes and hung his head in shame.

Around them, the emotional temperature shifted. Pockets of resistance faded. Nimur felt her hold over the others grow more solid. Then she sensed a mental presence, at once strange but familiar, and she remembered her flurry of vengeance in the caves.

It was behind her, lurking in the gathering darkness. She reached out and snared it with her mind. It struggled as she pulled it toward her, too stubborn to see it had no hope of escape. When at last her prey hovered before her, caught in her invisible grip, she looked him in the eye.

"Hello, Tormog. I thought you'd have run back to your sky-ship by now." He spat at her. The wet glob hit Nimur's cheek. She tightened her unseen hold on Tormog's body until he cried out. "Don't do that again." She turned him upside-down. "Why are you still here?"

He could barely breathe. "Mission . . . not done yet. Need . . . new subjects."

"What makes you think I'll let you abduct any of my

people?" She nodded at her mate. "He's plotting to kill me, and I won't even let you take him."

Tormog shook his head and gritted his teeth. "Doesn't . . . matter. Have . . . my orders."

"I'm sure you do." She looked up at the night sky and imagined the Klingons' sky-ship hovering there, concealed between the stars, spying down upon them. When she focused her mind, she could almost feel the sky-ship, but it was just too far away for her to touch.

Then she looked back at Tormog and saw the talking-tool tucked into a pouch on his belt. Holding him in place, she coaxed the device from Tormog's belt with a thought and floated it into her hand. She emulated one of the other strangers by flicking her wrist to open the cover of the small box. It buzzed gently in her hand, and a small crystal on its inner face glowed red.

She held it up so Tormog could see it. "How do I talk to the sky-ships?"

"You mean . . . my people's ship?"

"All of them. I want them all to hear what I have to say." She relaxed her hold on the Klingon to make it easier for him to answer her.

He drew a long breath and steadied his voice. "Turn the center dial so its red line points at the dot above it. Then rotate the left dial all the way to the right. Then . . . just talk."

Nimur did as he'd instructed and showed him the adjusted settings. "Like this?"

He nodded. "Yes."

"Thank you, Tormog. You've been very helpful." She tossed him aside and enjoyed the dull, heavy sound of his body hitting the ground. "Stay there until I call for you."

He wore a look of wild confusion—wide eyes, half-bared fangs, and a furrowed brow. "You're not going to kill me?"

"Not unless you give me no choice. After all . . . why would I kill a perfectly good slave?"

25

Khatami watched the northern hemisphere of Nereus II fill the *Endeavour*'s main viewscreen as McCormack announced the ship's updated status. "Standard orbit achieved, Captain. The *Voh'tahk* is keeping its distance on the far side of the planet."

"Very good, Lieutenant. Let me know if the Klingons make any sudden moves."

The navigator kept her eyes on the helm console. "Aye, sir."

Estrada checked in next. "Sir? Captain Terrell says his landing party is safely back aboard the *Sagittarius*. They're standing by to receive our medical and engineering teams."

"Glad to hear it." She glanced over her right shoulder at Stano. "Commander? Is our landing party ready to beam down?"

"Aye, sir. I've put Commander Yataro in charge of the team."

Selecting personnel for landing parties was the first officer's responsibility, but as the ship's commanding officer, Khatami reserved the prerogative to overrule the XO's choices. In practice, she was reluctant to do so. Second-guessing Stano might undermine her ability to do her job, which could lead to a breakdown of the chain of command. Regardless, Khatami harbored misgivings about letting the *Endeavour*'s new chief engineer lead a landing party into a tense crisis situation. It wasn't that he was a poor officer; he simply hadn't been tested yet—at least, not on her watch. "Belay that. Mister Klisiewicz, I want you to lead the landing party."

Klisiewicz traded a concerned glance with Stano before he replied. "Captain, I'm sure Commander Yataro is capable of leading a repair-and-rescue op."

"No doubt. But I want a command officer on the ground, just in case."

"Sir, I'm a *science* officer."

"You're also my third-in-command, which means you outrank Yataro on this ship." She swiveled her chair and quashed any further discussion with a pointed look. "Grab your gear and report to Transporter Room One, on the double. That's an order."

"Aye, sir." He nodded and walked toward the turbolift.

As Klisiewicz stepped inside the turbolift, Stano descended the stairs into the command well and stood beside Khatami's chair. Her voice was low and grave. "Captain, I—"

"Not now, Commander." Stano accepted the rebuff and returned to the sensor console on the upper deck of the bridge. Their truncated conversation cast a pall of tension over the bridge.

Estrada dispelled the air of disquiet with an excited declaration. "Captain, we're receiving an audio message from the planet's surface. It's a broad-spectrum transmission, but the signal appears to be coming from a Klingon communicator."

"Who's hailing us?"

The communications officer listened for a moment while adjusting the switches on his console. "Actually, sir, I don't think we're being hailed directly. The message isn't addressed to any specific person or vessel, and"—he fiddled with a few more switches and frowned—"well, I'm sorry, but this I can't explain. According to the universal translator, the person sending the message is directing it to 'the sky-ships above us.' I've checked the translation three times, sir. It says 'sky-ships' instead of starships."

Khatami feared the situation on the planet had just taken a turn for the worse—and that she was about to send her landing party into the thick of it. "Are the Klingons hearing this?"

He looked at his screens. "Yes, sir. They're receiving it now."

"I want to hear it, from the beginning. Put it on speakers." She sat back and waited while Estrada queued up the incoming message for playback.

A feminine voice wafted down from the overhead speakers. *"This message is for the people on the sky-ships above us. I don't know where you've come from, what you want, or why you've involved us in whatever fight you seem to be waging. But know this: You are* not *welcome on Arethusa, either of you. My name is Nimur, and I rule this world. Tell your people, and anyone else who might be foolish enough to come here: If you trespass on our soil again, you will do so at your own peril. Because as of now, Arethusa, and every living thing that dwells upon it—including your stranded comrades—are now* mine. *This will be your only warning."*

The transmission stopped, and a shocked silence settled over the *Endeavour*'s bridge. Khatami looked over her shoulder at Estrada. "Anything else?"

He shook his head. "No, sir. That's the whole message."

Stano grimaced. "I bet the Klingons are gonna *love* that."

McCormack let out a cynical harrumph. "I'm surprised they aren't glassing the planet."

"Give them time," Neelakanta deadpanned.

Khatami stood and strode forward, doing her best to project confidence and authority. "Lieutenant McCormack, keep our shields at maximum, and arm all weapons."

McCormack entered the commands as she asked in a shaky voice, "Am I targeting the planet or the Klingons?"

Neelakanta muttered with dry gallows humor, "With our luck? Both."

Khatami cursed her luck with a grim sigh. *So begins another glorious day in Starfleet.*

TO BE CONTINUED IN

STAR TREK®
SEEKERS

Point of Divergence
by
Dayton Ward & Kevin Dilmore

ACKNOWLEDGMENTS

Kara, my wife: Thank you for, as of this writing, suffering me to go on living under your roof. I'm sure my friends would all say that *suffering* is the operative word to describe your patient forbearance of my ongoing writerly foibles.

Dayton Ward and Kevin Dilmore: Thanks for agreeing to follow me on another damned-fool fictional crusade into the *Star Trek* universe. It wouldn't be the same without you guys at my side. Here's hoping our new mission to tell tales of strange new worlds and new life-forms in the twenty-third century is one that we'll continue together for years to come.

Rob Caswell, artist extraordinaire: Without your unique vision, and your inspired pairing of the cover-art aesthetics of James Blish's classic *Star Trek* anthologies from the 1970s with Masao Okazaki's masterful design for the *Archer*-class scout ship *Sagittarius,* we might never have conceived of *Star Trek: Seekers.* We all owe you a debt of gratitude. I salute you, sir.

My esteemed editors, publisher, and licensor: Thanks for letting us build another new corner in the *Star Trek* sandbox. We'll try not to break too many of your toys this time.

Lucienne, my agent: I promise I will get back to work on my new original novel manuscript very soon. (And this time, *I mean it*.)

Bourbon: You're perfect just the way you are. Don't ever change.

Lastly, I extend my gratitude to you, gentle readers, for all your kind support and encouragement. Here's hoping that *Star Trek: Seekers* exceeds your wildest expectations.

Ciao!

ABOUT THE AUTHOR

David Mack is a professional working on a closed course. Do not attempt to replicate his literary stunts without trained supervision. Learn more at his official website:

www.davidmack.pro